# FLIGHT SEASON

## ALSO BY MARIE MARQUARDT

*The Radius of Us*
*Dream Things True*

# FLIGHT SEASON

# MARIE
# MARQUARDT

WEDNESDAY BOOKS
NEW YORK

FLIGHT SEASON. Copyright © 2018 by Marie Marquardt. All rights reserved. Printed in the United States of America. For information, address St. Martin's Press, 175 Fifth Avenue, New York, N.Y. 10010.

www.wednesdaybooks.com

Designed by Steven Seighman
Illustrations by Emily Arthur

The Library of Congress Cataloging-in-Publication Data is available upon request.

ISBN 978-1-250-10701-5 (hardcover)
ISBN 978-1-250-10702-2 (ebook)

Our books may be purchased in bulk for promotional, educational, or business use. Please contact your local bookseller or the Macmillan Corporate and Premium Sales Department at 1-800-221-7945, extension 5442, or by email at MacmillanSpecialMarkets@macmillan.com.

First Edition: February 2018

10  9  8  7  6  5  4  3  2  1

Our spiritual awareness of ourselves and all that is around us; contact with the natural world and its beauties; sensing the sounds and smells and colors of our world; accepting the love of others and returning that love, these are the things that are important, and which I relearn I should relish each and every day.

—Frank Xavier Friedmann, Jr. (1940–1991)

*This book is dedicated to the memory of my father,*
*Frank Xavier Friedmann, Jr.,*
*who taught me how to find beauty in all of creation,*
*and who showed me how to love abundantly.*

# FLIGHT SEASON

Grasshopper
Sparrow

(Ammodramus
savannarum)

Migrating bird
Summers in Maine
or the Great Plains

Song:
Tick - tick - tick -
buzzzzzzz
Staring right
at me.
Should be long
gone by now.

May 29
12:37 PM

Is one of Nature's
best navigators
lost?

# CHAPTER ONE

## *VIVI*

BIRD JOURNAL

May 29, 12:37 P.M.

Grasshopper sparrow (*Ammodramus savannarum*)

*What is this little guy doing at a South Carolina rest stop? Is*
*one of nature's best navigators lost?*

Social Behavior: typically not in flocks, can be very
secretive, but often perch atop shrubs to sing.

Call: double or triple ticking note, followed by long insect-
like buzz.

Habitat: migrating bird, found during breeding season in
much of the northern and midwestern United States.
Winters in Mexico and the coastal southeastern US.

*It's a migratory bird, and it should be LONG GONE!*

**LATELY I'VE DEVELOPED** a fascination with birds. It started in
December, when a lovely little songbird perched above me in the
branch of an enormous oak tree and refused to shut up. At the time,
all I knew was that it was small and loud and incredibly persistent.

Now I know it was an American robin.

Birders give every bird's song a phrase, which is supposed to mirror the rhythm and tone of their sound. One of my favorite common birds, the barred owl, sings out in a low tenor, *Who cooks for you?* But the American robin doesn't ask questions. Instead it incessantly commands: *Cheerily, cheer up, cheer up, cheerily, cheer up!* Which is an especially frustrating thing to hear when you're sitting at an outdoor funeral in the blinding light of a Florida winter, trying to pay attention to the eulogy.

I don't remember much from that day, except for how bright blue the sky was, set against all of those dark suits, and how many people had crammed into my backyard—hundreds of mourners pressed against the edge of the still lake. And I remember hearing fragments of a traditional hymn, because everyone around me was singing about "awesome wonder" and "the greatness of God," while I was entertaining such not-so-awesome thoughts as: *I wonder where the ashes are* and *When will all of these people leave us alone?*

I stayed outside and sat in the shadow of that sprawling oak tree. I stared up at the Spanish moss, gray and dripping from every branch, waiting to feel something. Anything.

And that robin? He stuck around and kept me company. He sang to me, high and clear, until all the guests had gone back to their not-torn-through-with-grief lives (probably feeling quite anxious to *cheerily cheer up!*).

After that, I started to pay attention to birds, which wasn't terribly difficult. As it turns out, they were paying a whole lot of attention to me.

Take this little sparrow: I'm on my way home after having (barely) survived my first year of college, and I'm not even remotely surprised when I pull into the parking lot of a run-down gas station, only to encounter him watching me with beady black eyes. He's perched on a rusted-out handicapped parking sign, staring right at me.

I think he's a grasshopper sparrow, or maybe a Savannah sparrow. Either way, this little guy should already be at his summer home in Maine, or maybe hopping around the grasslands of the Great Plains, plucking up insects. He doesn't belong in the swamplands of rural South Carolina—not with summer fast approaching.

This poor bird has lost its bearings.

His stout neck flicks from side to side and he lets out a loud call: a triple ticking note followed by a long humming buzz.

*Tick-tick-tick-buzzzzzzzzzzz.*

His insect-like call gives it away. He definitely is a grasshopper sparrow, which means he definitely is lost.

Unless, of course, he stuck around to wait for me.

These birds may have pea-sized brains, but they are not dumb. They're incredible. They can make their way across continents with nothing but their own good sense. One time, a group of scientists packed up a few dozen sparrows in Washington State, took them on a plane to Princeton, New Jersey, and set them free. Within a couple of hours, they all were heading straight for their wintering grounds in Mexico.

*What kind of sparrows were those? White-crowned?*

I pull out my phone to do a quick search, but I'm distracted by a string of incoming texts.

The first few are from my roommate, Gillian. From the fragments I can see, it appears that she's reached Chicago, the first stop on our epic summer music road trip. We planned it together, and then I abandoned her before it even started.

Since I'm currently at a rest stop in the middle of nowhere, on my way home to repair last semester's epic mistakes, I can't muster the energy to look at her texts.

I scroll down to the next one, from my mom:

*I'm thinking maybe a little change of plans. . . . Call me!*

I watch the screen, forcing myself to take slow breaths, wondering if she'll tell me more. Nothing. When I look up, the sparrow has hopped over to perch on a metal pole beside a convenience store's entrance, like he's urging me to go in.

Maybe that bird is right. Maybe I should head in and get something to eat before I make this call—Twizzlers to gnaw on. They always calm my nerves.

I close my bird journal and put it in the passenger seat. I rest the binoculars on top and get out of the car. The door jangles as I go inside.

"Need somethin'?" a man behind the counter asks.

"Twizzlers?"

"Last aisle, on the right."

I walk along the gray linoleum floor, following the almost-white path made by hundreds of feet shuffling toward the candy.

"Look up," the man says. "See 'em there?"

I look up, but I don't see them. I'm squinting, scanning the brightly colored candies crammed onto metal shelves. I'm having trouble paying attention, because even through the thick plate glass, I hear that little sparrow's song.

*Tick-tick-tick-buzzzzzzzzzzz. Tick-tick-tick-buzzzzzzzzzzz. Tick-tick-tick-buzzzzzzzzzzz.*

The convenience store clerk comes out from behind the counter with, of all things, a baby strapped to his back—and a handgun attached to his belt.

*Yikes.*

He reaches beyond me and then hands me a king-sized bag of Twizzlers.

"Here you are, miss." He glances out the window at my car. "I guess you won't be needing gas."

My car's electric. It's also beautiful and sleek and near perfect. I know that teenagers shouldn't drive a car like this. I get it. So the amused tone in his voice and the way he looks back at me and gives me a quick once-over—they don't bother me. I understand where he's coming from.

And I can't exactly explain to this man, this kind stranger with a baby on his back and a gun in his belt loop, how much this car means to me—how much more it is for me than a status symbol for the environmentally conscious. Because, here's the thing about my car: no matter how bad things get, I can still climb in and press the start button. I can gently bring the engine to life, and I can remember the moment I got it—a moment filled with the bright possibility of a beautiful future. I'm clinging to that future, grasping for it, but I feel it slipping out of my reach, darting away with nervous, erratic, unpredictable jolts. It's like I'm trying to hold on to a hummingbird.

"Never seen one of those in person," the clerk says. "How far can you go without charging it?"

"Three hundred and fifty miles or so. It's amazing." I know I'm gushing, but I love that car with all my heart.

"And what do you do out here on the road when you need to charge it?"

"I have an app. It tells me where I can stop to charge."

"An app?" he asks, his eyebrows arching.

"Well, you know what they say." I shrug. "There's an app for everything these days."

He nods and pinches his lower lip, like he's thinking, but he doesn't ask anything more.

I'm tempted to tell him about the amazing birding apps I have on my phone—one of them can actually identify any North American bird from a photograph and a GPS locator. But he'll probably think I'm a basket case.

Down here on the ground, we barely ever give these feathered wonders a moment's notice, even though they have been on Earth for eons longer than we have. Most people don't know that birds are dinosaurs' closest descendants. They will, no doubt, outlast us all, and that's probably for the best.

Most people find my bird obsession weird. I get it. Six months ago, if someone had suggested to me that I'd be pulling over to the side of the road on a regular basis to strap a pair of binoculars around my neck and grab a journal from the glove compartment, or if someone had explained to me that I would sketch furiously while struggling to detect the subtle differences between two sparrows, or that I would know to focus my attention on the trill of their song and the hue of their underbellies, I would have said they were insane.

But the truth is this: I only started paying close attention to birds because they started paying attention to me.

I could offer any number of examples from the past six months. The horned owl that followed me home as I ran away from a dorm party where a junior I'd never met before cornered me and started to grope. The common raven that dive-bombed me several times as I attempted to enter the lecture hall where I was supposed to take an English exam covering a broad range of Canadian novels on the theme of refuge—most of which I had not managed to read.

And this one, from a couple of weeks ago: I was studying for exams, utterly sleep-deprived and subsisting on Twizzlers and Monster Energy drinks. During exams, space in the library is incredibly hard to come by, and I was feeling proud that I had managed to find a private desk by the window in the Southeast Asia Reading Room.

Yale's library is an astounding building—it looks more like a cathedral than a place to store books. In fact, when I first got to campus last fall, the space felt a bit overwhelming. It seemed almost too quintessentially Ivy League to be real. But any library with the motto A LIBRARY IS A SUMMONS TO SCHOLARSHIP carved on the walkway was exactly the place I needed to be that week. Up until that point, my second semester at Yale had been significantly lacking in scholarship, and I had three short reading days to make up for lost time.

I was camped out at a desk by the window, cramming the stability patterns of reactive intermediates into my exhausted brain. A small yellow bird came tapping on one of the windowpanes with its beak—so hard that I was sure it would shatter the leaded glass. And then the bird perched on a branch and started to call out.

That bird was an American goldfinch. Its call? *Po-ta-to-chip, po-ta-to-chip.* After enduring several minutes of unrelenting song, I finally gave up, slammed my textbook shut, and took the stairs down to the library's exit. Dazed, I emerged onto Rose Walk and into the sunlight. I followed the scent of buttered toast to the Cheese Truck and ordered the daily special, a grilled Caseus cheese with farm-fresh spinach, with potato chips on the side. I let my eyes fall shut and slowly breathed in the most comforting aromas of all time. Then I carried those chips and grilled cheese on sourdough to my favorite bench in a shady corner of Calhoun courtyard and devoured them.

It was one of the best sandwiches I have ever eaten. The chips were fabulous, too, with the perfect amount of salt and a satisfying crunch.

I'm almost certain that I tanked the exam. Remembering all those stability patterns was probably a lost cause from the start, but I'll never forget that perfect grilled cheese—and the goldfinch that made me stop to eat it.

I hang around in the candy aisle for another minute or two, pretending to study the shelves. I peer over a tower of chewing gum. The clerk is shifting his gun holster to transfer the sleeping baby into a Pack 'n Play. It's set up under the counter, behind the cigarette display. I don't want to interrupt him, so I wait until after the baby is settled to pay.

Standing there, desperate to kill time so that I won't have to make that call to my mom, I consider asking if he brings his baby to work every day. But then I worry that there's some tragic story behind it all—like maybe his wife left him for his brother, or she died in a terrible interstate accident involving an eighteen-wheeler. Maybe he was in the car too. Maybe it was his fault, and the agony of having killed his wife is almost too much for him to bear.

*God, what is wrong with me? Not everybody's life has to be in shambles.*

I decide that's enough death and destruction for today. His wife probably went to visit her mom in Beaufort or something. Or maybe she's at home, right around the corner, making tuna sandwiches for lunch. Maybe he just likes hanging out with his little girl at work—a way to pass the time.

My phone rings. Mom.

I say a quick thanks and head toward the door.

"Hi, Mom. I was just about to call."

I swing the door of the convenience store open, and a blast of sweltering hot air hits me at the same time as her voice.

"Good news, Viv!"

For as long as I can remember, my mom's voice has served as a precise barometer of her mood. With only a few words, I can tell how she's faring. It's hard to admit, but I've come to dread our phone calls. Because, when she's sounding bereft, and I'm several states away, doing everything I can to hold it together enough to keep from failing out of school, I have no idea how to talk to her.

But today she sounds good. Great, actually.

"My friend Anita is going to North Carolina for the summer. She's giving pottery workshops at an artist colony near Celo—"

I'm not sure how any of this is relevant to Mom and me. But I think I know what she wants me to say, so I say it. I interject with an enthusiastic "And?"

"She's decided to focus the workshop around roots, trees, leaves, and branches. . . ."

My voice rises. "And?"

"Oh, well, I just thought you should know. . . ."

It's a game we used to play when Dad came home from a day in court with another wild idea. He would burst into the kitchen, announcing a string of facts that appeared in no way relevant to our lives.

*Did you two know that Bhutan has extraordinary biodiversity? And an incredibly diverse range of climates. . . .*

*And?*

*The takin is Bhutan's national animal, but most people travel there to get a sighting of the Bengal tiger or the clouded leopard. . . .*

*And?*

*Oh, and there are some fabulous Buddhist monasteries there. I mean, if you're into that kind of thing. . . .*

*And?*

*I was just driving home from work and thinking about how you two might not know a whole lot about Bhutan, and perhaps you should. . . .*

*And?*

*And I've booked a trip. Vivi's spring break. How does that sound to y'all?*

So, even though it hurts, physically, to play this game with my mother, and a hole is opening up in my chest, I squeeze my eyes shut and make myself do it.

"And?"

"And she's offered us her beach cottage."

I lean against the wall and rip open the bag of Twizzlers.

"It's so adorable. Just a few houses from the ocean. You're going to love it."

I start gnawing on a Twizzler, watching the sparrow hop to the pavement and begin a little jig.

"Vivi?"

"Uh, that sounds like a great adventure, Mom."

I say it because that's how the game always ended. But what I really want to say is: *Can I please just come home?*

"I think we'll be happier there, Vivi," she says, a touch of melancholy creeping back into her voice. "I know it's last-minute, but are you willing to give it a try?"

I'm thinking so much about that subtle shift in her voice, and about what it might mean, that I can't seem to produce a response.

"If you don't like it," she continues, "we can always decide to go back home."

"Sure, I'm always up for an adventure."

I say it because I'm a Flannigan, and we are adventurers. But even as I'm saying it, I know that—for me—it's no longer true. I'm like a common pigeon these days—entirely sedentary and almost incapable of caring for myself. It seems like I've spent the last several months waiting around for someone to throw me any old scrap of food. The crazy thing? Common pigeons, the ones that prefer to stay put and

take scraps from strangers, are closely related to homing pigeons—
the most incredible long-distance navigators out there. Homing pigeons are heroes. They were bred for special bird battalions and
trained as spies during the World Wars. One brave World War II
bird-soldier nicknamed G.I. Joe saved more than a thousand British
troops when he swooped in and let the bombers know they needed
to call the bombing off.

"How far is it to my internship?" I gnaw on a Twizzler, savoring
the gummy sweetness and the way my teeth feel pressing against it.

I bet common pigeons eat Twizzlers too. They probably root them
out of garbage cans.

"That's the wonderful thing!" Mom's voice is light again, buoy-
ant. "It's actually closer to the hospital than home. Your commute
will be shorter."

*It's time to connect with my inner homing pigeon.*

Tomorrow I'm starting an internship at a university hospital about
an hour from where we live. And this time I can't screw up. It's the
reason I'm not chilling out with Gillian and a beer at a downtown
music festival in Chicago.

Well . . . it's one of the reasons, at least.

Getting this job required elaborate negotiations between me, an
old family friend who works for the hospital, my resident college adviser, and Professor Stipleman. I begged, I cajoled, I even consid-
ered blackmailing Stipleman. The man must have been a child
prodigy, because he looks like he's about twenty-five—and he's as
mean as a snake. I'm convinced he would have taken great pleasure
in failing me. But then my adviser stepped in and told him my sad, sad
story. I guess Stipleman *does* have a heart, because he agreed to the
plan: I successfully complete a summer internship at the university
hospital, and he waives my final exam, allowing my semester grade to
stand as it was before the exam period began.

In other words, I earn another perfectly mediocre B-.

"As long as I can get to the hospital," I tell her, "I'll live anywhere you want." I'm trying hard to sound brave and focused, just like that pigeon, G.I. Joe. "Text me the address."

"Right away!" she says. "I can't wait to see you!"

When we hang up, I take two Twizzlers from the bag, feeling grateful that they're king-sized, and shove them into my mouth.

*Tick-tick-tick-buzzzzzzzzzzzz.*

The sparrow hops toward me, lets out one last call, and then takes to the sky, heading due north.

"That's right, little guy," I call out to him as he flaps his wings with purpose. "You head north; I'll head south. Because you and I are pulling ourselves together. Starting right now!"

Sure, I'm giving a pep talk to a migratory songbird who appears to be lost, but despite this small piece of evidence to the contrary, I'm great. I'm ready. I'm gonna give those doctors the best damn intern they've ever seen. They'll be calling Stipleman to thank him for sending me. They'll be falling all over themselves to write my recommendations for the premed track.

I am getting back on course.

I climb into the car with renewed purpose, ready to pull onto the interstate heading south. Before I can even start the car, my phone dings with an incoming text.

82 A Street
St. Augustine Beach, FL 32080

St. Augustine. *Oh god.* My stomach does two quick flips. I swallow hard, and a gooey chunk of Twizzler lodges in my throat.

There are so many memories that I'm hoping won't fade. I cling to them all the time. But then there are the legendary disasters from the past few months, the ones I'm desperate to leave far behind. The disaster I most want to obliterate from my consciousness? It happened almost six months ago to the day in St. Augustine, Florida. And my mom, thank God, knows nothing about it.

Of all the beaches in Florida, why does our next "great adventure" have to be there?

I spend the rest of the drive alternately stressing out, pondering fate, and struggling to work out the mysterious ways of the universe. Before I've had time enough to come up with a plausible explanation for my new summer home, I'm off the interstate, driving due east through Anastasia Island.

I travel a short stretch of A1A that's flanked on either side by palmettos and oaks. It's a welcome break from the miles of outlet malls and fast-food restaurants I had to navigate after leaving the interstate. Plus, I'm driving *away* from Old City, St. Augustine, which is a very good thing. Old City is the site of those memories I can't bear, and it's already behind me.

The road makes a sharp right curve, and there it is.

The beach.

I roll down all the windows at once and let the salt air hit my face. I take in the sharp aroma of sand and sea oats. Up in New Haven, when I was hit with exhaust fumes or rotting garbage, I used to close my eyes and try to imagine the scent of the beach. It's nearly impossible to imagine, so now I breathe in deep, almost grateful.

Even though I'm going to a place I've never laid eyes on, smelling the ocean, feeling the warm briny air on my cheeks, makes me feel a little more at home.

My parents were wanderers. I didn't have much of a choice in the matter. We took advantage of every spring break, summer vacation, winter holiday, and even random long weekends to work our way around the globe. No matter where we traveled—and we traveled just about everywhere—I drifted toward the lake, the river, the ocean, the stream. I loved to lie down next to the water and stare up, listening to the lapping or roaring or bubbling of water moving beside me, and watching the sky open wide above. My dad joked that when we finally made it to North Africa, I'd be the first one to find an oasis in the desert and lie down beside it.

The only thing is, we never made it there.

I rest one arm on the open window as I navigate along a crowded A1A, counting down.

Fifth, Fourth, Third, Second, First.

A Street.

I turn left at the Blue Ocean Surf Shop and head down a cute beach lane, straight toward the ocean. Second house on the right.

I'm looking for Mom's silver coupe, but I don't see her car anywhere. Still, the numbers are clearly marked on the mailbox, so I ease onto the empty parking pad in front of number eighty-two.

Before I'm even out of the car, Mom bursts through the front door.

"You're here!" she calls, rushing to embrace me.

We grasp each other tightly, not wanting to let go. I feel her dark curly hair wild against my neck, her thin arms wrapped around me. I take in that earthy scent that is so uniquely hers—woodsmoke and rosemary. I feel shaky, suddenly, and I'm forcing back tears.

That can't happen. The last thing my mother needs is to see me cry. And, for God's sake, I'm not seven. I'm an adult. I can hold myself together for her.

I pull back, letting my hand rest on her shoulder. I notice that she's wearing a smock, which has the strange effect of making me feel like a kid again. I squeeze my eyes shut and turn away from her, so that when I open them again, I'm looking at the house.

"Isn't it so cute?" Mom exclaims.

The house is one of those strange little A-frames that was popular in the seventies. It's painted gray and the windows are trimmed in avocado green. Mom's friend Anita must really be into alliteration, because just in case an A-frame on A Street in St. Augustine Beach isn't enough, she decided to go ahead and build a little gate in the shape of an A on the porch that wraps around the front.

It is cute, but maybe a little *too* cute.

"When Anita brought me here, I knew this was the place for us, Viv. All these As reminded me of you!"

I'm speechless. My stomach starts doing those crazy flips again, and I feel like I need to sit down.

Mom looks at me, puzzled. "Perfect for a girl who hasn't ever earned a B!" she says, clearly surprised by my reaction, worried that I didn't get her joke.

What she doesn't know is that the joke is on me. I remember my first B very clearly—it was for my "unoriginal" interpretation of the relationship between the 1951 United Nations Refugee Convention and Alice Munro's "A Red Dress—1946."

I thought it was good, and by comparison to most of my work during second semester, while I free-fell into such a deep depression that I couldn't even drag myself to the dining hall for meals, the essay was *awesome*. By now, I've earned Cs and Ds and even one straight-up F, on a particularly abysmal calculus test. But Mom doesn't know about any of this. And she doesn't need to know—not yet, at least.

"It's really cute, Mom. I love it." I smile and nod, but what I'm really thinking is: *when my second semester grades show up, we'll be calling an agent to help us find a C-frame house.*

# CHAPTER TWO

## *TJ*

**IT'S 7:08 A.M.,** and this monster parking lot is already full. How is that even possible? I mean, how many sick people can there be in the middle of a Central Florida swamp?

I'm late. Again. Prashanti is gonna murder me. Or fire me.

At this point, I'm so desperate to keep my job that being fired and being murdered would have about the same effect on my life. This isn't exactly my dream job, but it *is* my only way out of that restaurant. And I've gotta get out of there soon, before I lose my mind.

I floor my piece-of-crap SUV and drive up onto the grass. I yank the keys out of the ignition, grab my backpack from the torn-up passenger seat, and take off running across the parking lot. I see an old man heading toward the revolving door, and I know I'm gonna have to find another way in. Not that I have anything against old people. Truth is, I love hanging out with old people. I just don't have time to get behind one of them this morning.

I jog past the revolving glass doors at the hospital's main entrance and enter through the east wing. I shove a heavy door open and head into the emergency stairwell. I'm running up the stairs, digging into my backpack to find the top half of my scrubs.

I should have brought Prashanti some of my great-aunt's *pão de queijo*. She can't get enough of my *tia*'s little cheese buns. I regularly bribe her to forgive my tardiness with a bag full of them. It's Tuesday, which means there would have been a bunch cooling on wire racks in the kitchen, next to the coffeepot. But since I woke up a half hour after my alarm, I didn't make it to the kitchen. I didn't even get my morning coffee. I barely had time to yank on the bottom half of my scrubs, brush my teeth, and slap on some deodorant. I bet my hair is sticking up in twelve directions.

I really need a haircut. And a shave. But who has time? Not me. That's for damn sure.

When I get to the third-floor landing, I drop my backpack and pull off the T-shirt I slept in. The same shirt I wore last night under my work uniform. It smells like *picanha* and *cordeiro*.

Great start to the workweek: I've got an itchy three-day beard, my too-long hair is flying every which way, and I smell like a walking grilled meat kebab.

I really need to find a way to cut back on my shifts at the restaurant, or at least stop working holidays.

I don't mean to sound judgmental, but it's a simple fact that people act like total idiots on holidays. Since my uncle built that bar last Thanksgiving and set up the little stage in the corner with the karaoke machine, tourists think they're supposed to get wasted on caipirinhas, sing bad seventies music at the top of their lungs, and do incredibly stupid stuff.

I get it. They're on vacation and they want to cut loose, relax a little. But who has to stay there until four A.M., scrubbing puke from the toilets and fixing broken chairs? Me. That's who.

I miss the old place, the hole-in-the wall with mismatched tablecloths—the place that locals came to because the food was great and they all loved chatting with my *ótima tia*.

*Enough.* It's pointless to dwell on the past. We all worked our asses off back then, too. It's not like we were living the dream or anything.

Maybe I'm just jealous. Maybe I wish I could spend every holiday singing classic rock ballads and getting wasted with my friends.

Or maybe not.

I don't even like Journey. Plus, the only "friends" I ever actually see are my cousins, and none of us drink. We've seen way too many drunk people doing way too many stupid things they'd regret.

In my family, we don't have time for regrets. *Christ*, I don't even have time to get dressed for work.

I throw the T-shirt into my backpack and pull out the top half of my blue scrubs. I'm backing through the stairwell door and I can't see a thing, because I'm wrestling to pull the stupid scrubs over my head.

I push through the door and head into the hallway, cold air prickling my skin and the smell of antiseptic hitting me hard. When my scrubs finally make it down over my face, I see that I'm inches from colliding with a huge paper cup of Starbucks coffee.

I stumble back. "Sorry," I say to the hands holding the giant coffee. Then I take off in a full sprint toward my unit.

"Hey!" a girl's voice calls out. "Can you tell me where ICU-3H is?"

I don't turn around. "Yeah," I say. "Follow me."

I slow to a jog and take two corners, fast. I push through the double doors of the heart ICU and hold them open for the girl, who's still trailing behind me.

"Sorry." I turn back to look at her. "I'm late for—"

*Wait. Do I know this girl?* She looks familiar, but . . .

"This is it," I say, studying her face. It's strangely familiar—the deep-set hazel eyes, the light smattering of freckles across the bridge of her nose. Her lips are thick and naturally rosy, set against her fair skin and dark brown hair, which falls in loose waves halfway down her back.

"What?" she asks, swiping her chin. "Did I dribble coffee or something?"

*Oh Christ.* Those freckles across her nose. Is this why I recognize her? Or is it the eyes?

*I know those eyes. I know that face.*

"I gotta go clock in." I let go of the door and it swings fast, practically knocking her down.

She stumbles to block the door as I head down the hall to find Prashanti.

Could she possibly be the same girl who showed up at the restaurant out-of-control drunk last Thanksgiving? The one whose tangled hair I pushed out of the way when I had to stop the blood gushing from her nose?

If it really is that girl—and I think it is—what is she doing in the ICU at seven in the morning? (Seven fifteen by now. *Damn.*) Maybe we got a new patient overnight. I'm really hoping it's a valve repair, or something else fast and easy. Because whoever *that girl* is visiting needs to get the hell out of my ICU as soon as possible. I don't need any more complications in my life.

Prashanti is heading straight for me, clipboard clutched tight to her chest, lips pursed and head wobbling from side to side. *She's pissed.*

I give her a weak smile and shrug. "I'm really sorry, Prashanti," I mumble. "Late night at the restaurant. Long holiday weekend, you know?"

But instead of launching into a painful scolding, Prashanti looks right past me and her face breaks into a huge smile.

"Richard! Bertrand!" she calls out to the other staff on the hall. "Sharon!" She grabs me by the forearm and turns me around so that I'm facing the girl directly. "I'm so glad you haven't left yet," she says to Bertrand, the night-shift charge nurse. "Come meet our new intern!"

*New intern? I guess this is just more proof that the universe doesn't give a crap what I need.*

Richard and Sharon rush over from their workstation, while Bertrand wraps the new intern in a hug.

Prashanti leans forward to whisper into my ear, "You and I will have a conversation about tardiness later." She's practically hissing. "Don't you doubt it for a moment."

Then she drops my forearm and turns back to face the girl, who everyone on the unit is gathering around to greet, all bright smiles and sparkling eyes.

I'm looking directly at the new intern's chest and my head is starting to spin. I don't make a habit of staring at girls *there*. The problem is, I've seen that chest before.

Up close.

Without the clothes.

In public.

I'm sure of it now. This is the girl—the pretty-faced hot mess from Thanksgiving. The one who went home with those asshole frat boys even though we insisted that she get a cab.

Of all the drunk tourists, of all the long nights. Why is this the one I can never get out of my head?

I shouldn't have let her go home with those idiots. But *Christ*, it's not my job to babysit every person who comes into the restaurant. I've got enough to worry about. More than enough.

She's talking about how happy she is to be here, but I'm too busy staring at my shoes, the wall, the mobile monitor—anything but her, our new intern.

"Vivi has come all the way from Yale University to spend the summer with us!" Prashanti is practically bubbling over with enthusiasm.

"Yale!" Richard exclaims. "We've got a smarty-pants on our hands."

*Smarty-pants. Who says that? And I don't care where she goes to college; I've seen this Vivi person do some incredibly stupid things.* I clench my jaw tight.

"Yes, she's very intelligent," Prashanti says. "Valedictorian of Holy Innocents!"

*This girl is no holy innocent.*

"And she wants to be a doctor!"

*Of course she wants to be a doctor. Who doesn't?*

Prashanti nudges me. "Where are your manners, TJ? Aren't you going to introduce yourself?"

I drag my gaze up to Prashanti, who is giving me the do-it-now-or-else look.

"We met already," I tell her.

And then, worried that the new intern might think I'm talking about that night at the restaurant, I stumble into a clarification. "Back in the hall, I mean. Uh, by the stairwell. A minute ago."

I offer the girl a quick glance. She looks confused but definitely not sorry. If she remembered me, she would be. I mean, I hope she would. I'm guessing that she doesn't remember any of it at all.

She thrusts out her hand, all formal. "I'm Vivi," she says.

I look down at her hand, knowing I have to take it.

"TJ," I say, shaking her hand once and then dropping it. "I'm a nurse's aide." And then I add, "I don't want to be a doctor."

She looks right at me with her big hazel eyes opened wide. Maybe she's pissed off or embarrassed about the whole "very intelligent" thing, because her cheeks turn pink.

"While it might appear that Mr. Five-O'clock Shadow and a Bed Head is working toward becoming a cologne model," Richard says, "he actually aspires to be a registered nurse—like me!"

*This is a three-day shadow,* I think. And I do not aspire to be like

Richard. He's a heart nurse who smokes a pack of cigarettes a day. *How is that even possible?*

I run my hand through my hair in a futile attempt to tame it. "Long weekend," I say. I'm sure that by now I'm looking almost as annoyed as I feel.

"It's hard work being chased around all weekend by *the ladies*," Sharon says. Well, she actually kind of sings "the ladies" part.

If Sharon weren't the sweetest woman I know, I'd tell her exactly what's on my mind. Instead I look down at my feet—again.

I love all these people. Really, I do. But they have no idea what my life is like.

"All right, all right," Bertrand urges with his honey-sweet voice. "Let's stop teasing TJ—the poor child looks exhausted."

It doesn't even matter what Bertrand's saying. Just hearing the cadence of his voice makes my heart rate slow down.

Bertrand has that effect on everyone. He's a natural. To be honest, he's kind of my hero. I know I'll never be as good as Bertrand, but if I can manage to keep this job and get through school, I hope someday to be *that* nurse—the one whose simple presence heals.

Seven hours into a quiet eight-hour shift, and things finally have started to look up. Prashanti gave me another scolding for being perpetually late, but I'm pretty sure she's forgiven me. (She always does.) The new intern has been shadowing Richard all day, so I haven't had to see much of her. I'm not sure how I'm going to last an entire summer avoiding her, but I guess I'm just gonna have to take it one day at a time.

I've got the good patients today: Mrs. Blankenship in 306 made me give her an extra-long sponge bath, which Sharon—predictably— gave me shit about. But Mrs. Blankenship's a sweet lady, and her kids are really nice. I mean, some kids treat their elderly parents like total crap, but not Mrs. Blankenship's. They take turns coming over from Starke. One of them is always here, waiting to give her what she needs. I guess she was a pretty good mom to them. She doesn't have a husband. Maybe she's a widow, or divorced. I don't know. I never ask questions. I just give baths, change sheets, check fluid levels, and make small talk with them if it seems like they might be in pain.

"Good weekend?" Mrs. Blankenship's daughter asks.

"Yeah, it was okay," I tell her, turning Mrs. Blankenship onto her side.

"Did you take your girlfriend out?" Mrs. Blankenship asks, teasing. "Dancing, maybe? Or to a beach luau?"

"You know I don't have a girlfriend," I tell her. *And if I did, I wouldn't be taking her to a beach luau. It's not 1964.*

"I find that impossible to believe," she says, looking back at me. "I mean, look at you!"

I can't *look at me.* Because I currently happen to be inspecting her bare ass for bedsores. And anyway, I have no idea what she means. Like, if I look in the mirror, I will magically *see* the invented girlfriend?

They always ask me questions—especially the old ladies. There are a lot of old ladies on the heart ward. They usually want me to tell them about my girlfriends, which is pretty much a dead-end conversation.

If I don't even have time for a shower, then I definitely don't have time for a girlfriend.

The patients also ask me where I'm from. I don't mind them asking, but I hate it when they try to guess—they're all over the place. Usually, they think I'm half something: half Indian? Half Japanese? Half Arab? Half Hispanic?

I think it's the blue eyes that throw them off.

I always reply with: "Nope. One hundred percent American, born and raised right down the road, in St. Augustine." Which inevitably is followed by: "But I mean where are you *from?*"

My parents are from Brazil, which makes me *not* Hispanic, and not any of those other things, either. There's a little Japanese in there, though. My mom's granddad. And some German, too. And, like most Brazilians, I've got plenty of African heritage. But I'm not going to dive into the history of colonialism while I'm giving these people a bath, so I don't bother to explain.

"We need you in 311," Prashanti says, sticking her head into the doorway.

*Room 311.* That's Ángel, aka the biggest pain in the ass in this entire hospital. He's got a pretty bad case of viral cardiomyopathy, and he's still a kid. I mean, I guess he's at least eighteen, since they sent him over here from the children's hospital, but he's, like, five feet tall and a hundred pounds. I'm not super-brawny or anything, but even I can pick him up with one arm. For real. I've done it before, while using the other one to block him. He was punching me, just for the hell of it. Or maybe because I touched his Johnson while I was bathing him. But *damn.* I have to. It's my job.

Anyway, Ángel is in really bad shape today, so he's barely even been awake. I only feel a little guilty to be relieved. I know the kid must be in a ton of pain, since his heart is swollen up like a balloon and his joints are all inflamed. They did another biopsy last week, and they're pumping all kinds of medicine into him to reduce the swelling of his heart, so he'll probably be back to his pain-in-the-ass self in a couple of days. I'm gonna enjoy the break while I can.

"Code Blue. ICU-3H, 308. Repeat. Code Blue. ICU-3H, 308. Clear the floor."

I hear the code blue over the loudspeakers and head out into the hallway to make sure the floor is clear. Since this is the heart ICU, it's pretty common to deal with cardiac arrest. But when they want the floor clear, it means they're heading into emergency surgery, so it's serious, and maybe ugly.

Yeah. This one's ugly.

Richard's on top of the patient from room 308—a quadruple bypass with some unexpected complications. Poor guy. Richard has the paddles going, and it looks like some of the patient's sutures have torn open, because he's bleeding pretty bad from the chest. Sharon and some resident I've never laid eyes on are pushing him around the corner, fast.

And then that Vivi girl comes sauntering out of the break room, holding a container of yogurt, clueless. Without thinking about it, I reach over and grab her by the elbow, pulling her toward the wall.

"Watch out," I say, nodding toward the gurney speeding toward us. She lets out a gasp and backs into me.

"We've gotta deal with this bleeding, people!" the resident calls out.

They stop in front of us, and Richard yells for Prashanti, who comes out of 304, holding a clamp. Richard tugs on the chest sutures, and Prashanti moves in to stop the bleeding from a busted artery, but not before a bunch of blood spurts from it onto Vivi, who's still got her back pressed against me, me pressed against the wall.

It all sort of happens at once: Prashanti calls out, "Go!" Richard hits the paddles again, the resident pushes the gurney hard, and the Vivi girl collapses, her yogurt spilling all over my thigh. I catch her, just in time for her to avoid being run over by a fast-moving gurney.

And here she is, passed out in my arms. Again.

*At least this time she has her shirt on.*

I pick her up and carry her to the empty bed in 302, trying to ignore the yogurt on my thigh, and call over my shoulder to Prashanti, "We're gonna need some salts over here!"

*So this girl wants to be a doctor?*

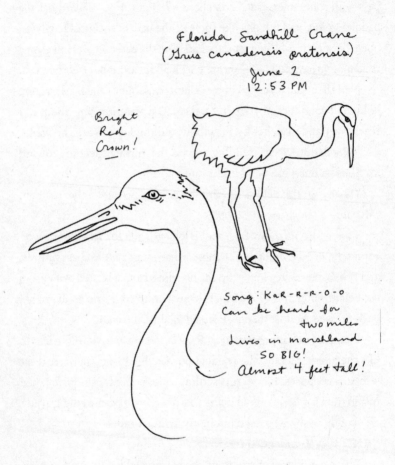

Florida Sandhill Crane
(Grus canadensis pratensis)
June 2
12:53 PM

Bright
Red
Crown!

Song: KaR-R-R-O-O
Can be heard for
two miles
Lives in marshland
SO BIG!
Almost 4 feet tall!

# CHAPTER THREE

## *VIVI*

BIRD JOURNAL

June 2, 12:53 P.M.

Florida sandhill crane (*Grus canadensis pratensis*)

*Today I shared my lunch with one of Florida's biggest birds! He*
*was sweet, even though he did steal some of my sandwich.*

Habitat: marshes, agricultural fields, freshwater prairies.

Unique Markings: adults have red crown.

Nesting Behaviors: both male and female participate in
incubating the eggs. Offspring begin traveling from nest
with both parents very quickly—just twenty-four hours
after hatching.

*This bird is enormous! Almost four feet tall.*

**"AND HOW DO *YOU* FEEL** about your first week with us?"

Prashanti is standing in the doorway of Room 308, watching me
avert my eyes as Richard changes Mrs. Blankenship's catheter bag.

"About my first week?" I ask. "Oh, um . . ." I look out the window, toward the pine bench on the retention pond. I've just returned
from a lunch break on that bench, where I shared a tuna sandwich

and some peaceful quality time with an enormous Florida sandhill crane.

I know I shouldn't feed wild birds, but this one stood so patiently beside me, waiting. He wasn't aggressive at all. So even though he was one of the biggest birds I have ever laid eyes on, I wasn't worried about getting close to him, or about reaching out my hand to feed him.

I'm not easily intimidated.

He's gone now, but not too far. I can still hear his loud rattling *kar-r-r-o-o-o*. They say you can hear the call of a sandhill crane from as far as two miles away. He may not have the most beautiful song (that would be the winter wren, in my humble opinion), or the most elaborate (that would definitely be the mockingbird, who steals and samples from all sorts of songs, like the EDM DJ of avian music). But wow. This crane makes up for it in sheer volume. His incredibly loud call is pulling my concentration from the conversation at hand.

"Vivi?" Prashanti snaps.

"Oh, uh, it was pretty good," I say.

Richard looks up at me and smiles encouragingly—because he's nice, and because by "pretty good," I mean "a total disaster."

"Well, that certainly is descriptive," Prashanti says, deadpan.

"Maybe a little more detail?" Richard asks, eyes bright, head nodding.

"I know I still have a lot to learn."

*Like how to not pass out at the sight of blood, for starters.*

"She'll be fine," Richard says, now inspecting Mrs. Blankenship's catheter tube.

I turn away, because I can't bear to watch. I feel woozy just thinking about it.

*Kar-r-r-o-o-o, kar-r-r-o-o-o.*

"Let's take a break and get a cold drink," Prashanti tells me, motioning for me to come with her.

"Absolutely," I reply enthusiastically. I need some distance from that rattling crane.

We ride the elevator in silence. It's afternoon on a Friday, and the cafeteria is practically empty. She buys me a sweet tea and leads me to a table in the corner.

"It's time for us to rethink your responsibilities, Vivi, in light of your weak constitution." She says it before I've even had a chance to sit down.

Yes. As it turns out, I have a *weak constitution*. In one short week, I have managed to produce sufficient evidence for a brief scientific case study on the topic, the outline for which would look something like this:

1. Proximity to any and all bags of fluid elicits in subject an immediate gag reflex. Such fluids include, but are not limited to:
   a) urine
   b) blood
   c) *oh God, I can barely even stand the thought*—runoff from healing wounds.

In summary: gag reflex exhibited in cases (a) and (b) results in full-on head-hanging-over-toilet pukefest in case (c). It's happened twice this week already.

2. Observing a broad range of mundane procedures results in both subject's eyes involuntarily squeezing shut, or, alternatively, in subject's entire torso turning away from the unsightly procedure. Such procedures include, but are not limited to:
   a) the insertion of IV needles
   b) the changing of catheters
   c) the drawing of blood.

In summary: Involuntary body motions exhibited in cases (a) and (b) may escalate into full shudder in case (c). This produces significant embarrassment on the part of the subject.

3. Contact with the partially or fully naked bodies of sick people appears to result in a sort of wince. Subject's wince includes, but is not limited to:

   a) shoulders shrug forward
   b) neck muscles contract
   c) eyebrows knit together.

Subject stresses that such physical reactions occur without her voluntary consent, and to the dismay of the nice patients whose bodies our subject can't bear to see. . . .

"There's no shame in admitting it, Vivi," Prashanti says. "All of us must come to terms with who we are."

I nod, staring down at the table.

"But it's also my responsibility to ensure your safety. To avoid any more . . . *incidents.*"

I prefer not to recall the worst of the incidents—the one that landed me in the arms of an incredibly surly nurse's aide who is *so not my type.*

Which begs the question: Why do I feel dizzy every time he looks at me?

TJ is buff, and incredibly sloppy. He has shaggy black hair that's always in need of brushing, and his jaw is stubbly—not in that sexy five-o'clock-shadow way, but more in the patchy forgot-to-shave way. His scrubs are always slightly wrinkled, as if he pulled them from the bottom of a laundry basket (probably still dirty).

His eyes, though.

They're haunting, almost translucent blue. And they're framed by clear mahogany skin and thick dark lashes.

I know girls who would auction their firstborn child in exchange for those lashes.

Despite those incredible eyes set against gorgeous skin, he isn't the kind of guy I'm usually into. He's too bulked up, and disheveled. I'm more drawn to willowy artists and musicians, of the skinny-jeans-and-a-buzz-cut variety.

But still, I feel an inexplicable vertigo every time I look at him.

When I woke up from the unfortunate incident with the squirting artery, I looked directly into his almost-translucent eyes while he gently wiped my face with a warm cloth. Then I let my own eyes fall shut again, feeling a strange, intense déjà vu and thinking, *This must be a dream.*

"Hey," he barked. "You need to get up. I gotta change these sheets." He grabbed my forearm and tugged hard. "A *real* patient is coming up from surgery."

I sat up, unsteady, as he thrust the bloodstained cloth into a bin. "You're cleaned up, except the clothes."

I looked down at my skirt. Blood was splattered across it.

*Why did I decide to wear a skirt, again? Oh yes, to impress my boss with my professionalism.*

My head started to spin. But then I felt his warm hand against my back, holding me steady.

"Put your head between your knees and breathe deep," he growled.

I nodded and let my head drop.

"You can change into those." I didn't dare sit up, but I turned my head and saw that he was gesturing toward a clean set of scrubs folded in a neat stack on the edge of the bed.

"Thanks," I said.

"Just doing my job," he mumbled, looking away. "Which, by the way, you're making a lot harder."

*Ouch.* That was cold but probably also deserved.

He hasn't spoken a word to me since, which is fine. The last thing I need in my life is to be obsessing over a surly guy. It is strange, though. He doesn't seem to be particularly surly with anyone else. I always overhear him laughing and joking with Sharon and Richard when he thinks I'm not around. And sometimes I'll go around a corner and catch him smiling. But his smile falters when he sees me coming, and he always turns away.

Whatever. It's a big unit. We'll keep our distance and things will be fine.

That is, if I can even keep my internship.

I take a long sip of my sweet tea and absently watch a cafeteria worker replenish the salad bar.

"You're a lovely young woman, Vivi," Prashanti is telling me. "And you have a bright future ahead, but are you quite certain that you want to spend the summer *here*?"

It's not an unreasonable question. My first week has been an unqualified disaster.

"I would be happy to help you find something more suited to your gifts," Prashanti says. "Give it some thought over the weekend, will you?"

I nod and smile, but I can't seem to produce any words.

Last August, it wasn't easy to decide to leave my parents—to travel a thousand miles away for college, when they could have used my help. I made a promise to myself on the day I left home. I promised that I'd do something that *mattered*, that I'd commit my life to making a difference. I'd heal people.

I'm starting to wonder whether this is a promise I can keep.


On the way home from the hospital, I decide to stop in at Kyle's—the fish market on the old Jacksonville highway. I ask the guy to give me the freshest fish he's got, and then I go next door to the produce stand for what I need to make a salad.

I'm growing tired of the Bait Shack. I love cold-boiled shrimp, and the Bait Shack has some of the best I've ever eaten. I love how it's served in a red plastic bowl, and how the communal tables are lined with half-full bottles of cocktail sauce and cheap rolls of paper towels. But we eat there every night, and Mom's not showing much interest in the kitchen.

Dad was the chef in our family. . . .

*Go big or go home, Vivi.* That's what my dad used to tell me when I was feeling overwhelmed. My father never did anything halfway. He worked hard; he adventured hard. He somehow managed to turn even the most mundane of activities into an experience.

*You won't believe this, hon! Vivi and I were heading back from her field hockey practice—out there on 301. We stopped in at a tomato stand that was advertising vine-ripe tomatoes. We picked up some swordfish down at the market, and we were reminiscing on that fabulous trip to Tulum, thinking maybe we could get some good heirloom tomatoes and make a pico de gallo to go with the fish, like we had at that little place down there last summer.*

*And this guy, working the tomato stand, shows us some of the most pathetic specimens of tomatoes I've ever laid eyes on. I told him I grew up on a farm, and I knew a vine-ripe tomato when I saw one. He looked me up and down and then he told me if I was willing to pay, he'd take us out to the farm himself, and Vivi and I could pick our tomatoes straight from the vine.*

*Vivi jumped right on in the back of his truck and said, "Let's go!" I pulled off my tie and suit jacket and hopped next to her. He took us out past that old clapboard church up 301, and we pulled up next to this big ol' greenhouse. Vivi and I jumped out and headed straight for the sweetest plum tomatoes I've ever seen, and cucumbers as long as my forearm, still on the vine. And inside that greenhouse, Vivi here picked up some of the most beautiful, delicate butter lettuce you could imagine. Didn't you, Vivi?*

*Growin' out there in the middle of a Florida summer, wasn't it, Vivi? Oh, girls! We're gonna eat well tonight!*

That's how my dad and I put together salad for a Wednesday night dinner. So, needless to say, when it came time for me to think about college, we were *going big.*

I took every AP class offered at my high school; I sorted musty clothes every Saturday morning at the Last Stop Thrift Shop; I was yearbook editor, class secretary, and president of the Key Club. I drove forty minutes one way to practice field hockey because the Ivy League loves that sport.

I know how to *go big.* My father taught me that.

When I get back to the house, I'm still thinking about that perfect farm-fresh salad, wondering if I can re-create it for Mom. I head through the A-shaped gate and into a dark hallway.

"I got some mahi from Kyle's," I call out. "I thought maybe I'd try making it with avocado salsa, like we had in Roatán. Remember?"

"Sounds perfect," Mom says, poking her head out from the bedroom. "I'll be right out to help."

The bedroom is behind the living area, with a soaring, pointed ceiling and a spiral staircase twisting through the middle of the room. I drop the produce bag in the kitchen and head back out to the car for the fish. I pause on my way back for long enough to notice a huge pile of bills stacked on the table by the door. The one on top is as bright red as the crown of that sandhill crane I shared a tuna sandwich with. *That can't be good.* I go to pick it up, but then I see a check from CarMax sitting next to the pile.

"Where did you say your car is?" I call out. "Back at the Winter Park house?"

"Oh no. I sold it!" Mom says brightly. "You know I never liked that car. And the bike is perfect for St. Augustine."

I pick up the red envelope. It's a water bill for our house in Winter Park, the Orlando suburb where we would be living if we weren't here in the A-frame. The water bill has FINAL NOTICE stamped across the top in bold letters.

Mom can be a little flaky sometimes. Dad loved that about her. He said she was like a moon, with many phases, but all of them beautiful. Sometimes she had everything together; sometimes she had nothing together. I didn't always love Mom's phases—particularly the ones in which she forgot to pack my lunch or send in a permission slip for the class field trip. But everything tended to work out okay. A kind teacher would share her lunch with me, or the principal would text my mom and she'd rush up to school to fill out the permission slip. I always knew she would phase back around and all would be well.

I guess she's in that phase where bills go unpaid.

I put the red bill back on top of the stack, and that's when I notice it—a letter from Yale.

Almost all of Yale's communication with students is by email. But I remember my resident adviser joking that, when the administration wants to be sure your parents see something, they send it the old-fashioned way. That usually means the news is bad.

Whatever this news is, I'm not ready for Mom to see it.

She comes out of her room, still fiddling with an earring. I hurry to tuck the letter into the waistband of my pants before she pulls me into a hug.

"Don't worry about all that right now," she says into my hair. "We'll take care of it later."

"I'll grill the fish if you'll make the salad," I say, giving a little squeeze and then stepping back. "With that white balsamic dressing?"

"Absolutely," she says. "Your wish is my command."

I follow her down the hall, toward the kitchen.

"Do I look sufficiently artsy?" she asks, turning to face me again.

She's got on a pair of cowboy boots that I helped her pick out on a trip to Big Sky, Montana, cutoff denim shorts, a fitted T-shirt, and a flowing vest with geometric prints. Her light brown hair is pulled up in a messy bun and she's wearing her moonstone hoop earrings.

"You look great," I tell her. It's true. She looks beautiful and vibrant and alive. I, on the other hand, look like the walking dead. It's been a very long week.

We wander into the small, open kitchen, and I look inside the fridge: milk, orange juice, and a couple of containers of Greek yogurt. That's it. There's plenty of room for the fish and the bag of ice that's keeping it fresh.

The linoleum counters are all covered with long stretches of thin cloth, dyed with angelfish, whales, manatees. I've gotten used to this—our kitchen doubling as Mom's art studio.

"After dinner Wendy and I are going to the Old City for the art walk—they do it on the first Friday of every month. Come with? There are some wonderful galleries."

*Oh no, I will not be going to the Old City.* I've been avoiding that part of St. Augustine like the plague, and I don't intend to stop avoiding it now.

"Who's Wendy?" I ask.

"She's the batik artist I told you about—the one who gave me lessons last spring. You'll love her—"

"I'm exhausted," I interrupt. "I want to meet Wendy, but not tonight. I've got big plans for a Netflix marathon on the couch." I discreetly touch my side, where the letter from Yale is tucked away. *And I have to read this letter. Alone.*

I make room on the counter for a cutting board, and I try to remember how Dad used to season fresh fish. *Keep it simple, Vivi.* That was always his advice on fresh seafood or produce. *Let the flavor come through.*

In this case, I don't have much of a choice, since the pantry is practically bare. I settle on a little olive oil, salt, and pepper.

Mom makes a salad while I grill the fish and cut up the avocado. We eat on the back deck, and even though we're a few houses away from the ocean, we can still hear the surf. It sounds loud tonight, maybe because we can't seem to come up with anything to talk about. So we sit in silence and eat our fish, lulled by the ocean's rhythm.

I overcooked it. I wish I had paid more attention when Dad was around to show me how. The avocado is good, though. Perfectly ripe.

A bright yellow vintage Checker cab pulls into the drive, and Mom stands to clear her plate. "That's Wendy," she says. "I'm off to the art walk!"

"Have a great time," I tell her, deciding not to comment on the unusual vehicle her friend drives. "I'll take care of the dishes."

I sit on the deck and watch her climb into the car. Wendy's cab pulls away, sputtering black smoke, and I take the envelope from my waistband to open the letter. No use putting off the inevitable.

## NOTICE OF ACADEMIC WARNING

I read quickly. The letter is short, and to the point: as a result of my grade in Stipleman's class (combined with a string of barely passing grades), I currently have insufficient course credits and, consequently, a failing grade point average. I've been placed on academic probation.

In other words, unless I successfully complete this internship, I will *not* be permitted to continue at Yale.

*Oh no. This can't happen.*

High school valedictorians don't turn into college dropouts.

College dropouts don't get into medical school.

And I will be going to medical school if it's the last thing I do.

I knew I needed this internship for the premed track, because I knew it would give me a passing grade in Stipleman's class. What I didn't know? This internship is the only thing that will get me back to Yale in the fall.

Part of me wants to cry, and another part of me feels like cheering, because—if I want to cry, it means that I care. And I haven't really cared about much of anything for a very long time. But I don't cry or cheer. Instead I pull out my phone and send Prashanti a text:

> So sorry to bother you on a Friday evening. I just want you to know that I am willing to do anything you need—anything at all. I love working on the heart ICU, and I really hope you'll let me stay! Have a great weekend! See you Monday!

*Go big, Vivi.*

I stare at my phone all weekend, but Prashanti doesn't reply to my text.

I do, however, get an enormous string of texts and several Face-Time calls from Gillian, who has moved on to the third stop in our epic summer music tour—without me. I guess she took advantage of the travel time between shows to send me a wide range of selfies summarizing the trip so far: Gillian with two dreadlocked hippies at the Firefly Festival. Gillian on someone's shoulders at Bonnaroo. Gillian pressed against a stage with the Boston skyline behind her, the lead singer of a band I don't recognize singing right at her.

Finally, on Sunday afternoon, I relent and pick up a call. I can barely hear her over the screaming fans and blaring music.

"Vivi!"

"Hey, Gillian. Where are you?"

"Vivi! It's your favorite band!" She's drunk. I've heard her drunk voice enough times to know. "We miss you! I wanted you to live vicariously!"

Then, just in case all of this isn't painful enough already, she lifts the phone in the air to reveal that, indeed, my favorite band is onstage ten feet in front of her, singing one of the best songs of all time.

It sounds like crap through the phone. After about ninety seconds, it's clear that she's forgotten she called, since I'm still hearing one of the best songs of all time, but I'm seeing a blur of feet and legs.

I hang up, drop my phone on the bed, and head out to the beach for a swim.

It's stifling hot, and the beach is crammed with people, but still. Maybe if I go out and let my head get slammed by a few big waves, I'll forget about the summer that could have been.


On Monday morning I arrive early. I wait next to Prashanti's locker, and as soon as I see her come through the door, tote bag in one arm and lunch box in the other, I launch in. "This ICU is exactly where I want to be. I'll do whatever it takes to prove it to you, Prashanti."

I swallow hard and smile wide.

"I really like it here. I think maybe I just need some time to adjust," I continue, watching her silently stuff the tote bag into her locker.

I worked too hard for this. I can't let it go. I owe that much to my dad, at the very least.

Prashanti turns and steps toward me. "Perhaps we can secure an administrative position. Or possibly something in the accounting office?"

"But you see, I have to do this. There's no other way." A strange stillness has descended on me. I speak slowly, my voice even. "Do you remember what I explained in my cover letter? About last December? How I couldn't go back to take my exams? And how my adviser made this agreement with my professor, because they knew I wanted to be premed?"

"Yes, of course, but—"

I need to try a new tactic. This isn't going anywhere. It's time to beg.

"You have to understand," I say, my voice rising and my heart starting to flutter. "I wasn't being irresponsible. I mean, I know you hate it when people don't take responsibility seriously. But that's not it. It's just—I had to help my mom." Now I'm rambling, pleading, tripping over my words. "We had to deal with the body and the funeral and she was so—"

I hate hearing myself say this. I despise it—I despise myself in this moment. Because *who invokes the memory of her dead father as a way to keep a job?*

*Apparently, I do.*

"Of course, of course." Prashanti's face goes all soft. "We'll come up with something," she says, taking my clammy hand in hers. "We can make this work."

"Really?" I ask. "I can stay?"

"Yes, yes. Now let me get my paperwork done before rounds begin. We'll talk after rounds."

Beaming, I head to the break room to pour myself a cup of coffee. As promised, Prashanti meets me there after morning rounds. She brings a thin stack of papers from her duffel bag and announces, "I have an idea!"

"Great!" I exclaim, layering on the positivity.

"I reviewed your résumé," she says, waving the papers toward me, "and I think we have the perfect position for you here on ICU-3H."

Richard and TJ are in the break room too. I watch as both turn to look at her, clearly wondering what might be the perfect ICU position for someone with a now notoriously "weak constitution."

"You're fluent in Spanish?" Prashanti asks.

"Yes." I nod vigorously. "That's right."

"Wonderful!" she replies. "We have a patient who needs extra attention, and he also speaks Spanish. You'll be invaluable as his interpreter."

"You mean Ángel?" Richard asks. "You're putting her on *full-time* Ángel duty?"

TJ grins. TJ is not one to smile often, at least not when I'm around. So I'm starting to sense how bad this assignment might be.

Prashanti glares at Richard and TJ, head lowered slightly, eyes on fire.

*This woman is a force of nature.*

"Sorry," Richard says, suddenly sheepish. "So, Vivi, where did you learn Spanish?" I think he's trying to change the subject.

"In Buenos Aires," I respond, unable to contain my genuine enthusiasm. "I spent a glorious semester there in high school."

"Well, that sounds really, uh—"

"Glorious," TJ says, deadpan, cutting Richard off midsentence.

And so begins my *glorious* first day as Ángel's babysitter.

# CHAPTER FOUR

## ÁNGEL

**"ALL RIGHT, ÁNGEL.** Let's try to make this as painless as possible."

*Let's do that, TJ. And, while we're at it, maybe you can find somebody who will tell me what the hell is going on.*

But first, let's you and me get this awkward part over with. I'm gonna go ahead and let you into my head.

Yeah, you.

*Why?* you ask. I dunno. I guess I figure maybe if I let a few more people up in here, it might keep me from losing my mind. Maybe you people can help me hold it together, you know? Or maybe not. Doesn't matter.

Honestly, it would be nice just to have somebody else know what I'm thinking. I mean, nobody around this place understands it, maybe because I need to explain in Mam. Yeah, Mam. It's a language. I figure you've probably never heard of it. No big deal. As long as you're up in my head with me, it really doesn't matter much, does it?

You don't believe me? Okay, try this. Look out of the nearest window, and just notice what's going on. I mean, really watch. What you're seeing, what your brain is telling you you're seeing—it's not happening in a language, is it? It's just happening.

So, that's settled. You're up in here with me and I'm letting you in on all of it.

Well, okay, not *all* of it. I mean, you don't need to know what it feels like for me to take a dump, or to . . .

Let's move on to other topics.

Those people—TJ and the pretty girl who showed up this morning—they have no clue. Nobody around here does. You want me to prove it to you? Yeah, okay. Check this out:

TJ is standing at the whiteboard, holding tight to a big blue marker. He looks down at his phone and reads, *"¿Cuál es su meta para el día?"* He butchers it, as always. I can't figure it out, but somehow his phone tells him how to speak bad Spanish.

Wanna know why I already know what he's asking me? Because he asks me the same incredibly stupid question every day.

Every. Single. Day.

I have no idea how to answer it. Since nobody has even managed to explain to me what I'm doing in this place, it's hard to know what I want.

*So, no, TJ. How about we* don't *make this as painless as possible.*

Hey, I never claimed to be an actual angel.

I lift my head and shoulders off the bed, which only kinda hurts my chest.

*"¿Mi mata? Me matas? Me vas a matar!"*

I start mashing hard on the nurse call button and pick up the stupid little phone attached to my bed rail.

*"Policía! Policía!"* I yell into the phone. *"Me van a matar! They kill me!"*

The pretty white girl with long brown hair, who was sitting in a chair by my bed when I woke up this morning, stands up and walks over to the board. I'm not complaining. She's nice to me, and I like watching her. But I can't exactly figure out what she's doing here.

"He heard you say *mata* instead of *meta*," she says to TJ, all patient and calm. "*Matar* means to murder."

He shakes his head slowly, looking down at the ground. "He knows what I said."

Yeah, sure I know. I speak Spanish, and a little English, too. I'll admit it: I understand more than I speak. But these people don't need to know any of that—not until I know what's happening around here. Let me tell you something: as far as I can figure out, they might be trying to kill me. For real. Oh, you think I'm being stupid? Paranoid? I hear you. But listen to this: I woke up in a room a few weeks ago with a bunch of strangers standing around. And I'm strapped into a bed with a metal railing. I mean, I can't even lift my arms because of these huge black straps over them. And machines are going crazy around me, making all kinds of insane noise, and a dude is standing over me with a knife. Okay, maybe not a knife, but I'm telling you, he was about to cut my chest open with whatever that thing was. Until I started screaming. What the hell else was I supposed to do? Then this lady comes at me with a massive needle, and the next thing I know, I'm in dreamland.

I wake up here, feeling like I've been sleeping for a month. I can barely catch my breath, even though I'm flat on my back in bed; I've got strange pains stabbing my chest and my shoulders, like a sharp knife digging in; and my legs are all puffy, so I can't even find my ankles. Nobody's telling me where I am or what's going on.

Every once in a while, a doctor comes in with a lady who speaks Spanish, and they start talking really fast.

Oh, wait. Don't go thinking I'm stupid or something. I get what they're saying. But then they're talking about all this stuff I've never heard of, and how serious it all is, and they're using some strange words that don't sound like English *or* Spanish.

All the while, I'm thinking: I spend my days chasing turkeys, for chrissake—twelve hours a day out in the brutal heat, taking care of scrawny little turkeys that the rich people call "heirloom." I guess they are supposed to taste better. Whatever. It's a job. But I'm doing this in Florida, where it's crazy hot and there's no shade. I'd been feeling a little weak, sure, but I was repairing the shed that day, and it was like kneeling on the surface of the freakin' sun up on that roof. I probably just passed out from the heat or something. No big deal.

Except I guess it is a big deal. Or, at least, they're all treating me like it is.

"I'll try asking," the new girl tells TJ.

"Be my guest," he responds, putting down the marker and heading straight for the window.

This should be good.

"What. Is. Your. Goal. For. The. Day?" She points to each word as she says it. Then she goes back and points to each word again. *"¿Cuál. Es. Su. Meta. Para. El. Día?"* She speaks each word really carefully, in a super-fancy Spanish accent. Then she looks at me, concentrating hard, her finger pointing again to one of the words on the board. "Your goal. *Su ambición. Su objetivo.*"

Girl's like a walking, talking Spanish dictionary! Which would be fascinating if I weren't feeling so incredibly annoyed. I mean, *my goal*? I'll tell you people what my goal is. Maybe, for starters, to figure out why they're keeping me here against my will, like a *criminal*.

Okay, yeah. As jails go, this place is pretty sweet. Sponge baths every morning, three free meals a day that I get to order from a menu. Three clean pillows. A comfortable bed that moves up and down with a button. Warm blankets whenever I want them. (I mean, they're, like, warmed up in an oven or something—super cozy.) But still. Until I figure out what's going on here, there's no way I'm gonna play their little "goal for the day" game.

TJ, who can't seem to bring himself to look at the pretty girl, keeps staring out the window. "I'm telling you, he knows exactly what I'm asking him." He's sort of growling at her. "We go through this every day. He's just being a pain in the ass."

TJ's right, of course. I'm just messing with them. I've gotta do *something* to pass the time in here.

"Where did you say he's from?" she asks, all concerned and stuff.

"Guatemala."

Her face gets all bright, and she steps forward so she's standing right by the bed.

"*Usted habla español?*" she asks.

I shrug.

"*O tal vez usted habla uno de los idiomas indígenas?*" she says.

I shrug again.

She bites her lip. "Maybe he doesn't speak Spanish," she says to TJ. "Some Guatemalans don't really speak much Spanish. There are, like, dozens of indigenous languages spoken there."

He's still staring out the window, looking mad. It's kind of weird, how angry he looks. Usually he doesn't really mind me messing with him. Most days I can get a laugh out of him.

"I'm trying to remember some of those languages," she says to TJ. "I mean, what they're called."

She lays her hand on my arm and says, "*Usted habla K'iche'? Kaqchikel? Q'anjob'al?*"

Dang. She's a walking, talking dictionary and encyclopedia of Guatemalan languages, too. I shrug again, but really soft, because I don't want her to take her hand away. It feels good. Warm like the blankets, but softer.

"Uh . . . Oh, wait! Mam?" she asks.

She guessed it. But there's no way I'm giving her the satisfaction of knowing that.

Okay, now watch this. Pay attention, because it's gonna be good: I put my hand over hers, which is still resting on my arm. Then I look the girl right in the eyes and say, *"Contigo, señorita, solamente hablo el idioma del amor."* I lift her hand and kiss it gently. That should mess with her plenty—me saying that, with her, I can only speak the language of *love*.

Her cheeks turn pink and she pulls her hand away, which knocks the oxygen tube from my nose. No big deal. It's not like I'm gonna die without it. I can breathe on my own just fine, at least for a little while. So I don't worry about it. Instead I look at her face. It's pretty and smooth.

Her eyes, though. I'll let you in on something about the pretty girl. From far away—she looks like the kind of girl who's never suffered a day in her life. But she has these big hazel eyes that look a little sad, like she's been through something hard.

Which makes me feel only a tiny bit bad for messing with her.

"Cut it out, Ángel," TJ says, walking back to the whiteboard.

"Should I try again?" she asks.

"I'm just gonna come up with one," he says, but not to her. "Prashanti will blame me if you don't have a goal for the day written up here." He's talking to me, but not really. Because he thinks I don't understand him. "And she'll be coming to change out your meds in, like, two minutes."

He starts to write, and that's not gonna be any fun. He'll probably write something pointless, like "to sit up in my bed without help."

I gotta stop him. If I don't, these people are gonna leave and I'm gonna be stuck in this bed all day, staring at a whiteboard where there's a stupid goal—that's maybe okay for, like, the eighty-year-old grandma next door, but not for me. I'm eighteen years old! *Eighteen*. And the messed-up thing: I can't even sit up. I don't know why, but it's like there's a pile of stones on my chest, and they keep getting heavier, and most of the time I can barely move.

*Why?* you ask? Your guess is as good as mine. . . .

"Ahem." I clear my throat loudly.

"Oh, you're actually going to cooperate?" TJ asks, all grumpy. He starts to erase whatever he was writing.

Then I talk all formal, trying to sound like the pretty girl with the sad eyes and fancy Spanish. *"Mi meta para el día es"*—I pause for dramatic effect—*"jugar al fútbol. Messi y yo contra TJ y Prashanti."*

TJ's holding the blue marker right up against the whiteboard.

"What did he say?" he asks the girl. He's still staring at the board.

"His goal for the day is to play two-on-two soccer. He and Messi against you and Prashanti."

TJ's empty hand flies to his forehead. "Jesus Christ," he says. And then: "Whatever."

He writes a bunch of words on the board in English.

"Who's Messi?" the girl asks.

TJ looks at her like she's sprouted a third arm or something (which, in this case, maybe she deserves). *Who doesn't know Messi?*

"The most famous soccer player in the world," he grumbles.

Then my monitor starts up.

*Beep. Beep. Beep. Beep.*

"What happened?" the girl asks. It's sort of sweet, the way she says it all nervous.

*Awwww,* she's worried about me.

TJ puts down the marker and walks over to my monitor.

"Pulse ox," he says, pointing to one of the thousands of strange numbers on that stupid screen. Nobody has thought to tell me what they mean—not a single one of them.

"His oxygen tube came loose." TJ steps toward me so that he's standing really close to the girl. He reaches across her so that he can get to my oxygen tube, which I'm completely capable of putting back in my nose myself. But why bother? I mean, that's why TJ's here.

"If his pulse ox drops below ninety, the monitor sets off an alert," he says.

*Who knew?* Now, if only I had any clue what "pulse-ox" was.

"You just have to make sure the tube is secure against his nostrils so the oxygen's flowing in." He leans in and adjusts the tube around my ears. "I think even you can handle this," he says to her. "Or maybe you'll faint at the sight of snot, too?"

Ouch. That wasn't a very nice thing to say to the new girl, was it?

The new girl doesn't say anything. She just leans forward; I guess to get a closer look at this oh-so-complicated oxygen tube procedure. Maybe she's slow or something. I don't know. She seems really smart to me.

TJ finishes arranging the tube and then pulls his hand away from my face. I watch his forearm brush against her side by accident. And then—you're not gonna believe this—her cheeks go pink again and TJ jumps back like he's been hit by lightning.

He turns and storms out of the room, not saying a word, never once looking back at the girl. Like she did something to make him really mad.

And that's when it hits me. These two are totally *hot* for each other!

*Aw yeah. This is gonna be fun.*

Like I said, people: I'm no angel.

June 7
5:16 PM

"Scrubland Survivor"
Habitat under constant
threat

Florida Scrub Jay
(Aphelocoma coerulescens)

Offspring
care
for
parents

Just shared
my LUNA BAR
with
this one!
Is he taking
it to his mate?

# CHAPTER FIVE

## *VIVI*

BIRD JOURNAL

June 7, 5:16 P.M.

Florida scrub jay (*Aphelocoma coerulescens*)

*Florida's most endangered bird just landed on my arm and stole a piece of my Luna Bar!*

Physical Description: bold-blue-and-gray jay

Habitat: lives only in the Central Florida oak scrub. Its unique scrub habitat, comprised of oaks, palmettos, and rosemary, is under constant threat.

Social Behavior: very social—stays in family groups to raise young. Offspring remain as adults to care for parents and future offspring.

Mating Patterns: mate with one partner for life. Male scrub jays are known to seek out their desired mate's favorite food and feed it to them as a courtship ritual.

Nickname: "scrubland survivor."

*I still can't believe this actually happened! These birds are classified as threatened under the Endangered Species Act!!*

## "¿LO PODRÍA TOCAR?"

I'm alone in 311 with Ángel, counting the moments until this eternal day ends.

"*Tu cabello bonito. ¿Lo podría tocar? Se ve tan suave.*"

*He wants to touch my hair?* This must be a misunderstanding. His Spanish is a little hard to comprehend. Maybe he's saying *caballo*. Maybe he's saying the horse looks soft. I glance at the TV to see if there happens to be a horse galloping across the screen.

No such luck. It's a cooking show.

"No," I say simply. But, of course, he does it anyway. He reaches his hand out and strokes my head, like I'm a horse. I jump back— rear back?—and hit the tower of monitors with my elbow.

*Ouch.*

And then, like my knight in shining armor, Bertrand glides into the room to save me.

The first time I ever exchanged words with Bertrand, he told me—unsolicited—that his life was "a gift." Bertrand grew up in Cameroon, and his childhood was filled with violence. He should have died as a child, he told me. But he survived and he left Cameroon, and then he was "blessed" with a family and a career he loves. Bertrand is like a lovely trumpeter swan. When he walks through the hospital, I swear that he glides, leaving calm in his wake.

"Time for me to take over!" he says pleasantly. At this moment, I am so thrilled to see him that I could kneel down and kiss his feet.

Assuming that, if I do indeed kneel prostrate before him, Bertrand will become embarrassed, I say a quick (and genuinely cheerful) "See you tomorrow!" and then rush out of the room.

I am *so* done with Ángel.

This is a problem, since I've only managed to live through the first three days of an entire summer I'll apparently be spending with him. Unless he gets well and they discharge him.

*God, I hope he gets well soon.*

And then, of course, there's TJ. For three straight days he's been calling almost everything he encounters in my presence "glorious"— from the flavor of that disgusting-looking beef broth I have to feed Ángel to the chlorine-laced scent of Ángel's freshly laundered sheets. (Oh, and by the way, Ángel is perfectly capable of feeding himself. But he loves making me or TJ do it instead, because he's a jackass. And a misogynist. I'm pretty sure they both are. But TJ just spends most of his time glowering, so I can't be positive.)

That's right. As if having Ángel duty weren't punishment enough for my "weak constitution," I also have to spend countless hours in a room with TJ, who's basically always assigned as Ángel's nurse's aide.

But I'm not a quitter. That's what I keep reminding myself. If hanging out with Ángel and the Glowering One is what it takes to keep my internship and finish my credits from last fall, then I'm determined to do it.

I finally leave the hospital, starving and exhausted. I've just torn into a Luna Bar and I'm shoving half of it in my mouth, when I see something blue moving in the scrubland beyond the last row of cars in the parking lot. I step out into the palmettos toward the flash of blue, hoping not to encounter a rattlesnake. I'm walking very carefully, as quietly as I can, toward the branch of a low oak tree. And then I stop and stand perfectly still, because a Florida scrub jay is staring right at me. A Florida scrub jay! The state's most extraordinary endangered bird!

My arm is stretched out a little, because I need to balance as I step over a huge palmetto frond. And that scrub jay—it jumps right onto my wrist and stares directly into my eyes. It darts its little beak toward my Luna Bar and tugs off a piece.

And then, just as quickly as it arrived, the scrub jay hops off my arm and makes its way, jumping and hopping with a hunk of Luna Bar balanced between its mandibles, back through the palmettos. I remain perfectly still, wondering if perhaps the whole thing was a dream.

*Did Florida's most rare and endangered bird really just land on my arm and steal my energy bar?*

Florida scrub jays are survivors. When, as a result of development, their entire world starts to collapse around them, when the scrubby forests they call home begin to disappear, scrub jays don't have the option of taking off. The poor birds can barely fly at all. So they stay put and they make do. The scrub jay will do whatever it takes to survive, even if it means cozying up with humans. Scrub jays are renowned for taking care of their families, too. They stay together and help out, no matter what.

And here's another completely crazy thing about scrub jays: the scientists who study these incredible little guys have determined that male scrub jays learn what foods their mates like best, and then they go out to get them. They bring their partners' favorite morsels back to them, hoping to win their favor.

I guess maybe there's a female scrub jay back in those palmetto fronds who really loves Luna Bars.

Or maybe this extraordinary, rare bird jumped onto my arm to tell me something. *I wish I knew what.*

I run to my car and pull out my bird journal from the glove compartment. I sketch and scribble furiously, before I forget the curve of its tail or the angle of its beak.

Fifteen minutes later I put away my journal and shift my car into gear, feeling grateful that my one amazing moment with a Florida scrub jay has made up for the brutality of this day.

But then I see TJ. He stands on the other side of the roundabout, his arms crossed in front of his chest—glowering, of course. I have no idea why he's so angry all the time, but I don't really care to know either. I just want to keep my distance from him. In fact, I want to drive away from him as fast as I possibly can. But I can't, because Prashanti is standing next to him, frantically waving her hands above her head.

I glance into my rearview mirror, hoping beyond hope that she's trying to get someone else's attention.

"Vivi!" she calls out, arms still flailing.

*No such luck.*

I pull up to the curb slowly.

"I'm so glad we caught you." I have to assume that the "we" to whom she refers includes TJ, but he's staring off into the distance as if I'm not even there, so I can't be sure.

"TJ needs a ride back to St. Augustine," she says. "He's having car troubles and he needs to get to work."

"Oh, uh—"

"You live in St. Augustine, yes?" she asks in the exact same tone of voice she uses with patients who refuse to comply with her demands.

"Uh, yeah."

"And, clearly, you have plenty of space in your car, yes?"

I nod, my eyes darting toward the empty passenger seat.

"I don't need a ride," TJ grumbles, staring at his feet. "My cousin said she'd come for me."

Prashanti turns to face him. "And that will take how long? An hour? Maybe more? And you'll be how late for work, when there's a perfectly good ride waiting for you right here at the curb?"

TJ shrugs. *Not a wise move, TJ.*

Prashanti launches into one of her signature scoldings. "As you know, TJ, being prompt is the clearest way to demonstrate one's respect for others, including—perhaps most important—one's employer."

"It's my *uncle*, Prashanti. I work for my uncle. Remember?" TJ is shaking his head, still looking at the ground.

"Oh, I see." She puts both hands on her hips. "You're not interested in showing respect for your elders? For your own family? Is that what you're trying to express?"

"No, it's just—"

"Tell me, Vivi," Prashanti says, turning to face me. "Would *you* take it so lightly if you were faced with the prospect of arriving an hour late to work?"

*Oh no. She's not going to drag me into this.*

"No, you wouldn't, would you? You most certainly would not, because you understand the value of hard work, of being prompt, of honoring your commitments, no matter how difficult they are, or how many natural obstacles you face. Am I correct?"

*Yes, clearly she intends to drag me into this. And now she's making reference to my pathetic job performance and my "weak constitution." Fabulous.*

"Get in," I say to TJ, leaning out the window. "It's not a problem. I'll give you a ride."

TJ clenches his jaw and releases a little huff through his flared nostrils. A huff! Who the hell does he think he is? I'm just trying to help him get to work—and to keep Prashanti from verbally assaulting him. I think a little gratitude is in order.

He walks toward the passenger side of the car, arms tightly crossed over his abdomen, like he's going to be sick. He leans in. "You sure?"

"Yeah."

"My POS truck broke down again." He's got his elbows on the edge of the open window, but he's looking away from me, across the parking lot.

*Who knows?* Maybe that's where his piece-of-shit truck is. I really couldn't care less.

"Door's open," I say.

He yanks on the door and slouches into the passenger seat, while I roll his window up to trap in the cool air. He slams the door shut.

"Sorry," he mumbles. "I guess I pulled the door too hard."

I don't say anything in reply.

"See you tomorrow," I tell Prashanti.

"Yes, tomorrow," she says. And then I roll up my window and she turns to march away.

Suddenly my perfect car is feeling very small. And I'm feeling very sorry for myself. It's as if TJ's sucking all the oxygen out of the air.

"Nice ride," he says. "Is this one of those electric cars?"

I pull out onto the highway and accelerate.

"Yeah, it's a Tesla."

He looks over at me quickly but then turns away just as fast.

"Damn," he says, drawing the word out. He's running his hand across the dash. "So, let me guess. Your daddy bought you this fancy car to drive to that fancy Ivy League school. Am I right?"

*He did not just say that.* I whip around to look at him, and he's grinning. Grinning!

*That's it. I'm done.* My face is burning hot. I stare ahead at the road and grip the wheel hard to keep my hands from shaking.

"You *are* right," I say, my foot pressing on the gas. "My dad bought me this car as a parting gift. And then he died, leaving my mom and me with nothing but crushing grief and a nearly new Tesla."

Silence.

"What?" I say, my voice rising. "No pissy response? Is that all too hard for your feeble mind to wrap around?" I'm launching the words at him, sharp and cold.

I refuse to look at TJ, but I can see from the corner of my eye that he is watching me.

"That was a crap thing to say," he mumbles.

"Yeah, well, I'm in a crap mood."

"No, I mean *me*. What I said."

"Oh."

"Sorry about your dad."

I want to look at him, because his voice sounds almost genuine, but I force myself not to.

"Me too," I bark back.

He doesn't say anything else. I lean forward to switch on some music. Acoustic guitar. Quiet, dark, just what I need.

He reaches down to open his backpack and then pulls out a phone and some earbuds.

"No offense," he says, "but I'm gonna—"

He's holding the earbuds out for me to see.

"Yeah," I say. "Fine."

He shoves his earbuds into his ears and fools with the screen.

And then I drive toward the coast, through scrubby pine forest and swampland, through forgotten half-empty Central Florida towns. And I try to listen to the mournful wail of the guitar, but TJ's earbuds emit a constant thumping beat, which distracts and annoys me to no end.


"Where am I taking you?"

I'm pulling into St. Augustine on 207, and—after almost an hour of stifling silence—I have to ask. I need to know which way to turn.

"Old City," he says. "Left here."

I really wish that hadn't been his answer. But I try not to think too much about it—Old City, and how little I want to go back there.

His fingers are drumming nervously on the dash. They have been for, like, ten minutes. I'm trying really hard not to look over at them.

*He's driving me insane.*

I head up Ponce de Leon and then turn onto King Street, toward the tourist district.

"Now what?" I ask, moving slowly past the fountain at Flagler College and then pausing in the road for a group of tourists to cross to the Lightner Museum.

"Can you go down to Charlotte and drop me at the corner of Hypolita?" He's pulling something out of his backpack. A shirt, maybe. "I'd say drop me wherever, but I'm already late."

"Yeah, that's fine," I say. "But I don't really know the streets up here."

A horse-drawn buggy pulls out in front of me, so I have to stop. I glance over to see TJ pulling off the top of his scrubs.

*He is undressing. In my passenger seat.* Why doesn't this boy ever change clothes in a bathroom or a bedroom or something? Like a normal person? An image of the first time we met comes to mind, against my will. That time I allowed myself to look at his abs. *Big mistake.*

"Left on San Marco," he says, his arms over his head, blue scrubs coming off.

Thank God he's wearing an undershirt. Still, it's a little too hard to drag my eyes away. He shoves the scrubs into his backpack. I'm starting to worry that maybe he's planning to wriggle out of his pants, too. But he zips the bag closed.

"And then left again up there, just before the city gate."

The city gate. That's the main entryway to the tourist insanity. It also happens to be where the most humiliating night of my life began—the part that I remember.

"Do you work on St. George Street?" I ask. I hate the way my voice sounds—worried, weak.

"Why?" he spits out. "You got something against St. George?"

"No, I just, uh—"

His fingers are drumming again, and now his foot's tapping too. I guess he's really stressed about being late, which is strange, in light of the fact that—before Prashanti's little intervention—he was planning to wait an hour for his cousin to come.

"Okay, turn here, on Charlotte."

I ease onto a pretty little side street, passing a weathered wooden house with a sweet courtyard beside it. Old Town Coffee. I'd never noticed it before.

"Do they have good coffee?" I ask.

"Wouldn't know," he grumbles. "At four bucks a cup, I'm not planning to find out."

*Ah, TJ. So charming.*

I resist saying anything, but I can't help letting my eyes roll. TJ watches me, and then he blurts out, "I know the owners, though. They're good people. So, yeah, you should try it."

"I'll keep that in mind," I say, not wanting to give him the satisfaction of knowing that I probably will—if I'm ever forced to be in the Old City again.

We pass a couple of run-down T-shirt shops, dodging tourists walking down the center of the street (when there's a perfectly good sidewalk a couple of feet away).

"You can drop me up there," he says.

There's an unusual store, or museum, maybe. The kinds of places that you only see in Old Town, St. Augustine. The sign says MUSEUM OF MYSTERY.

"By the decapitated wax pirate?" I ask. There's a disturbingly accurate wax figure blocking the sidewalk. Maybe that's why the tourists keep veering out onto the street.

"A little farther," he says. "At the Hyppo."

I pull to a stop under a bright blue sign in the shape of a Popsicle. I look inside the shop. It's cute, with distressed wood tables and walls covered in folk art.

"You work here?" I ask.

"Nope," he says, throwing the car door open. "Thanks for the ride."

*Why all the secrecy? Is he a male stripper or something?* I guess that would explain why he seems so comfortable taking off his shirt in strange places.

He grabs his backpack and jumps out of the car, slamming the door shut behind him. Part of me wants to squeal away, just to piss him off, but of course I can't. Another horse-drawn buggy has just turned the corner, and it's moving past me at an incredibly slow pace, with a sweating, heat-dazed couple looking out from the carriage's leather bench.

TJ turns the corner and drops his backpack on the sidewalk. He's standing close to the wall, like he's trying to hide from me, shrugging on the white shirt he was holding in a tight ball. I inch the car forward so that he's in full view.

I lean across the passenger seat and watch as he ties a red scarf around his neck and tucks it into his collar.

*Oh my god.*

I know that scarf.

*Oh my god.*

I know that shirt.

*Oh my god.*

I know that logo, with the red flames surrounding it.

*Sabor do Brasil.*

The very site of my most shameful moment—the one I can't remember.

The first time I came home from Yale was the Wednesday before

Thanksgiving. I hadn't seen my parents for months, but Mom called every day. She always asked about how my classes were going, whether Yale was everything I'd imagined it would be.

I consistently told her my classes were going great, that Yale was a dream. We had worked so hard to get me there, and I couldn't bear to tell them anything but the good parts. Even though it was nothing like I had expected it to be, there *were* good parts.

A few, at least.

I soon discovered that I wasn't the only one who avoided telling the whole truth on those daily calls. I came home to find my father very sick, much more than my parents had let on. They didn't lie to me exactly. They always offered brief updates on the promising alternative treatments he was trying, and the success rates that each of them had.

I guess they had decided to focus on only the good parts too.

I wasn't mad at them, not really. But I did feel blindsided, and worried. I was so afraid that my father might be dying, but none of us talked about that. We didn't dare.

By the Saturday after Thanksgiving, I felt like I would lose my mind if I didn't get out of the house.

Gillian was spending the holiday a couple of hours away, at Ponte Vedra Beach. She called on Saturday morning and told me she was meeting up with some friends in St. Augustine—Luke and David, her friends from boarding school. I had been at Yale long enough to know that the guys from Gillian's boarding school tended to be entitled pricks. Places like Gillian's school apparently feed Yale an endless supply of them.

But I was desperate to escape the house, if only for a few hours.

We met on the beach in St. Augustine, near the pier. The guys came stocked with plenty of beer and a couple of flasks filled with tequila.

We got wasted and then took a cab to downtown St. Augustine. Somehow we ended up wandering into Sabor do Brasil.

I remember a karaoke machine, a stage, and a small crowded dance floor. I remember singing "Low Rider" with two middle-aged bikers wearing black leather from head to toe. I remember one of them shared his frozen margarita with me and told Gillian he was from Connecticut too. Turns out, both bikers were investment bankers. I remember laughing about that with Gillian.

I don't remember much of what happened after that.

A week later, when I finally gathered the energy to let Gillian know my father had died, the story of our "epic" night in St. Augustine had traveled far and wide. All my social feeds were clogged with details of the night I can't remember—the terrible night I will never forget.

I read enough to know that I danced topless on the karaoke stage. Then I shut down all of my social media accounts. Gillian made them take down the posts, and then she told me what I needed to know. I begged her to spare me any extra details, so she did. To this day, I don't know all of what happened that night. I think, probably, I should keep it that way.

Now, months later, TJ is watching me watching him. He leans toward me, his expression—sad? Worried?

I realize two things at once: my hands are shaking so hard that I can barely grip the steering wheel, and for the first time since I met him ten days ago, TJ is actually *looking* at me.

Does TJ know what I remember about that night—and maybe also what I don't? Could he tell me? Could I bear to hear it?

*God, what if he knows? He must think I am a complete mess. He must see me as some irresponsible party girl with no respect for my own body. . . .*

A horn honks. In my rearview mirror I see the grill of a Chevy truck practically against my bumper. The horse-drawn carriage is already halfway to St. George Street, and the couple in the back has wrenched around to see what's going on. And I'm sitting here, breaking down, blocking traffic. I ease forward, rolling into the intersection, not daring to look back.

Driving along San Marco, over the Bridge of Lions, through the heart of Anastasia Island—all the way back to the A-frame—I squeeze my eyes shut at every stoplight, desperate to block the memories. After six or seven stoplights, I finally start to breathe evenly, and my hands are steady again. I try to convince myself that I'm reading way too much into things. But I still can't stop seeing that shirt, the flaming logo and the red silk scarf, and TJ's worried eyes. I can't stop remembering that terrible morning when I woke up on a pool deck outside of Gillian's condo, wearing nothing but beer-stained jeans and a shirt just like the one TJ wore. I don't know what happened to my own shirt, or my bra. I don't know where my sandals ended up.

"It's probably for the best." That's what Gillian told me. "Just stupid drunk stuff, Vivi," she said, her voice strangely cheerful. "Don't even give it a second thought!"

I *did* give it a second thought. In fact, I haven't stopped thinking about it. Maybe it's a survival strategy. Maybe by obsessing about this particular mistake, I can ignore all of the others.

There are so many.

I pull onto the parking pad to see my mom sitting on the staircase that leads to the A-shaped gate. The gate's still open, and so is the mailbox. There's a pile of mail spread on the ground around her—magazines and leaflets, envelopes and cards.

She stands up and walks toward me, holding a single sheet of red-tinted paper. She has this sort of stunned look, like she's walking through a dream, or maybe a nightmare.

*Is it possible that we got another notice from Yale?*

My heart starts to race again, and I remind myself that Yale would never send correspondence on red paper—the Ivy League is far too understated for that.

I step out of the car and walk toward her. "Is everything okay?"

"I should have told you," she says. "I should have told you earlier."

I take the sheet of paper from her hand.

## PRE-FORECLOSURE NOTICE

I look up at her. "What does this mean?"

"I was so overwhelmed, Viv. I mean, I couldn't even handle going to the grocery store."

And that's when I put it all together—all the red sheets of paper, all the avoided conversations. I can barely manage to form the words.

"Are we losing our house?"

"I just didn't deal—not with the lawn or the pool, not the bills."

"None of them?"

She looks down at the ground, silent.

"Since when?" I ask.

"Awhile." She goes back to the stairs and slumps down in the middle of the mail. "But then I came here and I started to make art and to get better, and now I'm trying." She picks up a red envelope. "Really, I am."

"Mom," I say, my voice sharp. "Are we losing the house? Is that why we're here?" I glance behind her, toward the strange A-frame.

"I'm working on it." She releases a single loud sob. "I'm trying."

I sit down next to her and take the envelope. Florida Power & Light.

"Please believe me!" she cries. "I'm doing my best."

"I can help," I say, gently taking her hand in mine. "I can pay the bills. I'm good at that kind of stuff. Just give me your bank passwords—I mean, do you know them?"

She doesn't answer.

"Did you forget? Is that the problem? Or did he not have time to tell you what they were?"

She shakes her head, her face twisted with worry.

"I'll go to the house," I tell her. My mind searches for a solution. "His office. I mean, they must be written down somewhere."

"Viv, it's not the passwords. It's the money." She tilts her head to the sky and looks up. She can't even look me in the eye. "We don't have the money."

"What do you mean?" I ask. "Do we need to move money from a different account? Deposit a check?"

"There are no checks left to deposit."

"We can cash out stocks, right?"

Mom pulls away from me, riffles through a stack of papers, and hands me one. A bank statement. I scan the columns, looking for the bottom line.

$123.81

*That's all?* I look again.

-$123.81

*Oh sweet Jesus.* It's a negative number. In Mom's bank account. Even my personal account has a couple hundred dollars, at least. How did Mom let this happen?

"That's impossible," I say, trying to remain calm and focused. "Dad made a lot of money, right? It must be in a different account or something. We'll find it."

"It's gone."

"All of it?"

"And then some."

And, I guess because I'm the most profoundly selfish person on the planet, all I can think about is Yale.

"My school. Next semester? You paid for it, right?"

She shakes her head. "I don't think so."

"You don't think so?" Suddenly my whole body is shaking and I'm angry as hell. "How can you not even know?"

I'm yelling. But I deserve to yell!

I killed myself to get into that school. I practically sold my soul to the devil. Grades and clubs, sports I hated and volunteer gigs I couldn't have cared less about. Sleepless nights, hunched over piles of SAT prep books. And now I'm working my ass off, putting up with all manner of bullshit in that godforsaken ICU so that I can go back in the fall, and my mom *doesn't even know* if we've paid for it yet? I mean, *what the hell?*

"I'll call the school. We'll work it out." Mom's begging again.

I drop her hand and stand up. "It's fine, Mom," I grumble, even though we both know it's anything but fine. I start gathering up the unpaid bills and cutoff notices. "I'll take over from here."

# CHAPTER SIX

## *TJ*

**"OI, PAI! I'VE GOT** that rump cap for you."

I drop the hunk of beef onto a metal table and my dad unwraps it. He inspects it silently, running the edge of his knife over the fat. Then he lets out a single grunt.

I know what's coming.

*"¿O seu tio que comprou essa?"*

"Yeah, Uncle João bought it."

I don't dare call him Jay, even though that's his preferred name. My dad hates it. I mean, it drives him nuts.

Another grunt, and then Dad's back to cutting tenderloin medallions.

I pull out a knife and start to sharpen it against a stone. Then I position the meat to prep it.

Back here in the butcher room, where Dad and I spend all our Saturday afternoons, we call this cut of meat a "rump cap." Out there, though—with the customers—I call it "top sirloin." It's for our specialty: *"picanha*, top sirloin seasoned with sea salt and grilled to perfection, the favorite churrasco meat of all Brazilians." Every night I repeat that phrase fifty times, at least. And no one ever asks me how it's possible that *all* Brazilians share a favorite churrasco meat. They also don't ask me why sangria is our specialty drink, when it's from Spain, or why the salad bar has potato salad and mac 'n' cheese among the "twenty-five Brazilian specialty items." I guess most of them are content to stuff themselves with all-you-can-eat meat and let it be.

"*Três dedos,*" my dad commands, holding up three fingers. "*Três dedos, não mais.*"

He says this as if it's maybe my first time preparing the *picanha*— as if I haven't been slicing this meat with him since I was ten years old.

"I know, Dad. Three fingers," I say.

I carefully measure the width of three fingers between each slice, even though I'm pretty sure that by now I could cut this meat to perfect proportions with my eyes closed.

Dad and I work mostly in silence, except when he's telling me, "*Mais sal! Mais!*" Even though I have already put plenty of salt on it. Or: "*Apertado! Bem apertado,*" as I'm already shoving the steaks onto skewers as tightly as is humanly possible.

Dad's sort of a perfectionist when it comes to churrasco.

When the meat is finally prepped for the Saturday night onslaught, I tell Dad I'm heading home. I'm just removing my apron when Uncle João comes around the corner and into the butcher room. My uncle's wearing a trim black suit and a white tie. I think he's trying to look like an Armani model. I guess he's pretty good-looking for an old man, but he's also incredibly full of himself.

And a player.

I have no idea why Tia Luiza puts up with him, and I really don't care. My mom, though. She cares. She's constantly yelling about how *she* would have divorced him fifteen years ago, how *she'd* take every penny he had in alimony and never look back.

"He thinks he's so American," Mom says. "Living the dream with his fancy car and his fancy restaurant. But he's the biggest *machista* there is." And then: "If that man wants to be a *real* American, he'd better learn how Americans treat their women!"

I'm not really sure how Mom became the expert on how Americans treat their women. But I am sure of one thing: she's spent my entire youth instructing me on how to be an "American man." To this very day.

And my big sister, Mariana, she's in on it too.

I guess, in a strange way, I have my uncle Jay to blame for all the talks Mom and Mariana have given me over the years. I mean, they lecture me about *everything*. From how important it is to do the dishes every night, to what I'm supposed to say when my woman asks if her ass has gotten fat.

No topic is off-limits for these women. Nothing is sacred. Once, when I was fourteen, they sat me down after school, fed me milk and Oreos, and told me about the importance of pleasuring a woman. *For real.*

I gulped down my milk, took a long shower, and spent the next several years feeling completely and totally grossed out that something my mother had said made me have *that* reaction.

As a result of all this, I'm pretty much incapable of entering into a normal relationship with any girl. I'm so neurotically worried that I'll mistreat her, that I'll get it wrong.

*Who knows?* Maybe that's what it means to be an "American man."

At least Mariana's in Miami now. She's got her own boys to lecture—a husband and an eight-month-old son. Poor kid.

My dad wipes his hands on his already bloodstained apron and launches in. *"Essa carne é de baixa qualidade."*

"The rump is fine," my uncle says. "It's good quality. No one knows the difference, anyway."

"I know the difference," my dad grumbles.

"And while you are back here, inspecting the meat, I'm out there paying the bills," my uncle says, gesturing toward the restaurant floor. "So why don't you let me make that decision?"

"Is this a restaurant or a bank?" my dad asks. "Because if it's a restaurant, then somebody should pay attention to the actual food!"

"This guy," my uncle says, turning to me and chuckling. "I mean, this guy! Back in Vila Velha, when we were kids, he couldn't even sell coconut water to a tourist on the beach." He throws up his hands. "Who can't get a tourist to buy a goddamned fresh coconut?" He's shaking his head. "The man knows nothing about business. Nada! Zero!"

This is my cue to exit. They'll be at it for at least twenty minutes, and I'm not sticking around for the theatrics. It's my first night off in eleven days, and I need a shower. I also need about fifteen hours of sleep. Maybe more.

"You're a meat runner tonight," my uncle says as I'm heading out the door.

I turn the corner, lean against the wall, and let my eyes fall shut. *Maybe he'll think I didn't hear him. Maybe he wasn't talking to me.*

"*Ouve!* TJ!"

I sigh and push off the wall. "I'm not on the schedule," I say, heading for the exit.

"Well, now you are. We've got a big birthday party tonight."

I whip around and shoot him a glare.

"Party of fifty. All hands on deck."

*Oh Jesus.* If I stick around, I'll have to play the freakin' *pandeiro* and my cousins and I will stand around and sing "Happy Birthday" in Portuguese to some stranger. Because, *yeah, stranger. There's nowhere me and my cousins would rather be on a Saturday night than at your very special birthday dinner.*

"What about Frankie? He could use a break from working the

salad bar," I say. Frankie's the youngest of the cousins. He just turned thirteen, which—in this family—makes him old enough to handle a sharp knife.

"This night's important. We need experienced *churrasqueiros*," he says. This place always needs family. "You got somewhere else to be?"

*Honestly, no.* And even if I did, my uncle wouldn't care.

Doesn't matter. I need the money anyway.

"Okay," I say. "But can I borrow your car? I've gotta run home and take a quick shower."

"Where's the Durango?" he asks.

"In the shop."

"What's the problem?" my dad asks, looking up from a lamb loin.

"Don't know. I'm still waiting for Travis to call me and drop the news."

"Get it taken care of," my dad says. "We'll need it for the Costco run next week."

Of course, he doesn't mention that I'll need it to get to work. To my real job—the one that I actually need if I ever want to finish school. The one that's gonna get me out of this restaurant for good.

Uncle Jay throws me the keys to his Mercedes.

"Be careful with my baby," he says.

I catch the keys and mutter, "Thanks." I guess maybe it's appropriate for him to call that car his "baby." I'm pretty sure he takes better care of it than he ever did of his four kids. As far as I can tell, my cousins and I were all brought into this world to be cheap labor—nothing more, nothing less.

Twenty-five minutes later I'm back at the restaurant. My hair is still wet from the thirty-second-long shower, but I'm already sweating again because I'm standing over the mesquite coals, stoking the fire.

*Why do I even bother?*

"Hey, TJ," my cousin Sabrina calls to me from the restaurant floor. "Come move this table for us."

I leave the poker and head out to the floor. She's standing around with three girls I've never seen before, all of them wearing tight sweatpants and tank tops.

"We're gonna have to make more room here," she says, pointing at a two-top table. "For the wings."

"The what?" I ask, picking up the table.

"For the costumes," she says, "for the dancers." She gestures toward the three girls in sweatpants. They smile, and one of them winks.

*Is this some sort of joke?* I'm so confused.

"What dancers?" I ask.

"You know," she says. "Samba Saturdays. We're starting tonight."

"Oh hell no. For real? I thought Dad said we were gonna bring back the 'family-friendly' vibe."

"Well, *my* dad wants to bring in the making-money vibe," Sabrina shoots back. "Restaurants don't pay for themselves, you know?"

"Are *you* gonna samba dance?" I ask my cousin. I'm thinking there's no way Uncle Jay would let his daughter parade through this restaurant wearing nothing but a sparkly bikini, a headdress, and wings. But that man is full of surprises these days.

"No," she says brightly, gesturing toward the three girls. "They are! We've been working on the choreography all week. They're great!"

They look nice enough, but they don't look like samba dancers. Or maybe they do. I wouldn't know. I've never even been to Carnival.

"Hi!" One of them gives a little wave. "I'm Alisha."

I put the table down a few feet to the left of the door. "I'm TJ."

Alisha smiles big. "I like your costume," she says. "You look really cute in it."

I ignore the comment, because I'm not wearing a costume. I'm wearing my uniform.

"So, where did you three learn samba?" I ask.

"Oh," Alisha says. "We're belly dancers, actually. We teach at the studio down on Catalina. But I mean, it's pretty much the same thing, you know?"

I nod and keep my mouth shut.

"I mean. The costumes are different," Alisha says. "And the arms . . ." She starts to wave her arms around. I guess to demonstrate the subtle differences between samba and belly dancing.

I must be looking skeptical, because Sabrina is glaring at me.

"It's hard to find samba dancers in St. Augustine," she says, her voice sharp.

"Yeah," I say. "I get that."

Of course it's freaking hard to find samba dancers here. I mean, we're the only Brazilians for fifty miles in any direction! What's next? Come February, is Uncle Jay gonna make us all parade down St. George Street in our own little *desfile de Carnival*? Is there anything he *won't* do to bring in tourists?

"So what's your story, TJ?" Alisha asks.

"My story?"

"Yeah," she says, stepping closer. "What do you like to do when you're not wearing that cute costume and serving up meat?"

I'm not liking the direction of this conversation.

"TJ is studying to be in the medical profession," my cousin Demetrio says from behind the bar.

"Oh wow," one of the other samba/belly dancers says. "That's so great. You want to be a doctor?"

"Oh no!" my cousin Carlitos calls out. "TJ here wants to be a *male nurse*."

*And I'm out.* I turn to walk away, because I know exactly what's coming. When it comes to my career choice, my cousins are nothing if not predictable.

"He's very *nurturing*," Matheus says from the other side of the restaurant floor.

"Our TJ," Demetrio calls out from the bar, his voice thick with sarcasm. "He loves to dream big."

"And you?" I say to Demetrio, still heading for the kitchen. "What are you dreaming of back there? How to make the perfect lemon drop martini?"

That one gets laughs from Carlitos and Matheus.

"Nah, man," Carlitos says. "Demetrio—he's all about the mai tais!"

"I'm just gonna go back to quartering my limes," Demetrio says. "And later on tonight I'll be laughing all the way to the bank."

He's got a point. The bartender makes more money in one night than the rest of us put together.

"I mean, who even needs college when you've earned *that* beautiful certificate?" Carlitos asks, pointing at the health inspection report that's framed behind the bar.

"That's what I'm talkin' about," Matheus says. "Ninety-nine percent. That's an A plus right there."

Matheus actually did really well in school. When he was a senior, I tried to help him with some college applications. He worked on them for about a week, and then he quit. He actually said to me, "Why waste my time in college when I can start out at 40K a year, serving up caipirinhas?"

"You're an idiot, Matheus," Carlitos says. "You'd better get your ass to college next fall, or you'll have me to answer to."

"And me." Demetrio reaches over the bar and smacks Matheus on the side of his head—not hard, though. He's just playing around.

"Ow! Damn, y'all stop messing with me!" Matheus grabs the side of his head like he's been mortally wounded or something.

"Kid doesn't even know a joke when he hears one," Demetrio mutters, shaking his head.

A bunch of idiots. All of them. Here they are threatening to hurt their little brother if he doesn't go to college, but they make fun of me endlessly because I want an actual profession? I love those guys, though. They're family, and I know they don't mean anything by the teasing. That's just what we do—we give each other shit.

I turn back to the girls and smile. "It was nice to meet you," I say. "I look forward to seeing your, uh, performance."

All three smile big.

"I've, um—I've gotta go set some tables."

I wander off to prep for the dinner crowd and my phone rings. It's Travis, the mechanic.

"Hey, Travis."

"Hey, buddy. I've got some bad news."

"Seems to be the only kind I get these days." I shake my head and let out a breath. "So what is it? The ignition switch?"

"No, man. It's the transmission."

"No way."

"Would I lie to you about this?"

He wouldn't. Travis and I have been friends for fifteen years. This man and his dad took me alligator hunting when I was eleven. I mean, you've gotta trust the guy who takes you out to a swamp to search for giant mammal-eating reptiles in the pitch-black dark.

"I've got a buddy up in Jacksonville," he says. "He's gonna look for a rebuilt one. But it'll cost you. Even the rebuilt ones aren't cheap."

"How much?"

"Don't know yet. I'm guessing eight hundred to a thousand."

"What? Is the old girl even worth that much?"

"Unless you've got a wad of cash stashed somewhere that's gonna buy you a brand-new car, you're gonna have to take care of that Durango."

"Yeah," I say. "I get it."

"Plus, she's the only girl you got."

Leave it to an old friend to remind me how pathetic my love life is.

"How long?"

"No idea," he says. "I'll keep her here until we get that part."

I hang up and then immediately start to stress. How am I gonna get to work? There's no way my cousin can take me every day. She has her own day job. I've gotta come up with something. I'm not going to let a broken-down SUV keep me from getting out of this place.

I stare at my phone for a full minute, while my cousins move around me, getting the restaurant ready for another Saturday night.

And then I do the only thing I can think of. I start to compose a text to Prashanti.

Can you give me Vivi's number?

My thumb hovers over the send button. Do I really want to do this? Do I have any choice?

I hit send.

Uncommon
and local.

Distinctive
forked tail

June 16.
7:43 PM
Swallow-tailed Kite
(Elanoides forficatus)

Graceful, a joy to watch.

Extraordinary flight
pattern, circled me & TJ!

## CHAPTER SEVEN

*VIVI*

BIRD JOURNAL
June 16, 7:43 P.M.
Swallow-tailed kite (*Elanoides forficatus*)
*Oh wow. This swallow-tailed kite is an absolute joy to watch! I
can't tear my eyes away from him.*
Habitat: uncommon and local. Often seen soaring over
swamps and along the edges of woods.
Physical Description: a beautiful bird of prey, striking in its
shape and pattern. Extraordinarily graceful.
Flight: hanging motionless in the air, swooping and gliding,
rolling upside down and then zooming high in the air
with barely any motion of its wings.
Mating Patterns: usually involves aerial chases by both
sexes; male may feed female.

**"WHAT ARE YOU DOING?"** TJ practically barks from the passenger seat.

"What does it look like I'm doing?" I ask. "I'm pulling over."

I pull onto the shoulder of the two-lane highway, grab my journal from the center console, and get out of the car. I can feel TJ watching me, which makes me feel incredibly unsettled. But I ignore his stare and look up at the sky.

I've never seen a swallow-tailed kite, but I've read plenty about them. They used to be common throughout much of North America, but now they can only be found in Florida, only at certain times of year, and rarely as far north as St. Augustine.

Here he is, right above me, the "coolest bird on the planet," according to the Cornell Lab of Ornithology. And he's calling out with that high-pitched squeal, like he's talking directly to me.

*Klee-klee-klee. Klee-klee-klee.*

TJ gets out of the car and slams the door.

"Shhhhh," I hiss, pointing up to the sky as the magnificent kite soars and swoops and dives.

"What?" he asks. "Why are we being quiet?"

*The bird*, I mouth. Then I whisper, "It's a swallow-tailed kite."

He smiles, a gorgeous, crooked smile, which has the strange effect of really pissing me off. Then he loud-whispers, "Oh okay. Sure. Let's make me late for work so you can sit out here in the middle of the swamp and watch a bird fly in circles."

The kite is circling around and around like he's riding the edge of a corkscrew, that distinctive forked tail and pure white breast clearly visible. I ignore TJ (I'm getting good at that) and start taking notes in my journal.

He lets out a long sigh and leans into the hood.

*Klee-klee-klee. Klee-klee-klee.*

"Listen," I hiss. "That's his warning call."

And he should consider this mine. I don't care what TJ thinks. I'm going to spend a few minutes observing this incredible creature's extraordinary flight pattern, even if it means enduring the scorn of my passenger.

Yes, it's come to this. My beautiful Tesla now serves as a vehicle for hire. And my paying customer? None other than TJ Carvalho. His text came in last Sunday morning:

It's TJ from the hospital. Need ride. Will pay for gas or electricity or whatever.

How much? I shot back immediately. I happened to be three hours into an all-day marathon of working through our dismal financials. Let's just say he caught me in a very weak moment.

Thirty a week.

It only took me a second to do the math. That would be $120 a month. That would, at least, ensure that Florida Power & Light would keep the electricity going.

*Text me your address.*
101 Fletcher—near San Marco & Castillo.
*Next to Fountain of Youth?*
Yeah—between that and Ripley's.
*Be ready at 6:05.*
Okay.
*If you make me late even once, we're done.*
Okay.

That last line might seem cold, but it's not. It's self-preservation. If I've learned anything about TJ, it's that he's notorious for being late. And if I know anything about Prashanti, it's that she has a very low tolerance for tardiness.

So far, TJ has managed to be ready on time every day for a week, which is about the only good thing I can say about this arrangement. With each passing day he becomes both more dismissive of me and— it pains me to say—better looking. I keep waiting for the terrible attitude to ruin his looks for me. I mean, that's a thing. You think someone is beautiful until you realize that it's just on the surface, and the ugliness inside begins to reconfigure the exterior.

But here I am, having endured a full week of driving back and forth through swamps with a mostly silent and brooding TJ Carvalho, and I still can't look directly at him without having to swallow hard and turn away.

*Why won't this boy turn ugly?*

On the upside, it's become abundantly clear to me that I was imagining all of the drama last Friday. TJ probably got the job at that Brazilian restaurant a month ago. Considering his track record with being late to the hospital (until he started riding with me), I can't imagine that he keeps a job for more than three or four months at a stretch. So I've stopped worrying about it. He doesn't know anything about that night. I'm sure of it.

It doesn't really matter, anyway. That's in the past, and I've got plenty of things to worry about in the here and now.

I'm going to need to find work—a paying job. And the job will have to be nights or weekends, since I also have to keep my internship. I've been searching desperately all week, and I haven't found anything yet.

The situation is getting dire. I need a paycheck before the end of the month. If I can earn enough to pay off the water bill in Winter Park, or at least to pay something toward it as a sign of good faith, we should be okay until the end of July. And even though Mom can't seem to wrap her head around the future right now, I'm beginning to worry obsessively about the fact that she may not have a house when I go back to Yale.

*If I go back to Yale?*

On Monday I snuck away from Ángel duty for thirty minutes and called the office of financial aid. It only took a few words out of my mouth, and they were bending over backward to give me my own personal aide counselor. I'm quickly learning that "My father died" tends to be an effective way to garner the attention of bureaucrats. My counselor, a lovely woman named Alice Thistlethwaite, assured me that Yale would do everything possible to ensure a smooth transition into my sophomore year. Then she directed me to two websites where I would find—and eventually need to fill out—two incredibly complicated forms. For one form, alone, I have to pull together about forty documents, most of which I have never heard of. She told me that my mom would be able to help. I couldn't find the words to explain that—unless the documents needed to be dipped in vats of dye and hung from a clothesline, Mom's not likely to be of much assistance right now.

I'm on my own.

*Klee-klee-klee. Klee-klee-klee.*

I watch the swallow-tail kite pump its wings twice and fly away.

"Can we go now?" TJ asks, standing up and heading toward the passenger seat.

I nod, a little surprised that he was even paying enough attention to notice that the kite had moved on.

Half an hour later, we're pulling into St. Augustine.

TJ looks up from his phone. "You can drop me at the Alligator Farm," he says.

"The Alligator Farm?"

"Yeah. You live out there, right?"

I nod. Okay, I'll drop him at the Alligator Farm. I'm not about to ask questions.

I turn off A1A and pull in front of the building, a Spanish Colonial with a red tile roof and a tall tower in the center. The Alligator Farm is one of St. Augustine's oldest tourist attractions, and—from what I can gather—one of the city's lamest, too. The parking lot bears some evidence of this: a camo-painted military-style truck with enormous wheels is a permanent fixture here. The flatbed has an enormous plastic gator in it, its arms wrapped in rope, its jaw wide to reveal row upon row of gleaming sharp teeth.

If this lovely little sculpture offers any evidence of what's inside, I'd prefer not to go in.

A girl emerges from the entrance, waving. Long, lean body. Wavy dark hair cascading halfway down her back. Clear sun-kissed skin and deep brown eyes.

*Oh God. That's probably his girlfriend.* They look like they were made for each other.

TJ mutters, "Thanks," and starts to get out of the car, but before he can close the car door, the girl has reached out to hold it open.

"Hey!" she says to me. "Thanks for putting up with my stupid cousin every day."

*Cousin.* Okay, so I jumped to conclusions.

I nod and shrug. "It pays pretty well."

TJ heads across the parking lot, as if we're not even there. The girl glances at him, puzzled, and then back at me.

"Does he always act like that?" she asks, squinting a little.

"Like what?"

"Like, *rude.*"

"Oh," I say. "No, he's a perfectly charming gentleman most of the time. I think maybe the gator scared him away." I gesture toward the gaping mouth to my right.

"Hmmm," she says. "Weird."

"I'm Vivi," I say.

"Let's go, Sabrina!" TJ calls out, clearly annoyed. "It's a thousand degrees out here."

"Well, somebody's hot and bothered," she says. She looks me over one more time. "He doesn't usually act like this. Sorry."

"No big deal," I say. "I'm used to it."

She waves and smiles a gorgeous smile—one that somehow also manages to be kind and approachable. I wave back and start to pull away. She's standing in front of TJ, and it looks like she's teasing him or giving him a hard time about something. He has his arms crossed over his chest (which I now identify as his signature stance) and he's shaking his head, frowning. He must sense me watching him, because he glances up as I drive by, and he looks right at me.

It's utterly pointless for my body to react like this, but still, my breath catches.

Trying hard to ignore the acceleration of my heart rate, I turn to look away. That's when I see the sign across the street in front of the lighthouse entrance.

## HELP WANTED (NIGHT SHIFT)

Twenty minutes later I'm standing in the gift shop of the St. Augustine Lighthouse, pretending to inspect the extensive collection of Christmas tree ornaments. Darren, who runs the Darkest of the Moon paranormal tour, is reading my job application, which stresses me out immensely.

I *need* this job. The hours are perfect, the pay is decent, and I am so incredibly desperate.

"How old did you say you were?" he asks, looking me up and down, but not in a creepy way.

"Nineteen."

"And you've never worked a day in your life?"

*Okay, Darren.* That's what I want to say, but I keep my mouth shut. I've worked my butt off for almost as long as I can remember. A 4.9 GPA doesn't just materialize out of thin air. But I have a feeling that telling him I took four SAT prep classes my junior year of high school won't be the answer he's looking for.

"I was a professional dog walker," I say. "See, on the application?"

"You mean Pumpkin?" he asks, looking up from the application.

"Yes, the labradoodle. Mrs. Tipton paid me to feed and walk him. I'm sure she'd be willing to give a recommendation. And I had other clients in the neighborhood—"

"Right," he says. "In addition to Pumpkin. When you were thirteen."

*When I was thirteen.* That was the moment before everything started to matter so much—grades and clubs and activities and sports I didn't even care about playing. It all felt so important. Every class, every yearbook or newspaper I edited, every varsity letter in fencing and squash and field hockey—they all were bringing me one step closer to my goal: the Ivy League.

Now it's all in danger of slipping away. And I'm begging for a job on the ghost tour. Because if that's what it takes to hold this all together, then that's what I'm gonna do.

"Anybody else I can call for a reference?" he asks.

I don't tell him about the internship, because (a) it's not a paying job and (b) I don't want him to call Prashanti. She doesn't need to know I'm trying to moonlight. My situation at the hospital is precarious enough.

"Ever been on a ghost tour?" he asks.

"No," I reply. Honesty is the best policy, right? "But I know a ton of history, and I have a great memory for details."

"Like, what kind of details?" he asks.

"Well, I know that the current lighthouse was built in 1874, and that it's the oldest brick structure in St. Augustine." I stand up a little straighter. "And I believe I once learned that the first female lighthouse keeper in the US worked here. Her husband died, and she took over, maybe?" I look at Darren, whose jaw is hanging open. "It was right before the Civil War, before the current structure was built, right? What was her name? Uh, Delia? No, no. I remember now. Dolores. And the last name, it starts with an A."

"Dolores Andreu," he says.

"That's right," I say. "Dolores Andreu, keeper of the lighthouse from 1859 to 1862. But she's probably not one of your ghosts, since—as I recall—she was buried in Georgia."

Darren nods. "You're good," he says. "I'll admit it."

"Should I tell you more?" I ask. "Maybe about some of the shipwrecks? The most interesting, of course, were during the post-Revolutionary era—"

He stands up and throws his hands into the air, as if in surrender. "Oh no," he says. "I think you've made your case. Can you start tomorrow?"

It's everything I can do to keep from throwing my arms around Darren. Instead I clear my throat and don my most professional voice. "Absolutely," I say.

"Lord knows we need some new stories—tourists are grumbling on TripAdvisor about the same old, tired ghosts. Think you could drum some up?"

"You mean, like, historical research?" I ask—I know my voice sounds a little too nerded-out and excited.

"Something like that," he replies, shrugging. "Just dig around the archives and find me a few stories, some dead folks we haven't thought to resurrect yet."

"Will do! What time do you need me?"

"Night shift starts at seven thirty P.M."

"Perfect!" I exclaim, feeling really glad that I spent that ten minutes in the car before I came into this place, reading up on the St. Augustine Lighthouse's very informative website.

I always come prepared.


There's no one here, since the museum closes at six and doesn't re-open for the ghost tour until eight thirty. I'm in no hurry to get back to the A-frame and that stack of incomprehensible financial aid paperwork, so instead of getting in my car, I head down a gravel path toward the lighthouse keeper's residence.

It's that perfect time of evening when the light is starting to soften and the wind picks up off the ocean to push away the damp heat. The path is lined with low oak trees, their narrow trunks twisting and curving, their branches dripping with Spanish moss. It ends at the edge of a broad lawn. From the back of the lawn, the lighthouse rises, impossibly tall. I crane my neck to follow the twirl of black-and-white stripes painted around it, to the red-roofed structure where the huge lens spins, constant and slow, still lighting the way for ships on the ocean. I think about that light, and it makes me feel calm somehow—to know it's been throwing its beam across the water for almost 150 years.

I don't walk toward the lighthouse, though. I head to the top of the lawn, where the keeper's house stands. I pause and listen for a while to the songbirds in the trees around me. The low, throaty *jeer* of the blue jay; the repetitive *birdie, birdie, birdie* of the cardinal; the Carolina wren's lovely, sweet *teakettle*.

The keeper's house is a two-story redbrick structure, with a big, wooden wraparound porch painted white. I guess it's supposed to be haunted, but to me it looks warm and inviting—like a place that's been filled with life. I stand on the grassy field behind it, and I imagine the families who lived here, the lighthouse keeper resting on the back porch after a long day of trudging up and down those stairs, kids chasing one another other across the lawn, calling out to each other, their high voices piercing the island's quiet.

This was a home. It must have been a lovely place to grow up.

All those families, long gone now. And tourists clamoring to this place to try to find them again—to catch a glimpse of how they lived, to try to convince themselves that, somehow, they're all still wandering around here, desperate to communicate with the living.

Why is it that we don't want to let the dead be gone?

# CHAPTER EIGHT

## *ÁNGEL*

**"OKAY, ÁNGEL, I NEED** for you to work with me today. When TJ gets here, we're going to make this goal thing fast and painless. . . ."

Ah, Vivi. She's always so *nice.* Honestly, between you and me, I don't know how she stays so cheerful all the time. What with TJ being so strange and grumpy around her.

"I can't handle him today, Ángel. I just don't have the emotional energy for it. We need to get him in and out of here as quickly as we can."

What, and ruin the only fun I get to have today?

"I worked all weekend. A real job." She's walking around my bed, picking up empty ice cups and throwing them away. "Yeah, I had to get a paying job—nights and weekends. My first one ever."

Girl's never had a job? That's kind of weird. I think I've been working since I could walk. Maybe that's why I'm losing my mind in here. I need something to do.

"My mom's suffering some sort of mourning-induced psychosis, which entails dipping sheets into dye all day, and in the meantime, our entire financial situation is in massive disarray. We're about to lose our house in Winter Park, and she hasn't paid any of the utility bills for months." She crushes a paper cup in her fist. "And I spent all day yesterday looking for insurance policies, bank statements, W-2 forms. I still can't figure that one out—I mean, it does not exist. Honest to God, if I have to call one more person and sound like a total idiot, asking what all these forms are . . ."

She pauses and looks right at me. I smile all innocent. You know the smile I'm talking about—the poor-clueless-sick-boy smile.

"I sort of forget that you don't understand what I'm saying."

Oh, she's wrong there. I don't know about all those forms, and I'm not sure what exactly her mom is suffering from . . . something about not liking the mornings, I think. But the rest of it? Crystal clear. You might think it's mean for me not to let her in on the fact that I'm crazy smart when it comes to picking up languages. A certifiable genius, I'm pretty sure.

I've decided that Vivi needs this. Girl's under a ton of pressure. I feel kinda sorry for her. So, every morning when she gets here, I pretend to be half asleep and I let her wander around, tidying up the room, and unload it all. I've got nothing better to do than listen to her problems.

I gotta tell you, though, I'm really tired today. She's talking and talking and my eyelids are feeling like they've got rocks in them. They're closing down on me, and also pushing in, so my eyes ache. Like the rest of my stupid body. I don't know if it's because I've been in this bed for, like, a month, or what, but I want to sleep all the time. And you know what really sucks? I can't, because everything hurts, and because when I finally do relax a little, somebody comes in here and makes me take a pill or wants to change my sheets . . . or asks me what my goddamned goal for the day is.

Right on cue, TJ walks into the room and grabs that stupid blue marker from the whiteboard.

*"Buenos días, Ángel. ¿Cuál es su meta para el día?"* Then he sighs. Okay, first, this guy speaks Spanish like he can't feel his tongue.

It's like all thick and floppy in there, and it sends these weird slurs out. Second, what the hell is up with that deep sigh? Like, he's all, *My life is so hard.* I don't mean to be too self-absorbed, but he's not the one who can't get out of bed! And, third, how about some manners, Mr. Carvalho? He hasn't even acknowledged that Vivi exists. Not so much as a sideways glance in her direction.

"Ángel?" Vivi touches my arm really soft-like. *"Despiértate, Ángel."*

I open my eyes slowly and pretend to be waking up. I look right into her eyes and throw her another one of those poor-clueless-sick-boy smiles.

*"Tienes que decir a TJ—¿cuál es su meta para el día?"*

TJ starts tapping his foot all impatient-like and stares out the window. You wouldn't believe how much that guy stares out the window when Vivi's here. It's like he's waiting for one of those airplanes to come by with a big banner attached to the tail. Like the kind I used to see down on Daytona Beach, with signs about some Burger King special, or a lizard trying to sell people car insurance.

*Aw, man. I miss the beach.*

Anyway, like, maybe a plane will fly by and the sign will say: JUST DO IT ALREADY! ADMIT THAT YOU'RE INTO THIS GIRL AND BE NICE TO HER. I guess that would be a long banner, wouldn't it? Maybe it should say something short and sweet like: GET ON WITH IT, TJ!

But you know what? That's not gonna happen. And since TJ isn't going to have the assistance of incredibly obvious messages waving from the back of an airplane, I'm just gonna have to help this man out.

I have a plan, and it's probably gonna surprise you to learn that this plan of mine involves a goal for the day.

Step one: shock the crap out of him by playing nice.

*"Mi meta para el día de hoy: quisiera hacer los ejercicios que me die-ron en terapia. Diez veces por pierna."*

Vivi's eyebrows shoot up.

"What?" TJ asks her, looking at me. "What did he say?"

"He said he wants to do the exercises that the physical therapist gave him. Ten times for each leg."

"What?" TJ asks, finally looking at her. "Really? I mean, are you sure you understood him?"

"Yeah," she says, all surprised. "Really."

You wouldn't believe the look on this guy's face.

"Jesus, TJ, just write it down before he changes his mind," Vivi says, understandably annoyed.

So TJ turns to write and Vivi watches him, even though you and I both know that she wishes she could resist the temptation. But the girl can't. Her shoulders sink a little. She crosses her arms and bites on the edge of one finger, studying how the muscles flex in his bare forearm while he writes my goal for the day. I mean, you've never seen anything like this, people. I'm telling you.

So you might think that I'm doing all this to be nice to Vivi, because she asked me to get him out of here fast. But no. I've got a better plan for our entertainment today.

Y'all ready for this?

Step two: sit up on the edge of the bed.

*Okay.* This part sucks. Because I am telling myself to sit up and move to the edge of the bed, but "myself" doesn't really wanna lis-ten. On the bright side, this might make my plan even better.

*"Ayuda, por favor,"* I say to TJ. He leans over me and points to his shoulders.

I know the drill. I rest my arms on his shoulders and he grabs on to my forearms. He braces his legs behind him.

One. Two. Three.

TJ leans back and tugs on me so that I'm sitting up. Now, you and I both know that once I'm up, I'm fine. I can sit up—I'm not some old dying man or something.

But let's keep that between you and me, okay? Because I'm planning to go total deadweight here.

"Tell him I'm letting go," TJ says. "Ask him if he's ready."

*"¿Listo?"* Vivi asks. She's standing on the other side of the room, too far away for this plan to work.

"No," I tell her, shaking my head once. *"No puedo."*

"He needs your help to sit up," she says.

*"Pero tengo que hacer mis ejercicios, Vivi."* I'm using my sad voice. *"Es mi meta para hoy."*

*"Pues, sí!"* she says, her face all concerned. *"Te ayudo."* Then she says to TJ, "He still wants to do the leg exercises. He wants to achieve his goal. But you'll have to help him stay sitting up, okay?"

"Okay," TJ says, and nods. He slides his hands down from my shoulders to the top of my arms and grips tight. Then he takes a small step back to make room for my legs to extend.

Perfect. This is all coming together, people. Check this out:

Step three: enthusiastically begin the leg exercises.

Oh, or don't. Because where's the fun in that? I look down at my legs dangling helplessly over the edge of the bed, and then I look up at Vivi with my best sad-puppy eyes. *"¿Me ayudas?"* I ask.

*"Sí, por supuesto,"* she says. Then to TJ: "He needs help lifting his legs."

He scowls. "I'm holding him up with both arms. I can't grow another one to help him lift his leg."

"I can help," she says.

He throws a nervous glance at her, and then back down to my legs, which are dangerously close to him. Then he does it again. You and I both know what's coming. And it's gonna be awesome. Here goes:

"No way." He shakes his head. "He's supposed to be doing this on his own."

"But it's his *goal*!" Vivi says, all emotional. "He finally gave us a *real goal*. We should help him get there."

*Absolutely they should.*

TJ nods once and takes another half step back, still holding tight to my upper arms while I concentrate really hard on continuing to be 100 percent dead weight. Vivi walks over to stand on my right side.

"*Listos?*" she asks, reaching out for my foot.

*Are we ready?* TJ definitely is not ready. He closes his eyes, clenches his jaw twice, and lets out another sigh.

Me, though? Yeah, I'm ready.

Standing as far away from TJ as possible, Vivi reaches over to grab my foot from the side. I pretend that I'm trying to lift my leg.

"*De atrás,*" I say, motioning my head toward TJ. "*Agarra la pierna de atrás, por favor.*"

"He wants me to move behind him so that I can get a grip on his leg," she says.

TJ tries to scoot over to make room for her, so I slump over a little, because that's not gonna work. He moves back and says, "This is the best I can do." He looks back out that window. I'm telling you, the man is using every ounce of his effort to keep from looking at her, and she is getting dangerously close.

Step four: let the entertainment begin.

I don't let my leg lift more than a quarter of an inch until Vivi is standing very close to TJ—so close that I'm pretty sure we could light up this entire ICU with the energy moving between those two. Vivi's biting her lip and TJ is clenching his jaw and I'm telling her to scoot over just a little . . . just a little . . . perfect! And then she's up against his side and he's sort of half hugging her, his arm wrapped over her shoulder so that he can keep holding me up while she helps me lift my leg. And I smile and move very, very slowly because her cheeks are turning pink and I'm pretty sure that if we listen carefully, we'll be able to hear his heart thumping.

And the beauty of it? I'm having so much fun with all of this that I almost forget to worry about my stupid heart and my legs that don't want to move and how tired every single one of my muscles is. I'm telling you, people, this little exercise may not be helping my body, but it's doing wonders for my mood.

I keep throwing these crazy instructions at them, and they keep following them. And when I've managed to get her hand resting on his bare forearm for support, and her face about three inches from his, TJ finally gives in. He lets himself look at the curve of her neck for five seconds, closes his eyes, and then reopens them and looks right at me.

You see that look? Okay, yeah. I'm so busted. He knows exactly what I'm doing, and he knows that I know exactly what he's feeling. And he's pissed.

"We're done," he says quietly. "That's the last one."

Well, that was fun. Wasn't it? Which is a good thing, because the rest of this day is gonna suck.

Starting . . . now.

Prashanti turns the corner with an old man in a long white coat. I've never seen that old man before, but one look at Prashanti's stony face and I know this is not good.

I can't figure it out. The old guy is obsessed with turkeys. I'm telling you people. He cannot stop asking me about the turkeys. It's the strangest thing.

I'll do whatever it takes to get this doctor out of the room, and if that means describing how to dispose of dead turkeys, then fine.

"He said that his employer asked him to remove the dead turkeys. He used a shovel to load them all onto the back of a truck—like, a dump truck—and then the owner drove them off. He doesn't know where they took the dead turkeys."

Vivi's talking to the old doctor, and he's rubbing his chin, looking all concerned. Prashanti scowls and asks Vivi, "Was he wearing protective gear? A face mask? Gloves? Anything at all?"

I wait for Vivi to translate, and then shake my head. Where do they think I was working? Some big fancy turkey distributor like Butterball? Linda and John could barely afford to put gas in the tractor. They were freaking out because they woke up one morning and half the turkeys were dead. Those fancy organic turkeys were the way they earned a living. They weren't gonna be using their last remaining dollars to buy me protective gear.

"Did he have extended physical contact with the turkeys? Did he have to kill any of them himself?"

Vivi translates, and I nod. They made me kill the rest of them, and then I dumped them in the truck too. John drove off to I don't know where. All I know is that he came back with an empty dump truck, parked it in the yard, and made me hose it down. It took forever to get all those feathers out, since the blood was sticking to them, and they were all sort of glued to the sides of the truck.

That was one nasty day's work.

"How did he kill the turkeys?" the doctor asks.

I'm looking at that doctor, and I'm thinking that man has never in his life had to kill the animals he ate. He's got a big potbelly, too. I bet he eats a lot of steak, huge steaks, still bleeding red. I wonder if he even knows what animal those steaks come from.

*How did I kill the turkeys?* That's a stupid question, but I guess I'm gonna have to answer it.

I lift one finger and slide it across my neck, then I let my head fall to the side, tongue drooping from my mouth. I pop back up and shrug.

"Did he come into contact with blood?"

TJ, who has been standing next to Vivi this whole time, saying nothing, lets out a quick laugh, and then covers his mouth. Yeah, I bet TJ knows where his food comes from.

Vivi translates. I nod and shrug again. Hell yeah, I came in contact with blood. I was covered in it, head to toe. I bet I looked pretty scary that day. Like one of those guys in a movie who goes on a big murder spree.

"Was Ángel aware that the turkeys had died from avian influenza-HPAI? Did his employers explain the risks involved?" The doctor tugs on his lip and knits his eyebrows.

"I don't know how to say avian influenza," Vivi says. She's starting to look super stressed, poor girl. "Can I just say bird flu?"

"Do we need to get an official translator on the phone?" Prashanti asks.

"No," Vivi says. "I think I can explain it."

*Good girl, Vivi.* I hate those telephone translators. They all speak with weird accents and they talk too fast. Plus, I can't *see* what they're saying. It helps to see the words.

"*Te explicaron porque los pavos murieron? Te dijeron que la enfermedad era grave? Que fue la influenza de aves?*"

She did a fine job translating. I knew she would.

I shake my head. It's true. They didn't tell me a thing. All Linda and John said was, "We gotta get rid of those turkeys fast or they're gonna shut this place down." So I got rid of the turkeys. It was that simple.

But then, a few days later, I was up on the roof of the shed, clearing away pine straw, and I started to feel dizzy, like I was gonna pass out. My legs collapsed under me, and I slid right off that metal roof and landed in the middle of the dirt yard. I think maybe I fainted from the heat, or I hit my head or something, because when I opened my eyes again, Lucy the pig was up in my face, using her big snout to shake me awake.

I miss Lucy. She was a good pig, as smart as they come. I used to let her sleep with me sometimes, when she seemed lonely. I don't know. I guess since I'm being honest with you people, I'll go ahead and admit it: I think I was the lonely one. John and Linda were nice and all, but I spent every day out there alone with those animals, and every night sleeping alone in that room by the barn. Still, it was better than living with my uncle, and Lucy was a good friend to me. For real, she was.

Anyway, that was a long time before all this crap went down— a couple of months, at least. I took some pills and got better. Until I got really sick and landed here.

I'm tired of talking about those scrawny dead turkeys. I want to sleep. I wish this old doctor would go away.

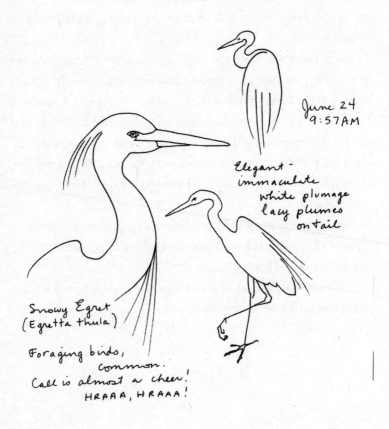

June 24
9:57 AM

Elegant -
immaculate
white plumage
lacy plumes
on tail

Snowy Egret
(Egretta thula)

Foraging birds,
        common.
Call is almost a cheer!
    HRAAA, HRAAA!

# CHAPTER NINE

## *VIVI*

BIRD JOURNAL

June 24, 9:57 A.M.

Snowy egret (*Egretta thula*)

*A gorgeous snowy egret cheered me on today! I wish I could believe in myself as much as this beautiful girl does.*

Physical Description: the most elegant of the herons; beautiful white plumage that appears almost lacy.

History: once almost endangered. In the late 1800s, egret plumes were used for clothing and were valued more highly than gold.

Social Behavior: male and female take turns incubating eggs, and they both care for young when they hatch.

Call: *hraaa, hraaa!*

**I'M SITTING ON A BENCH** at the entrance to an extraordinary national historic landmark, trying not to think about massacred turkeys. I can't seem to get that image out of my mind—piles of them, loaded into a truck, their tiny bald heads and blue skin, the bright red gobblers tucked above their huge bodies. Paying attention to the way a turkey looks, I absolutely trust all those scientists who say that birds are descended from dinosaurs. They are incredibly strange-looking creatures. Honestly, turkeys might be the only birds I don't enjoy watching.

Just thinking about those heaps of dead turkeys is making me sweat. Or maybe it's that I'm dressed in an incredibly hot costume. And by "hot," I don't mean *hot*. I mean vaguely nineteenth century, consisting of a blousy white shirt, an itchy wool skirt with tiny red flowers on it, a wide leather belt, and a leather satchel. I'm guessing the satchel probably was a castoff from some former Pirate Museum employee. It comes in handy, though. It's the perfect place to tuck my K2 EMF meter. That's an electromagnetic flow meter, an absolute necessity for my summer job—the one that pays.

I'm fairly certain that the kids tumbling past me, grasping neon-green glow sticks and screaming hysterically, aren't aware that this lighthouse is a national historic monument. They probably don't know that the beacon, a nine-foot-tall Fresnel lens, was brought to St. Augustine from Paris and installed in 1874. And I'm absolutely certain that their parents, now diving into their third or fourth beer, couldn't care less about the history of this maritime treasure, or about its remarkable beacon. They're too busy scrolling through the dozens of pictures they took climbing the lighthouse stairs, searching for any sign of paranormal activity.

A woman shuffles toward me, looking down at her screen. "Do you see this?"

She reaches the phone out to show me, but all I see is a gray screen.

"Yes." I nod knowingly. Under different circumstances, I would tell her she accidentally took a picture of the floor while she was up there in the dark. Instead I give her what she wants to hear. "I think you've got something there. Let me take a look." I scroll back and then forward, glancing at photos of dark stairwells, of her kids swinging "eerily" green glow sticks.

"The upper landing," I say. "That's where the EMF was picking up so much activity."

"The ghosts don't like to be in pictures," her husband says. "I've studied it on the internet—it happens all the time."

"You're right," I say. "They don't." I neglect to add "because they don't exist." I also decide to hold my tongue about the dangers of conducting research via internet surfing.

"In April we went to Savannah," the wife says. "We were on that ghost tour that takes you through the old cemetery, you know?"

*No.* I've never been on a ghost tour. I nod encouragingly.

"And—honest to God—we heard that little boy calling out for help."

"I had my recorder on," the husband says. "And all it picked up was a bunch of fuzz."

"Wow," I say, not knowing what else to say.

I now spend four nights a week with people who are desperate to believe that spirits hang around after death. I don't really get it—their obsession.

But if that's what they want, that's what I'll give them. This weekend, I came up with a new story for Darren—two pages, single-spaced. Captain Coxteer, a Confederate sea captain whose ship ran aground in 1861. My script was packed with authentic period details. I listened to three scholarly lectures on Civil War ships from the Florida Humanities Council. I went to the lighthouse archives and read journal entries from lighthouse keepers.

I thought his story would be perfect—I mean, who wouldn't be terrified of a Confederate sea captain who spent decades running slave ships?

My ghost story bombed.

All the kids' eyes glazed over; their dads wandered off to get another beer. Darren watched my epic fail, and then he came up and whispered in my ear, "Great work, but maybe stick with women and children next time—nobody wants to get too political on vacation."

Maybe he's right. Maybe it was too political. Or too scary. I don't know, but I guess it's back to the archives for more research.

In the meantime, I really should let this family borrow my K2 EMF. Seeing this thing light up would be the highlight of their vacation, without any doubt. But it's expensive. If I break it, I have to buy a replacement, and currently my mom and I are flat broke. Unless I aspire to a long and illustrious career as a ghost hunter, I need to save every last penny for my next tuition payment.

And some groceries. We really need groceries.

It appears that my mom has stopped cooking. And shopping. And maybe also eating. *Who knows?*

All I know is that she spent the entire week on the covered patio behind the A-Frame, hunched over a boiling pot of wax and dipping old sheets into plastic bowls filled with bright dye. She strung the fenced yard with crisscrossed strings of clothesline. I watched as the week progressed, and the lines filled with brightly colored squares of fabric, flapping in the wind like Tibetan prayer flags.

But here's the thing: we're not meditating on the top of a mountain somewhere. We're a block from the beach, and we need to eat something besides shrimp.

Last night she sat across from me at the Bait Shack and peeled her shrimp with dye-stained hands, telling me about the color variations of octopi and sea stars and triggerfish. Every time I tried to bring up our financial situation or ask her about one of the dozens of forms I need to track down for those complicated financial aid applications, she somehow managed to veer the conversation back to undersea creatures.

When the bill came, I grabbed it from her and used my debit card to pay. The waiter whisked it away and I told her, "That's it, Mom. No more Bait Shack. We can't afford it."

She shrugged and went back to talking about the wonders of the octopus. The woman's obsessed. She's also in denial. It's time for one of us to break down and go to the grocery store. It looks like I'll be that person.

I stand up and smooth my skirts. "Ladies and Gentlemen!" I call out. "We hope you have enjoyed your ghostly experience. The park will be closing in fifteen minutes." I lift my right arm and gesture toward a dirt path. "Please be sure you have gathered all of your belongings, then make your way through the lighthouse museum store to the park exit."

"Is there time to get me another beer before we head out?" the dad asks.

"Depends on how fast you can drink it," I say.

He chuckles and heads toward the concession stand.

I don't drink anymore, not since last Thanksgiving. Right now, though, I would kill for a cold beer. I would kill for a cold anything. It's eleven P.M. and still probably eighty-five degrees out here.

Darren heads toward me, fumbling with ten or twelve discarded glow sticks that he's picked up from the grass and bushes.

"I need you to check the tower," he says. "Make sure no one's hiding out in there and then lock 'er up."

I glance up to the top of the lighthouse: 219 steps.

"Yeah, okay. I'm on it." I hike up my skirts and head in.

I really should look on the bright side. I definitely can't afford a gym membership, so two or three times up and down these stairs every night is a good thing, right? That's what I'm telling myself at first, but then the rhythm begins to take over: my feet striking against each metal stair, the sound reverberating through the tower. I'm all alone in here; I can feel it.

By the time I reach the top, the sound of leather soles striking against metal has combined with the heaving of my breath and the rapid beat of my heart. I throw open the door to the viewing platform, relieved to feel wind, heavy against my face. I step out into the night, still grasping tight to my electromagnetic flow meter. I start to walk along the narrow platform, checking for stray tourists. But once I see the light come sweeping past, those ugly turkeys somehow return to my mind, and something inside of me caves. I lean against the wall of the lighthouse for support, and then my legs give out. I slide into a crouch and wrap my arms around my knees.

It's not exhaustion I'm feeling—at least it's not physical exhaustion. It's just . . .

I can see Ángel's face, surprised at first, and then crumpling into agony, when that no-nonsense doctor stood at the foot of his bed and told him that his heart would quit on him. I can feel my own heart speeding up, working harder—as if to compensate for his own heart's slowing. I can feel my hand on TJ's arm. Grasping for something solid, something warm and alive. I can sense the presence of TJ's own hand, covering mine, for just a few seconds. And I can feel his face lifting up, the slightest bit, and his eyes squeezing shut.

And then we pulled apart, and Ángel smiled, shrugged, and said, "Well, I guess we're gonna have to find me a new one."

He said it in English—mildly accented but perfectly understandable English.

He sat up a little and looked right at the doctor. "You do that, yes? You find new hearts?"

The doctor winced, as if Ángel had poked him with something

sharp, annoying but not painful. "It's not quite that simple, son," he said.

I started to translate, but Ángel raised his hand to stop me.

"It can't be so hard," he said. "Everyone has a heart, yes? You'll find one for me."

The doctor stumbled and mumbled something about talking through his options, and then he fumbled with his phone for a moment and rushed out of the room. Prashanti, clearly frazzled, followed behind him in a flurry of nervous energy and white coats.

Ángel looked over toward me and TJ, both frozen against the wall. "Well, that sucks."

Incapable of forming a single word, I said nothing in reply. But TJ jumped right in. "Yeah, it does," he said. And then, without missing a step: "And, by the way, asshole, when were you gonna tell us you speak English?"

I watched TJ and Ángel laughing together. And I realized something: I couldn't remember the moment that I learned my father was sick. I had no recollection at all—where I was, who was there with me, how I felt, what I said.

None of it. It was gone.

But now here it is—the memory of sitting beside my father on the swing out by the lake, his arm wrapped around me, hugging me close. The air was cool, and a breeze came off the water. We moved together back and forth, and he told me not to worry. He told me it would all be okay—he would be fine. *We would be fine.*

But I'm not fine. I'm not even close. And Mom? I can't even . . .

I wake up on Saturday morning, determined to pull myself together, to pull our lives together—starting with our finances. Mom finally gave me the bank information so that I can start filling out the financial aid forms, but I need Wi-Fi to access the forms. The internet constantly blinks in and out at the A-frame, and I'm not going to risk getting halfway through a thirty-five-page form and then having it all be lost.

I pull on a clean tank top, call out good morning to Mom—who is hanging sea anemones out to dry in the backyard—and head to Starbucks. On the way, I stop at the ATM and deposit my first-ever paycheck, feeling incredibly proud and accomplished.

When I get to Starbucks, I order a straight-up coffee for the first time in my life. Feeling equally proud to have saved two dollars, I pour out a third of the cup, fill it with (free) half-and-half, and add four sugars. Then I sit at a large table, boot up my computer, and dive into the complete and utter nightmare that is a College Scholarship Service PROFILE form.

I think I have listened to the interactive guide a dozen times, but still I have no idea what the hell half of these documents are or where to find them. I send Mom a long and detailed email, listing each of the documents we are missing, all of them some strange combinations of numbers and letters. I hit send on the email, also sending out a little prayer to the universe that my mother will be able to gather enough focus to help me through this. I don't think I can do it alone.

After begging the nice Starbucks barista for a free refill, I find the courage to pull out the stack of mail that Mrs. Pennington, our neighbor from Winter Park, sent from our real house.

I sort through the pile efficiently, separating the bills from the junk, and I come across the letter from Costco. Our membership expires in four days, and we can't afford to renew it. When I see the flyer filled with Costco coupons among the junk, I decide I need to seize the moment.

I pack up my laptop and head out to the car, flyer in hand. I'm going grocery shopping.

The door swings shut and I come face-to-face with a majestic snowy egret perched on the railing outside of Starbucks. He stretches his neck slowly and gracefully swivels his head from side to side so that I can admire his elaborate, ruffled plumage. He turns to face me directly and nods. Then he spreads his enormous wings and takes to the air, calling out his familiar song:

*Hraaa, hraaa!*

My own personal cheerleader, waiting outside of Starbucks, sending me off to Costco with renewed confidence.

*Hraaa, hraaa! Hraaa, hraaa!*

A half hour later, I'm pushing an enormous flatbed cart down the aisle of Costco, feeling utterly overwhelmed. When I reach the toilet paper display, I turn into the aisle. Why not start with the essentials?

I stand in front of a few thousand rolls of toilet paper, trying to calculate how much we need to get through our summer in the A-frame. Two months. That's about sixty days. Mom and I are two people. How many rolls of toilet paper will we go through in sixty days? Maybe, like, a roll a week for each of us? Okay. I guess I need the twenty-four-pack just in case. I flip through the coupon book. *Charmin Ultra Soft 24-Pack for $13.99.* Two dollars and fifty cents off. *That's not bad, right?*

Of course, the twenty-four-pack is at the very top.

I lug a stepladder across the concrete floor so that I can get to the highest stack of toilet paper. I'm on my tiptoes, reaching with both hands, when I see—of all people—TJ. He's coming around the corner with his own flatbed cart filled to overflowing. He's wearing surf shorts, flip-flops, and a white T-shirt with the sleeves cut off. His hair is damp, and I swear his biceps are glistening—like he's out in the midday sun instead of under the fluorescent warehouse lights. He's with another guy about our age, who also looks like he just hopped off his longboard. His jaw has the same curve as TJ's, and he's even more buff. I'm guessing he's a cousin too.

I grab the toilet paper and hug it to my chest, ignoring the strong instinct to hide my face with it, because I'm almost certainly blushing. I'm also remembering that moment yesterday, when I instinctively grabbed that now-glistening arm.

TJ looks down at a list and then points to the Brawny paper towels.

"We need some of those," he says.

*Is it possible that he hasn't noticed me?* Of course, it's possible. I'm all the way at the other end of the paper goods aisle in an enormous store. And I'm not exactly glistening. I'm sleep-deprived and sweaty, I haven't brushed my hair, and—in my enthusiasm for pulling our lives back together—I left the house without changing out of my pajama sweats. Overall, I'm looking perfectly forgettable.

"Those Viva ones are on sale," the other guy says, pointing to a placard above his head.

"Yeah, those work," TJ tells him. And then, because the heavens are conspiring against me, he looks down the aisle, searching for a stepladder, and finds me instead—hugging a jumbo pack of toilet paper.

"What's up?" he says, nodding once. He says it in the way that means, *I really couldn't care less what's happening in your life, but I'm obligated by this situation to say something.*

I scramble down the stepladder and try to shrug, which is a little awkward while holding twenty-four rolls of toilet paper.

"Not much," I say. "Just getting some stuff for home."

The other guy looks at my cart, stacked with—among other things—two enormous cans of black beans, a five-pound bag of rice, a three-pound bag of lentils, a six-pack of Lysol wipes, a box of individually wrapped ramen noodles, two cases of LaCroix water, and a handful of Luna Bars. Those last items are extravagant, I know. But I don't think my mom can live without her LaCroix and Luna Bars, so I've decided to wean her off slowly.

"What are you gonna do with all those beans?" he asks.

"I'm a vegetarian," I say, hoping that will suffice.

It's true: I *am* a vegetarian, as of yesterday. After our farewell meal at the Bait Shack, I went into Publix to buy some groceries and realized how incredibly expensive chicken breasts are. And beef? Don't even get me started. I decided, standing beside the meat coolers, to put Mom and me on a vegetarian diet. We will experiment—just like the great blue heron. Those birds are notorious for eating just about anything that comes their way. Once, scientists in Mississippi watched a great blue heron eat a stingray. A stingray! If one of those guys can figure out how to get sustenance from a stingray without killing himself in the process, then I should at least be able to figure out how to cook a bag of lentils.

*It will be good for us.*

"That's cool," he says, walking toward me. "I'm Demetrio, by the way. TJ's cousin."

*I knew it.*

"I'm Vivi," I tell him, dropping the toilet paper on top of the pile. "I work with TJ at the hospital."

"Yeah," Demetrio says, reaching out to balance my toilet paper, which is about to topple off the cart. "I know who you are."

I steal a glance at TJ, who is studying the paper towels intently. I sort of wish I knew what exactly he knows, but mostly I'm terrified by the thought that TJ talks to his cousin about me.

"Yeah, well, uh, I gotta . . ." I get behind the cart and give it a shove, almost sending the LaCroix toppling to the ground.

I'm balancing LaCroix with one arm, pushing the cart with the other arm and my hip, and practically unable to breathe because—apparently TJ sucks the oxygen not only out of my car, but also out of this enormous warehouse. I decide this shopping adventure is done. Not looking back to say good-bye, I carefully maneuver the cart toward a checkout aisle with no line.

It goes without saying that a line starts to build when my debit card gets rejected. And Mom's Costco card and the "emergency" debit card Dad gave me when I left for college. The first time it happened, the bored-out-of-her-mind checkout lady took one quick glance in my direction and asked, "Got another card?" But with each subsequent rejected card, she simply shakes her head once, not even looking at me.

And now I'm out of cards and the two kids who have been swinging off the cart of the lady behind me are screaming, "Mommy, I'm hungry! Mommy, what's wrong? Mommy, why is it taking so long?" Which means that every one of the hundreds of people who are spending their Saturday morning in Costco knows that my mom and I are completely broke.

*I am going to die of embarrassment.*

"Vivi!" I peer past the two kids using their cart as a jungle gym, and there's TJ, standing alone in the middle of the Costco checkout area, waving his list at me.

"Hey, Viv!"

In all of these weeks, he's never once called me by my name. He usually just grumbles "What's up?" or, when he's being particularly charming, he deadpans "Hey, glorious" (he's not gonna let me live that one down). But now here he is, almost jumping up and down to get my attention, first saying my name and then giving me a little nickname.

"Hey, Viv! We're not done yet. You forgot pickles—" He's pointing at his list, and I'm feeling incredibly confused. "And I've got the money, remember?"

The checkout lady waves me through, and I push my cart forward and then maneuver it carefully back toward TJ. With the exception of the bored checkout lady, the people in every line are watching me and TJ.

He steps behind the cart and starts to push it back toward the soda aisle.

"Pickles?" I ask, practically jogging to keep up with him.

He glares at me, still leaning into my cart and pushing it toward the drinks.

"Two questions," he says.

"Huh?"

"I've got two questions for you. One: Have you ever been to Costco before?"

I shake my head.

"Two: How much money do you have in your checking account?"

"I don't know what happened," I say. "I just deposited my paycheck."

"Your paycheck?" he asks. "The hospital's paying you?"

He asks as if it's absurd that I would be remunerated for my work there, since I'm useless.

"I got a job," I grumble. "At night."

"Hmm," he mumbles. "And you just deposited the check?"

"Yeah, I mean, I have the receipt and everything," I say, fumbling in my purse to get it.

He squints at me, concentrating. "It's not available right away," he says. "You know that, right?"

*No, of course I don't know that. But I can't seem to find a way to answer.*

He nods and looks down at my phone. "Check your bank," he says. "If the money's pending, you can't spend it yet."

I pull out my phone and look for my banking app.

"There's free Wi-Fi here. You should use it." He stops in front of the LaCroix display. "And while you're figuring out how much money you have to spend, I'm gonna do you a favor and get rid of this insanely expensive water."

"But my mom—"

"Yeah, my sister loves this shit too. I get it, but the generic brand is just as good, at a third of the price." He's heaving the second case of LaCroix off my cart. "She likes the açaí." He shoves the cart forward to another drink display. "And the lime's not bad." He stops the cart and looks at me, still fumbling with my banking app. "Which do you want?"

I look up at the display, still trying to figure out what TJ is doing here, pushing my cart and recommending flavors of sparkling water. I'm feeling disoriented, wobbly. And the way it sounded when he called me Viv, it's still there, sort of echoing through my head.

"Uh." I name the first one I see. "Passionfruit?"

*Oh sweet Jesus.* And now I'm blushing.

His eyebrows raise almost imperceptibly. "Passionfruit it is," he says. He grabs two cases at once and drops them onto my flatbed cart. "Come on."

I stumble along behind him until we get to the canned goods.

"Here's the thing about Costco," he tells me, grabbing one of my cans of black beans. "The proportions are all off, cuz this place is so big."

"I'm not following."

"This," he says, pointing at the can, "would last you and your mom about three weeks *if* you ate black beans for breakfast, lunch, and dinner. Are you planning on that?"

I shake my head, feeling like a complete imbecile.

"And once you open this huge-ass can, there's no going back. You gotta eat them or they'll go bad."

I nod.

"So I'm putting them back." He takes the second and puts them both on the shelf. "You can get a normal-sized can of these for eighty-nine cents at Winn-Dixie."

I nod again, feeling like a child, like TJ might be about to reach out and pat me on the head.

He steps away from the cart and assesses the contents. "I'm thinking about two-eighty," he says. "Do you have that much?"

I'm staring at my phone and my eyes are going watery because I don't and I'm embarrassed and I hate that TJ is treating me like an idiot, but I also have this weird urge to hug him, because I'm so incredibly lost in here. And TJ knows exactly what he's doing. He's so *competent*. Why does he have to be so infuriatingly sexy and so incredibly competent at the same time?

I let out a tiny squeak, like an abandoned hatchling. I'm lost, adrift in Costco.

"Hey," he says quietly. "Hey." He puts his hand on my shoulder, against my bare skin. "Look at me."

So I do. I look up at him. He's staring directly into my damp eyes, so close that I can smell the salt on his skin.

"It's just money," he whispers. "You're okay. It's just money."

I nod, feeling the tears gather in my eyes, not wanting to look away, though. Because he feels so *solid* and I feel like I'm fading away, and watching him watching me, feeling his hand warm against my shoulder, I'm here. I'm okay.

It's just money.

# CHAPTER TEN

## *TJ*

**IT'S JUST MONEY.**

To be precise, it's the money I was saving to get my stupid broken-down Durango fixed. And, of course, Travis called yesterday to let me know that he found a part, but I don't have the money for it, because I bought Vivi and her mom two cases of generic sparkling water, among other completely unnecessary items. So now we have to wait until another used part comes along, and who knows how long that will take?

*What is happening?* Two days ago I bought a coworker three hundred dollars' worth of groceries. And now I'm down in the restaurant at six A.M. on a Monday morning, making her a *café com leite.*

I pour hot milk into two to-go mugs and add two shots of espresso to each. I add two large scoops of sugar to hers and stir. I know Vivi likes her coffee with tons of sugar, because I have to sit there every morning in the passenger seat as she drives through Starbucks and drops four bucks on a cup of coffee. And then I have to wait as she methodically tears open four packets of sugar in the raw, pours each in, and stirs.

For, like, ten minutes.

The girl is completely clueless. And she's driving me nuts.

I can't figure her out. She's obviously crazy smart, but she's also utterly helpless, like a little kid, who's never had to pay a bill before or buy goddamned groceries. How can she be flat broke and still drive through Starbucks for her coffee? In a Tesla, for chrissake.

And the other thing? She's so *kind*. She's so nice to Ángel, and so patient. She's nice to everyone, and I've been a total ass to her, all because I can't get over how she acted that night at the restaurant. She was a complete train wreck, no doubt. But I mean, everybody has bad nights, right?

Everybody makes mistakes.

Uncle Jay had put the new stage and karaoke machine in the weekend before Thanksgiving. He advertised the hell out of it on all the tourist sites, so the entire Thanksgiving week, the restaurant was a madhouse.

Tourists came to stuff themselves with food, and then they stuck around to get wasted and sing karaoke.

By Saturday I was over it. I was over the spilled drinks, the lost phones I had to track down owners for, the sticky bathroom floors, the guys deciding to take a piss by the shrubs on the back patio.

As soon as Vivi stumbled in with the blonde and the two frat boys, I knew it was gonna get ugly. Demetrio denied them drinks—told them they'd had enough. Plus, their IDs were for shit. But they kept sneaking into a dark corner behind the stage and sharing swigs from a flask. Thinking no one saw what they were doing.

They were all over each other too. Groping and sloppy kissing in the middle of the dance floor.

Uncle Jay should have kicked them out, but he didn't. And that wasn't my job. I had a ton of other things to do around there. I had no intention of volunteering to be a bouncer, too.

That night, at the end of an incredibly long and exhausting holiday week, all I wanted was to go home and fall into bed. It was almost two A.M.—almost last call. The end was in sight. Trying to get a head start on closing, I went upstairs with a mop and bucket to clean the bathroom.

Upstairs was the restaurant only, and it had been long shut down. When I threw open the bathroom door, mop and bucket in hand, Vivi startled me. She stood hunched over the sink, sobbing.

"Hey!" I said. "Are you okay? Do you need some help?"

She looked up into the mirror and she saw me standing right behind her. Her face was a mess—mascara running down her cheeks, eyes red, neck blotchy with patches of pink. We made eye contact for a brief moment, and then she swung around fast and pushed past me. She knocked against my bucket of soapy water, and half of it sloshed out onto the floor.

It took everything I had not to call her a name, not to yell at her as she stumbled down the stairs.

For *chrissake*, I was just trying to help.

"*Bom dia.*" My dad interrupts the memory, which is fine with me. I'd rather not go back to that night.

"*Oi, Pai,*" I say. "Need some help?" He has several boxes of sea salt stacked in his arms.

"*Sim,*" he says, nodding once.

I take two boxes from the top of the stack and follow him into the storage room.

"*O que é isso?*" he asks, glancing at the two coffee mugs.

"For the girl who drives me," I say. "You know, to the hospital."

His lips curve into a smirk. "*Bom,*" he says. And then, thank God, he lets it go.

Dad pushes aside two sets of glittery wings from the Saturday samba dancers to make room for the boxes we are carrying. I can't help but notice that he sighs and shakes his head as he does it.

"*Pai,*" I say, before I lose my nerve. "Can I ask you something?"

He nods again. My dad is a man of few words. He sits down on a stack of boxes and rests his head in his hand. I hadn't really noticed, but my dad is looking older these days. He's got more gray in his hair than I remembered, and it's like he's shrinking or something.

"Do you ever miss it? I mean, the old place?"

"*Sempre,*" he says simply. "Every day."

"Why did you let him do it, *Pai?*"

"Let him?" my dad asks.

We still talk about the whole thing like it was a miracle.

Dad and Uncle Jay had been running the little place on Hypolita Street since before I was born, barely getting by, but with a steady customer base that knew good food when they came across it. Most of them were locals, but—like everyone in Old City, St. Augustine—we relied on the tourists, too. When the lease ran out, the owner decided to sell the place to an ice cream chain (as if St. Augustine needs another ice cream shop). We thought it was all over. Real estate in Old City is impossibly expensive, and we'd never be able to afford our own place.

But then, one Thursday afternoon, a regular named Paul Simpson took my uncle Jay by the arm, walked him out of our little place, and pointed to the big house across the street. That place was nothing like our little hole-in-the-wall. It was a two-story Spanish Colonial, dripping with charm, a balcony overlooking the cobbled street, and a big, beautiful rear courtyard. It was classic Old City, St. Augustine. And it had been on the market for more than two years.

"It's yours if you want it," he said. "I bought it. We'll be partners."

Paul's retired, from I don't know what, but whatever he did earned him a shit ton of money. Because Paul was willing to pay 1.2 million dollars to keep drinking his morning *café com leite* with *pão de queijo da minha tia-avó*, and to keep having his Thursday churrasco nights with three other rich retired guys who also live down on Crescent Beach.

For real. This stuff happens. My great-aunt's cheese bread is really good and all, but I don't think it's worth buying a crazy-expensive house for.

I guess Paul would disagree.

Uncle Jay said we were "living the American Dream." "Work hard," he told us, "and opportunity comes to you."

So we all worked our asses off through the down season, sanding the wood floors, building the place out with fancy lighting and old distressed wood tables. Mom and Mariana filled the rooms with *artesanato* from all around Brazil, and Uncle Jay ordered the best of the best churrasco grill from São Paulo.

As it turns out, living the American Dream requires going into deep debt—and for our family, this was a first. We had never before carried debt. Not one cent.

But now we are living like true Americans, and this restaurant is like a leech, sucking the life out of us. Things were slow at first, since our regulars (who remain loyal to this day) could only fill about a quarter of the huge space, but after Uncle Jay set up the bar and the karaoke machine, business picked up fast.

Suddenly Sabor do Brasil wasn't known for my dad's tender *picanha* or my great-aunt's savory cheese bread. Instead it was the place where all the tourists came for a fun party.

And we have all been killing ourselves to feed the beast—filling the tables with birthdays and bachelorette parties, creating an ever-more-fun and "exotic" Brazilian experience for our guests.

Yeah, we are slowly climbing our way out of debt, but none of it feels quite right. And now here I am, making coffee for the same disaster of a girl who danced topless on the stage and then launched herself into the pavement. The same girl who has no idea how to shop at Costco, who's so clueless that she thinks she can make an ATM deposit and then go out and spend the money right away, who incessantly talks about random bird facts, speaks Spanish like a native, wraps that long wavy hair of hers into a messy pile on top of her head and still manages to look a kind of innocent-pretty in scrubs and no makeup . . .

*What the hell am I doing? This has to stop.*

I force myself to remember her face the first time I met her, reflected in the mirror of the restaurant's upstairs bathroom.

After I finished cleaning the bathroom, I headed downstairs, mop and bucket in hand.

I don't remember what song was playing. It doesn't really matter. I do remember seeing Vivi unhook her bra, swing it over her head, and toss it across the room. Her shirt was already off, and Carlitos was launching himself across the bar, trying to get to the stage to stop her.

He was too late. She took off into a sprint and threw herself into the small crowd gathered at the edge of the stage. I guess she expected them to catch her. I guess she expected to fly.

She didn't fly. She fell flat on her face, onto the brick pavers.

Everyone on the small dance floor stepped away to give her room.

And who rushed in to scoop her up off the pavement? I did. That's who.

Blood ran from her nose, and her left cheek was filled with tiny abrasions.

"Move!" I called out.

I carried her to the kitchen and held her head back. I compressed her nostrils with a clean dishrag. Sabrina grabbed a *churrasqueiro* uniform shirt from the rack in the break room and helped her put it on while I pressed the rag hard against her nostrils.

I must have asked her again—if she was okay, if it hurt. I'm sure I tried to determine whether she had broken her nose. But she didn't say a word. She leaned into my arms and cried silently while I stopped the bleeding and cleaned the abrasions with warm soapy water.

Sabrina went out to find Vivi's friends. They came stumbling into the kitchen, still laughing and singing.

"Let's get out of here!" one of the asshole frat boys said.

Vivi struggled to sit up and wiped her eyes with her forearm.

"She's done for the night," I said. "I'm calling a cab."

"Whatever, man," the other asshole frat boy said. "Look at her. She's all good!"

"She needs to go home," I growled. "She lost a lot of blood, and her blood-alcohol level is through the roof. She needs fluids—electrolytes—and she needs a bed."

"Who do you think you are, a doctor or something?" idiot frat boy said. "How about you stick to being a waiter and let us take care of this, buddy?"

"Dude," the other one said, gesturing toward my abandoned mop bucket, "I think he's the janitor. Doctor Janitor, M.D.!" They both laughed, doubled over.

I actually grabbed my right wrist with my left hand to physically prevent myself from punching both of those assholes in their faces.

"Sabrina." I clenched my jaw together tight. "Call her a cab."

As soon as Sabrina walked out of the room, Vivi's friend—the blond girl—came in and pulled her to stand up. She locked arms with Vivi and dragged her out of the kitchen.

"We'll take care of her!" the girl half slurred. "Won't we, Vivi?"

All four of them stumbled out of the restaurant and into the night. I figured I'd never see that girl again.

I hoped I'd never see any of them again.

My dad stands up and pulls a box of sea salt from the top shelf.

"Please answer me, *Pai*. I want to understand this. Why did you let him do it?" I know that, with Dad, I don't even need to explain what I mean by *it*—the stage, the karaoke machine, and now the samba dancers. He knows better than anyone what *it* means, and how far it's all taken us from where we want to be.

"I didn't *let* your uncle do anything, Tomás. We all thought it was the right thing to do."

Dad's the only one who calls me Tomás. It's not even my name, technically.

"Do you still think that?" I ask him.

"Bigger isn't always better," he says.

I guess that's his answer, because he starts to walk away. When he gets to the bar counter, he puts the box of salt down and grabs a leaflet from the top of a stack.

"For the girl who drives you," he says, handing it to me.

I look down at the leaflet. It's one of those inserts you find in the newspaper, with coupons from local restaurants. This one is for ours, a 50-percent-off July 3 special for local residents only. Uncle Jay decided to run the special as a way to fill the place on an off night. For once, he and Dad agreed on something—Dad just wanted a way to thank the locals for their loyalty (or, in other words, for putting up with all the wasted tourists).

"She's a vegetarian," I say.

He shrugs and smiles wide. "Salad bar—twenty-five items."

"Brazil's best," I say, and we both smile, because I say it a hundred times every night, and because: *When, exactly, did macaroni salad become Brazil's best?*

"What's up, my homeboy'?"

Did Ángel just say what I thought he said?

"Excuse me?" I ask, lifting the corner of his bedsheet.

"Just keepin' it real over here. So waaas uuuuuup?"

I walk to the front of the bed, where Ángel is sitting upright, holding one hand by his face in a crooked peace sign or a gang sign or some shit like that.

*I mean, what the hell?*

"Let's get this clear, Ángel: I am not your 'homeboy.' That's not—I mean, just *no*."

"Yeah, all right, my *vato*. We cool."

"Turn on your side," I say as I fold the sheet under his hip. He turns away from me.

"Tell me 'bout your weekend, homie," he says.

"Other side," I command.

He turns toward me.

"So, uh, Ángel, before I tell you about my weekend, maybe you should tell me where you learned English."

"Same place I learned *el español*, yo! Music, *la música*. Videos, mostly. Reggaeton, gangsta rap, but I like kickin' it old-school, too, homes. I'm all up in that—Big Daddy Kane, Slick Rick . . ."

I can't help myself. I'm trying to pull the bedsheet out from under him, but I'm doubled over, laughing my ass off. "For real? Slick Rick?" I manage to cough out between laughs.

"You got a problem with my boy Ricky?" he asks, whacking me on the shoulder.

I shake my head. "You're a piece of work, Ángel."

"Fo' real, TJ, I'm dyin' over here without my music. Can you help a man out?"

"What? You want me to bring you, like, an old iPod?"

"Yeah," he says. "Or somethin'!"

"Do you promise never to call me your homeboy ever again?"

"Yeah, okay, homie."

"Dude! I mean it, you can't go around talking like that. It's just—it's *weird*."

Ángel's face drops and he looks down at his legs hanging motionless from the end of the bed. "Go around? I'm not going anywhere, TJ," he says, suddenly serious. "I can't even stand up."

I nod and ease him back down onto the bed. "I'll try to hook you up," I say. "But none of that old-school rap bullshit. I think I've got, like, some Calle 13."

"I'm down," he says. "You got 'Uiyi Guaye'?"

"Never heard of it," I say.

He shrugs. " 'La Vuelta al Mundo'? Cuz I'm gonna play that one for you and Vivi."

"What are you talking about?"

" '*Yo no creo en la iglesia, pero creo en tu mirada.*' " He's singing, sort of. At least, I think that's what he's doing.

I have no idea what he's saying. Sometimes, just by looking at me, people think I speak Spanish. It bugs the shit out of me, how people assume that. I kind of wish I did speak some Spanish, though. I mean, it's close enough to Portuguese that I can read it okay, but my pronunciation is for shit, and I barely understand a word of it when I hear it.

"Where is she, anyway?" he asks.

Now that we know Ángel speaks English—messed up as his English may be—and that he understands most of what we're telling him, Prashanti has Vivi helping out with other stuff—nothing that's gonna make her puke. More like checking on the inventory of linens and restocking supply closets. She still hangs around for most of the day with Ángel, and whenever someone's trying to tell him something important, we make sure Vivi's there to translate, but she's not in here all the time anymore.

I think Ángel misses her.

At first I thought she'd have a fit about all that mundane work. I mean, little Miss Ivy League stacking rolls of toilet paper and stuff. But she's been totally cool about it. She never complains, no matter what Prashanti throws at her. The weird thing about Vivi is that she does every task like it *really* matters. Last Friday she was cleaning out the fridge in the break room, which is always super skanky. First she cleaned it really well, with bleach and stuff. She had these big-ass yellow gloves on all the way to her elbows, and a red bandana wrapped around her head. She had taken the top of her scrubs off, and she was wearing a black tank top. Her hair was piled up on her head and all sticking out in every direction and she was scrubbing away with a Brillo pad.

She looked kinda cute like that, if I'm being honest.

She came up with a system, for us to label all our food with different-colored sticky notes before we put it in there. She even went out and got the sticky notes and a marker, and she attached the marker to a little red string so it wouldn't disappear.

It's only been a couple of days, but her system is working so far. Maybe it will keep the fridge from turning into a petri dish again. Maybe that girl will start bringing her own lunch—save some money by not eating that crap cafeteria food.

*Christ*, I'm probably gonna be packing her a lunch every morning too, the way things are going. I need to pull myself together—grow a spine.

"Dunno." I shrug. "Last I saw her, she was sorting towels."

"No, I mean, what happened to Vivi to make her sad?" he says.

*Oh, so I guess we are getting real here.* I'm not sure it's my place to say, and I don't really know much. But for some reason, I feel like I should tell him what I do know.

"Her dad died. I don't know when, but not that long ago. And she and her mom are alone, and I think they're having a hard time, like with money and stuff."

"You got a dad?" he asks.

"Yeah," I say.

"And a mom?"

I nod. "Yeah, I've got a mom."

"You got a big family, I bet."

"Uh-huh," I say. "Too big, if you ask me."

"Nah," he says. "That's cool. Havin' a big family. I don't have a family. I mean, one drunk-ass uncle, but he don't count."

I figured Ángel didn't have anyone, since he's indigent, and since no one has ever visited him—not one person since he got here almost two months ago. But I'm not one to ask questions, so I didn't know for sure.

It seems like he was pretty close to the people he worked for— the owners of that turkey farm. He talks about them sometimes. I think he really likes them. I think maybe he wishes they would visit. But from what I know about Ángel's situation, there's not a chance in hell those people will show their faces here. Everybody here knows it was their negligence that got him in this situation. They used him to cover up all those sick turkeys so the state wouldn't shut down their farm. He was covered in blood by the end of the day, and I bet those people didn't even have a drop of it on their own hands. *Assholes.*

There's a soft knock on Ángel's door. I straighten the sheets to cover his scrawny legs, and his social worker, Mrs. Rosales, walks in with a guy in a uniform. The guy looks like police or something. Mrs. Rosales is standing extra tall, like she's stressed.

"How are you feeling today, Ángel?" she asks. Her voice is all forced cheerful.

"I'm all right, just chillin' with my boy TJ," he says. "How *you* doin', girl?"

I'm still having trouble getting used to Ángel's English. He's got a thick accent and all, but he strings together words like they're right out of some song or video. It's hilarious.

*At least he didn't call her "homegirl." That would have been a shit-show.*

Mrs. Rosales is very good at her job, but part of what makes her good is that she is no-nonsense. She doesn't let patients get away with acting all helpless. She tells them they need to be their own advocates, which—if you ask me—is some seriously good advice.

"I'm just fine, Ángel. Thank you for asking." She turns to the man in the uniform. "I'd like for you to meet Officer Talmadge, from Immigration and Customs Enforcement. That's part of the Department of Homeland Security, Ángel. Officer Talmadge has a few questions for you."

*Oh hell.*

Ángel doesn't say anything. I nudge his calf gently. "You want me to get Vivi?" I ask.

"No, thank you," he says, his voice firm. "Please, no. I not need help. I do not wish her to be here."

And just like that, Ángel's English has gone all proper, and a little broken. I guess if it doesn't come from a song or video, he doesn't quite have it mastered yet. Honest to God, that kid's *smart*. I think he could pick up just about any language you throw at him as long as he can mimic what he sees and hears—I mean, give the kid a couple of Bollywood movies, and he'd be talking Hindi in no time.

"Could you close the door behind you, TJ?" Mrs. Rosales asks.

I guess that's my cue to leave. I nod, throw a weak smile at Ángel, and head out of the room, closing the door almost completely. Then I take two quick glances down the hall and lean in to listen.

*Because Department of Homeland Security? That's not good.*

Scarlet Macaw
(Ara macao)
July 3
8:05 PM

Rita can
say HELLO!
HELLO!
and Amazing!

Habitat: Native to
South America
found worldwide
in captivity
Mimics human speech
Monogamous, travels in pairs
(I bet Rita is lonely)

# CHAPTER ELEVEN

## *VIVI*

BIRD JOURNAL
July 3, 8:05 P.M.
Scarlet macaw (*Ara macao*)
*Rita is the coolest! Not only is she drop-dead gorgeous, she's*
  *bilingual. This amazing creature talks English and*
  *Portuguese!*
Physical Description: a large red, yellow, and blue South
  American parrot.
Habitat: native to evergreen forests in tropical South
  America, found worldwide in captivity.
Social Behavior: monogamous birds, observed to maintain
  one partner throughout life.
Call: captive macaws are adept mimics of human speech.

**"BEM-VINDO AO SABOR DO** Brasil."

A distinguished-looking man who seems to be about Mom's age steps out from behind the host's stand and takes my mother's hand. He's wearing a black suit, European cut, a white shirt, and a black tie.

*"Obrigada,"* my mom replies, smiling.

*"A senhora fala português!"* the handsome man exclaims, bowing slightly and releasing her hand.

*"Um pouco,"* my mom says. "We picked up a little Portuguese in Ilha Grande, right, Vivi?"

Incapable of producing any words, I stand dumbfounded beside her.

I'm not sure I can handle being back in this place. I try to remind myself that it's better than sweating it out at the ghost tour, in my nineteenth-century getup.

Last night featured another bombed ghost story—this one a feminist tale of the first female lighthouse keeper, who took over from her husband in 1859, after he managed to plunge from a high scaffolding while trying to whitewash the lighthouse walls. I was three minutes into my carefully crafted account of the challenges faced by nineteenth-century women in Florida when a tourist lunged from the stairwell into the middle of the group, screaming about how a ghost had tied his shoelaces together—which precipitated a fall down a short flight of stairs. Darren was less than pleased with my suggestion to the gentleman that the six-pack of beer he had consumed over the course of the hour might have been to blame for the fall. He gave me tonight off—told me I needed to "unwind a little, maybe."

Anyway, I'm trying to muster up gratitude that I'm here, on a night out with my mom. And I'm trying to remind myself that there's no way anyone will recognize me from one night eight long months ago.

"Ilha Grande—a spectacular part of my native country," the host says. "Perhaps you ran across a cousin of our darling Rita?"

He gestures toward the stairwell, where an extraordinary scarlet macaw poses for tourists. She's an amazing specimen—all bright red and deep blue, a lovely streak of turquoise along her upper tail feathers.

"Say hello, Rita," he calls out.

"Hello," she replies. "Hello. Hello."

I bet Rita is lonely. Macaws are incredibly social birds, and they almost always travel in pairs.

"And is this your first time dining with us?"

Mom nods and glances over at me, but, thankfully, the host is still focused entirely on her, so he doesn't notice the way I shrug and wander over to see Rita.

Mom found the flyer on the floor of my car yesterday—50 percent off a full meal, tonight only. TJ put it on the dash before he got out of the car, after I gave him back the mug that he brought me coffee in. That coffee was so good—it made my daily Starbucks taste like burnt dirt by comparison. And, as if bringing me coffee isn't strange enough, when he got out of my car the other day, he mumbled something about a coupon and me being a vegetarian and probably not wanting it, and then he shoved the flyer onto my dash. He didn't even look at me when he did it.

*Ah, TJ. Pleasant and charming, as always.*

When Mom saw that flyer, she got very excited. "I am so grateful for what you're doing, Vivi—I mean, to keep us on a budget," she said, grabbing my forearm. "But wouldn't it be great to have a night out? To eat some meat?"

*At Sabor do Brasil?* I thought. *No, that would be far from great. That would be utterly humiliating, and it might in fact result in some sort of panic attack.*

But I couldn't say what I was thinking because—thanks be to God—Mom doesn't know anything about my one spectacularly terrible night at Sabor do Brasil.

I'm hoping TJ has the night off. I don't have the energy for his attitude tonight.

"I have the perfect table for you two lovely ladies," the handsome man says, gesturing toward the rear courtyard.

He leads us through the entrance to the old house, which has been converted into a tasteful, modern restaurant with just the right number of rustic and artisanal touches—distressed wood tables, sleek white lights, photographs of Brazilian landscapes in brightly colored frames, interspersed with colorful textiles and handwoven baskets. We leave through a set of French doors and emerge onto a cobblestone patio strung with white globe lights overhead.

I had forgotten how lovely this space was—or maybe I never even saw these parts of the restaurant. I definitely don't remember a gorgeous, smart macaw. But by the time we got here on that awful night, I was already a handful of beers and a few shots of tequila gone.

He leads us to a small table in a dark out-of-the-way corner, for which I am feeling very grateful. He pulls out my mother's chair and takes the napkin from in front of her to place it in her lap.

*Quite the chivalrous one.*

"Would you like to see the cocktail menu? Or perhaps a list of our finest wines?"

I shoot a not subtle glare at my mother, reminding her of our deal. The coupon covers food only, and we can't afford to drink anything but water.

Mom shakes her head discreetly.

"Tap water, or perhaps sparkling?"

"Tap's just fine," she says. "With lemon, please, and no ice."

"Of course, *senhora.*" He nods, smiles a charming smile, and turns to walk away.

I take my own seat and put my own napkin in my lap.

"Doesn't it smell divine?" Mom asks, pulling in a deep breath.

The air smells distinctly of burning flesh, but—I have to agree with my mom—in an incredibly mouthwatering way. Maybe she was right. Maybe we *did* need a break from the vegetarianism.

Five minutes later we are both standing in front of the most beautiful salad bar I have ever seen: hearts of palm artfully arranged on a platter, enormous piles of artichoke hearts, black and green olives, fire-roasted peppers, and sun-dried tomatoes. Beautiful hand-painted ceramic bowls stand filled to overflowing with delicate balls of fresh mozzarella, stacks of sliced tomatoes, thick spears of asparagus, and hunks of Manchego cheese. All I can think about is how much these things would cost if I tried to buy them at Publix. I mean, a single can of artichoke hearts is almost four dollars. And fresh mozzarella? It's so far out of our budget right now that I've learned to avoid the fancy cheese display altogether. It's too painful.

Arriving at the end of the salad bar, I encounter a young man—a boy, really. He looks to be about thirteen. He's standing beside a vast array of bottles, wearing that uniform—the same one I saw TJ in the first time I dropped him off for work, the same one I somehow ended up wearing.

I swallow hard and look down at my food, suddenly feeling nauseous. *He can't have been here that night. There's no way. He would have said something. I would have remembered him.*

Or would I have?

"Fresh pepper?" the boy asks, his voice still the high voice of a child. He holds a large wooden pepper grinder toward my overflowing plate.

I nod, and the boy begins to grind pepper over my food.

"Oil and vinegar?" he asks.

I shake my head, not feeling able to speak quite yet. I need to let go of this feeling. No one here knows what happened. No one could possibly recognize me in this place filled with people and activity, where a dozen waiters and waitresses swarm like bees throughout the restaurant.

I make my way back to the corner table, where a waiter is standing, poised, his hand on my seat back, waiting to pull it out for me.

His back is turned to me, and in the dim light of the courtyard, it takes a moment for me to recognize that the waiter behind my chair is TJ.

My heart starts to race and my fingertips go numb. TJ looks at me and smiles, an enormous, beautiful smile. He's never smiled at me before. It creates a strange and not entirely unpleasant sensation in the pit of my stomach.

*"Senhorita,"* he says, looking down at the ground as he pulls my seat from the table.

I come to a standstill in front of the seat. "You don't have to . . ." I mumble, sounding as nervous as I feel.

"Actually, I do. It's my job, and my uncle is watching us."

"Your uncle?" I ask, looking up to see the handsome man in the black suit, observing us.

"My boss," he says, by way of clarification.

"Oh, sorry," I tell him, sitting down quickly, putting my plate on the table, and yanking my seat forward.

My mom comes along behind me, and TJ does exactly the same for her—same broad, beautiful smile, same humble gesture of holding the chair back and looking downward as my mother takes her seat.

When she says, *"Obrigada,"* he looks up at her and smiles for real. Then he darts a sideways glance at me and strides off toward the kitchen.

I wonder what it would take for *me* to earn one of those smiles from TJ—the real ones. Considering how he acts toward me, I have a feeling that simply saying thank you in decently accented Portuguese wouldn't be nearly enough.


Almost two hours later it has become clear to Mom and me that we weren't cut out to be vegetarians.

I kept trying to muster the willpower to turn the square card in front of my plate from green to red. But here's the thing: when the card is on the green side, cute waiters constantly stop by our table, each one carrying an enormous skewer of freshly grilled meat—sirloin, rib eye, skirt steak, delicate little tenderloins wrapped in bacon. And, as if this isn't enough, they also come by with tiny lamb chops, chicken medallions, shrimp, even lobster.

In short, this meal is a far cry from the rice, beans, and ramen on which Mom and I have been subsisting. For this, I will gladly endure the occasional arrival of TJ at my side, carrying a big stick of meat and an incredibly sharp knife. Plus, he has been a total gentleman all night, so kind and warm.

The first time he arrived at our table, carrying meat, this is how the conversation went:

"I'm sorry I didn't introduce myself earlier," he told my mother as he gently carved a thin slice of sirloin. "I'm TJ. I work with your daughter at the hospital."

"So nice to meet you, TJ," my mother said, gingerly removing the slice with her silver tongs.

That's how TJ's cousin Sabrina instructed us to do it. As it turns out, just about everyone working in this restaurant is related to TJ, and Sabrina is our waitress. When she first came to the table, she reminded me that we had met weeks ago, in the parking lot of the Alligator Farm. Sabrina's the one who instructed us that when our card is green, the *churrasqueiros* (cute waiters who apparently are also cooks) will come by with meat options. "If you'd like some," she explained, "just use the small silver tongs to remove the slice." Or—in my case—slices. "And," she told us, "if you need a break, or if you'd like to return to the salad bar, simply flip your card to red."

I did take a short break, for a second trip to the salad bar. I couldn't resist getting another huge pile of fresh mozzarella and artichoke hearts. But now my card is green again and TJ is back at my side.

"Vivi?" TJ asks. "May I offer you some more *picanha?*"

I nod, trying not to look too ravenous, trying not to think about that subtle accent he placed on *more*.

"And remind me how you like it?"

"Rare," I say, looking down at my plate. "I like it rare."

"Of course," he replies, a tiny smirk playing at the corner of his mouth.

My mom is in love with him. I think maybe she's in love with *all of them*. And, really, what's not to love? Handsome men bringing succulent meats to your side, gently slicing the tastiest morsels just for you, and doing it all with impeccable manners.

That's a formula for success.

And so, even though we are gently slipping into a meat-induced comatose state, I can't bring myself to flip that little card to red.

Finally, while I'm holding my gut and groaning gently, Mom leans forward and flips the card for me.

Sabrina arrives by my side almost immediately and offers to remove my plate.

"Dessert?" she asks. "Coffee?"

I'm so tempted to order one of those Brazilian coffees, but it's not included in the price of the meal, so I shake my head.

"Shall we just take a look at the dessert menu?" Mom asks.

"Mom," I say under my breath, hoping she will remember our deal. She turns to Sabrina. "We're so full," she says.

"Of course," Sabrina says. "It happens."

I watch her walk through the bar area, which by this time of night is filled with gregarious tourists. I look away, feeling nauseous again. I decide instead to focus on the live music, which started around the same time I made my second trip to the salad bar, on a small stage that's tucked into the corner of the courtyard. The music is lovely and soothing—a guitarist plays while a percussionist gently beats out a soft rhythm on a range of strange handheld instruments, and a woman begins singing in a deep voice.

"Bossa nova," my mom says, letting her eyes fall gently shut and leaning back in her chair. "Oh, how I love this place."

Sabrina arrives at our table with a plateful of bite-sized sweets and two Brazilian coffees. "On the house," she says, smiling. She places a coffee in front of me. "This one's for you," she tells me. "Extra sugar."

And just like that I feel tears pricking at the corners of my eyes, and I have to press my lips together and let my eyelids flutter shut. Mom and Sabrina are chatting about the different desserts she brought to us, but I can't pay attention because I'm thinking about how strange it is—how this place that I so dreaded, that I was so desperate to avoid—how tonight, the one place that I thought I'd never be able to return has become, for me, something entirely different.

I pull in a deep breath, savoring the damp, briny air. I lean back in my chair and sip my perfectly sweetened Brazilian coffee. And I relax.

*Oh my God, I relax.*

I can't remember the last time I felt this content. And I know that my mom feels the same way. We sit together at the table, soaking in the atmosphere, in absolutely no rush to go anywhere. Sabrina doesn't even offer to bring us the check, because I think she understands that we have nowhere else to be, except for here.

Some of the tables around us empty, and the bar fills. The music continues, but the band is playing more lively songs now. Mom tells me the music has shifted to samba, but I wouldn't know.

And then the music stops and the handsome host, who I guess is TJ's uncle, steps onto the stage and takes the microphone.

"My dear friends . . . ," he begins, in a booming voice. "The clock has struck midnight."

Two of the *churrasqueiros* step onto the stage, and they start to unfold a piece of cloth.

"Which means that we have arrived on this most special of days," TJ's uncle continues.

I lean forward in my seat, because I'm realizing that they are stretching a huge American flag across the stage.

"Independence Day, for this great country that my family now calls home. So please stand and join me in singing our national anthem."

*Is this guy for real?* My mom looks at me and shrugs, and we both stand. The entire staff comes out onto the patio, and the woman who was just singing samba leads us in a rousing rendition of the national anthem. I glance back into the bar to see several drunk patrons who have formed a long swaying line of people, holding on to one another's shoulders.

But the staff—they all look dead serious, and they're all holding their right hands over their hearts.

When the song ends, the group in the bar claps and cheers and whoops. TJ's uncle gestures for them to lower their voices, and then he continues with his patriotic monologue.

"My family came here from Brazil more than twenty years ago. For most of the Carvalho clan, this is our adopted country, but it is ours!"

The drunks in the bar clap and cheer and whoop some more.

"This day is also a very special day for our family, because it is the birthday of the very first Carvalho to be born on American soil." He gestures toward the wait staff. "So please join my family in singing 'Happy Birthday' to my nephew Thomas Jefferson Carvalho!"

The entire restaurant launches into "Happy Birthday"—not the

Portuguese version that I have heard the *churrasqueiros* gather around tables to sing several times throughout the night, but the good, old-fashioned American version. I turn to see the other *churrasqueiros* pushing TJ forward toward the stage.

*TJ. Thomas Jefferson.* Somehow I find that both completely cheesy and utterly adorable.

The other waiters push TJ onto the stage, smiling and laughing as the song continues. An older woman wearing an apron brings flan to him, with tons of candles stuck into the top. The singing stops and she holds the flan in front of his face.

He stands still in front of the row of candles, and he looks across the courtyard, directly at me. He smiles. A *real* smile. I can't help smiling back.

I'm still sitting perfectly still, feeling my heart beat hard in my chest, still seeing TJ's smile for me, lit up by birthday candles, wondering what I did to finally earn it.

Soon Sabrina is back at our table, laughing about how her dad is such a sap, and how poor TJ has to endure that spectacle every year. And my mom is telling her how sweet it all is, and how wonderful it is that the Carvalho family feels such warmth toward this country. I want to join in on the conversation, but I'm still sort of floating, trying to ignore my rational self, which says that the smile was not for me, that TJ probably couldn't even see me back here in this dark corner.

But then TJ and his cousin Carlitos are standing at our table too. Carlitos has Rita the macaw perched on his shoulder.

"Did you meet Rita?" TJ asks. "I mean, uh, I know how into birds you are."

"Yeah," I say. "We met earlier. She's amazing."

"Amazing. Amazing. Amazing," Rita mimics.

"Wanna hold her?" Carlitos asks.

"Sure!" I say. I reach out my arm and Rita hops on as if we're old friends.

"Hello again, pretty girl," I coo.

"Hello! Hello!" she replies.

"Hey," I say, turning to look at TJ. "Happy birthday."

"Thanks." He shrugs and looks at the ground, suddenly shy.

*TJ. Shy. What is happening?*

"We're going out to celebrate later," Sabrina says. "Wanna join?"

"Me?" I ask, sounding like a total idiot, and to make things worse, I realize that I'm actually pointing at myself—directly at my chest.

TJ looks up—first at my chest, for a split second, and then at my face.

"Yeah, you," Carlitos says. "It'll be fun."

I hand Rita back to Carlitos while imagining a wild party—drunk people taking shots off each other's belly buttons, upside-down keg stands. In other words, I'm imagining exactly the kind of environment that I want—no, *need*—to avoid.

"You should go!" my mom urges, nudging me. "I haven't had a drop to drink, so I'll drive myself home. You can take a cab later."

A cab requires money. That's what I want to say to my mom, but I resist.

"Thanks so much for the invitation," I say, looking at Sabrina and Carlitos, and at the incredible Rita, looking gorgeous on his shoulder. "But this is about as much party as I can take for one night." I gesture toward the bar, which is getting more boisterous by the minute. "I'm not really up for—"

"You think we're gonna stay here?" Sabrina says. "Not a chance. We're going out to Guana Reserve—full-moon kayaking."

"Have you all ever been out there?" Carlitos asks. He's looking at my mom.

She shakes her head.

"It's a nature preserve—an estuary. It's incredible," he says.

"And you don't need to worry, Mrs. Flannigan. It's not like we will be partying or anything," Sabrina says. "I mean, we're not really into all of that." Sabrina smiles and nudges TJ.

"We're the clean-living Carvalho clan," Carlitos says. "All we need for a good time is some coconut water and a full moon."

"Sounds wonderful!" my mom exclaims.

"We can give her a ride home," TJ blurts out, and then he bites down hard on his lip and looks away from us both.

Maybe he's just trying not to be rude. I don't know. All I know is that I want another chance to see that smile tonight—the real one.

"Okay," I say. "Sounds fun."

# CHAPTER TWELVE

## ÁNGEL

**OH, I'M SORRY.** Did I wake you?

I don't sleep much these days. The nighttime is the worst. It's so quiet in here. You wouldn't think a hospital could be quiet, would you? Yeah, the machines are still beeping and sighing, but still, it's quiet.

Too quiet. Too calm.

And it must be a full moon, because there's lots of light coming in through the slats in the window blinds. If I could get up, I'd go over there and twist that plastic stick to make the blinds close, but I can't get up. And I don't want to call Bertrand.

He'll come in to close them, but then he'll leave without saying anything. And I'll feel even more lonely.

The night nurses tiptoe around, trying really hard not to wake us up, but I'm not asleep. It seems like I'm never asleep anymore. I need somebody to talk to. I need some way to get out of my head, because it feels like it's about to explode.

I guess I'm gonna have to talk to you people.

Sometimes, at night, when I can't sleep because I'm too busy pushing away the thoughts, or I'm listening to my heart and stressing about why it's beating so loud or so fast or not loud enough or not fast enough—sometimes I look up at the ceiling tiles and I imagine that I'm back at that place in Texas. It had ceiling tiles just like this. Before I got there, I had never seen a ceiling pieced together with big white rectangles. Most of the ceilings back where I'm from are made of thatch—a bunch of leaves woven together. And I guess, technically, they're roofs. Because they're the only thing separating a kid who's trying to sleep from the wide-open sky.

So when I got to that shelter in Texas, that ceiling looked so *solid* to me.

It only took me three weeks to get to the border. I had to sneak into Mexico from Guatemala, and then I had to walk and catch rides all the way through Mexico. It wasn't that bad, but I slept outside the whole time, on the ground, with a bunch of strangers who were also trying to get to the U.S.

When I got to the border, I was really scared, but I did what everyone I met along the way told me I should do. I walked past all the cars lined up to get into the *Estados Unidos*. And I went to the man sitting at that little window, and I told him this:

*I am fifteen. I am from Guatemala. I am an orphan.*

He called another man over to the little booth, and that man took me to a room where a woman asked me questions. She didn't speak Mam, but she called somebody on a telephone, and that person did. I took the phone, my hand shaking, and I held it to my ear.

*"Je'k, a nbiye' Leslie. Ti tb'iya?"*

She told me her name was Leslie, which I had to ask her to repeat a bunch of times. I'd never heard the name Leslie before. Once I got her name, I told her mine.

She asked a lot of questions, and I answered them. Then another man came, and he put me into a police car.

When that happened, I got really scared. Because when I was in Mexico, I met people who said they sometimes take you to jail. But he didn't take me to any jail. He took me to a nice complex of sturdy buildings made out of brick. It had flowers planted by the front door and trees in the garden and a pretty courtyard. A woman named Mrs. Richmond, who I later learned was the director of the children's home, took me to a room with two beds, and she said one of them was mine. Then she gave me some soap and some clean clothes, and she told me to take a shower.

So here's the thing: where I'm from, we don't have showers. When we want to get clean, we take a bucket of (cold) water and *estropaj*, which is a plant that's kind of like a sponge. We put some soap, called *q'e'q*, on the spongy thing, and then we scrub down and freeze our asses off.

You have no idea how incredible that first hot shower felt. I love showers, and hot-water heaters. Hot-water heaters are the absolute best.

And now I'm gonna be real with you, because it's the middle of the night, and what do I have to lose?

Lying in that bed in Texas, all clean and smelling like soap, covered with a cotton sheet (I'd never seen one of those before) and a soft brown blanket and another blanket that had bright red stripes on it, my head resting on not one but two fluffy pillows (I love pillows!), and looking up at that ceiling, I felt safe. For the first time in weeks—okay, maybe years or maybe for the first time in my entire stupid life—I felt like it was okay to sleep, because nobody would mess with me there.

Oh, how I slept. For sixty-three nights I slept. I woke up bright-eyed every morning, and I almost skipped to the kitchen for those eggs and bacon.

Eggs and bacon and toasted bread with as much butter as we wanted.

Every. Single. Morning.

Or, if we weren't in the mood for eggs and bacon, they gave us cereal with milk from a big silver machine. All I had to do was put my cup against a lever under that machine and push, and the milk came flowing out. It never stopped. Not ever.

I had tasted milk before, but I mostly drank *q'o'tj*, which is like a mash of corn, and also is way less creamy and delicious than milk.

The kids from the cities—from San Pedro Sula and San Salvador, from Tegucigalpa and la Ciudad de Guatemala—they just filled their cups with milk and went to the table, like it was nothing. That's how I knew which ones of those kids came from the *aldea*, like me.

Because, I'm telling you, we stood there like idiots, staring at that silver milk machine. And I know what they were all thinking, because I was thinking the same thing.

Do you know how long it takes to coax a cup of milk from a hungry cow? Or how many scrawny chickens you've got to have to gather a dozen eggs for breakfast? And bacon—I'd never even seen it until I got to Texas. Because: Who has a pig? And if you do have a pig, you're not gonna kill it so you can have a few strips of bacon on a Tuesday morning, are you? Nope. At least, I don't think you are, but I've never had a pig, so I wouldn't really know for sure.

I spent two near-perfect months in that place, where the milk came from silver machines, and where every night I slept like a baby under cotton sheets and a pile of blankets, my head on a couple of soft pillows. And five days a week, after that miracle of a breakfast, I went across the grassy courtyard with the other kids, and we sat at desks, in classrooms with whiteboards and markers in four colors. And a nice woman named Mrs. Jiménez, who spoke Spanish but with a funny accent, taught me English and math and other stuff too—like what to do with deodorant and how to brush my teeth with toothpaste.

You probably think that's bad, that Mrs. Jiménez taught me about toothpaste. You probably think maybe I should feel offended, like that means she thought I was uneducated or something. But you're wrong. Because I *love* toothpaste. I'm obsessed with toothpaste. I love the way it makes my mouth tingle and how smooth my teeth feel when I run my tongue across them. And deodorant's pretty cool too. And, it might seem weird to you, but I needed for Mrs. Jiménez to explain them to me, because I didn't use them before. But now I do. Twice a day, every day.

And on the weekends, we did a few chores, but they were easy—sweeping the kitchen or pulling weeds from the grassy courtyard. And then we got to *hang out*. We went into the living room and watched movies, or we kicked a ball around the courtyard.

There was this bulletin board down the hall from my bedroom. I learned those words when I got to the shelter: *bulletin board*. Mrs. Richmond would cover it every week with a new brightly colored paper, and she decorated it with these strips of cardboard—sometimes curvy, sometimes straight. And if there was a holiday, like Easter or something, she put little decorations on that bulletin board, brightly painted eggs and rabbits with big ears and stuff. And every week she put information up there about special "activities" and sometimes "outings."

I'm telling you, we all ate that stuff up. We loved it. Even the toughest kids from San Pedro Sula—the murder capital of the world—even those kids were all about hunting around the place for plastic eggs filled with candy, or playing that game called Pictionary. We played games after dinner—a big dinner, every night at the same time, always with meat and a vegetable. It was like we were living in some alternate universe, some fantasy life where we didn't have to eat the same steamed corn mash every night, where we got to pretend that we hadn't watched our father and our brother get shot in the chest, point-blank. We hadn't climbed over the still-bleeding bodies of our parents to run away. We got to forget about all that stuff. Except when we went into that one room, with Mrs. Ramirez.

She made us sit down on a yellow sofa and talk about it all. When I went in there, she even had a nice *gringa* named Julie with her. Julie spoke Mam. I still don't really get why. She said she lived in Huehuetenango for a couple of years. She worked for something called the Peace Corps. That's what she told me. I don't know what the Peace Corps is, but I liked Julie, and her Mam wasn't bad. She's still the only *gringa* I've ever met who knows how to speak Mam. And yeah, in there, Mrs. Ramirez made me talk about what happened. But it was all like a dream, like I was telling her about a nightmare I once had a long time ago, and then I woke up with my head on those fluffy pillows.

Julie told me that was okay. She and Mrs. Ramirez said that if I wanted to remember it all like it was a *pesadiy*, if I wanted to believe it was a bad nightmare, I could do that. Mrs. Ramirez said that, for now, that's the way my mind is helping me so that I can keep on going.

So I do. Most of the time, I think of myself as a *mox*—a kid who never had a family. Which is fine. Lots of kids don't have families.

Just at night, sometimes. Sometimes at night I wake up, and I forget to forget.

Anyway, that place was the best. I wish my stupid uncle had never come to pick me up.

THE OWL
 SWOOPED down
   in front
of our boat!
All will be well.

July 4
2:39 AM

Barred Owl
(Strix varia)

Usually Solitary
Not Strictly Nocturnal
Common, found in
  hardwood swamp
     areas

Call: Who cooks for you?
   Who cooks for you?

# CHAPTER THIRTEEN

## *VIVI*

BIRD JOURNAL

July 4, 2:39 A.M.

Barred owl (*Strix varia*)

*My favorite of all the owls led us through the marsh tonight. He*
*swooped and danced through the sky; he landed in a tall tree*
*like he was there to bring me a message.*

Physical Description: streaked belly, orange yellow bill.

Flight: heavy and direct.

Activity: not strictly nocturnal, sometimes active during the
day.

Social Behavior: usually solitary.

Call: *Who cooks for you? Who cooks for you?*

*When the barred owl asked me, "Who cooks for you?" he also*
*told me this: All will be well.*

**"HEY, VIV!" TJ CALLS** out to me. "Over here!"

I walk along the gravel path toward the sound of TJ and his cousins. The stones glow under the light of a full moon, and palm fronds rustle in the gentle breeze. The path widens and I see them, launching kayaks into the still water one by one, sending moonlit ripples across the lake.

I head toward TJ, awed that this is all happening—that I'm in the middle of a marsh with TJ and his family on a breathtakingly beautiful night, that they prepared and fed me and my mother the most fabulous of meals, and that now they *want* to be with me.

Sabrina lent me a bikini, a white tank, and some board shorts. The bikini has significantly less material than any bathing suit I've ever owned, and I've never worn board shorts before. When I went to the bathroom stall to change out of my jeans and silk top, it felt strange and exhilarating—as if I were letting go of much more than an outfit.

TJ is calling me over to his boat. He watches me walk toward him, clearly noticing that I'm not in my own clothes anymore.

"Have you been kayaking before?" For a brief moment I wonder what he thinks of me wearing his cousin's clothes. But I don't want to think about that.

"Yeah," I say. "A bunch of times."

Honestly, I don't want to think about that, either. Everything feels too good right now—too right for me to dive into those memories of kayaking with my parents—shooting through caves in Costa Rica, gliding along the edge of Alaska's Glacier Bay.

"Wanna drive?" he asks.

I shrug and hop into the rear seat—which is the seat of control in kayaks. He grabs the front of the kayak and starts to run, splashing through the deepening water at the edge of the lake. When the kayak gets going, TJ gracefully lifts himself out of the water and slides into the hull.

"Did you and your mom like the dinner?" he asks.

He's smiling at me. Again.

"It was so incredibly good," I say. "Everything!"

"I gotta say," TJ tells me, "for a vegetarian, you really know how to throw down the steak." His eyes gleam in the dark. "And you're definitely not afraid of a lamb chop. I mean, gnawing on the bone—that's a bold move."

"Yeah, okay." I laugh. "I admit that we are reluctant vegetarians, at best."

The other kayaks are well ahead of us, but the raucous sounds of laughter and splashing travel across the water toward us.

"Wanna catch up?" I ask.

"Nah," he says, looking out across the lake. "Let's hug the shore for a while. My cousins are too damn loud."

I steer toward the west shore of the lake. "They're *all* your cousins?" I ask.

"Every last one of them," he says. "Well, except Dougie—he belongs to Sabrina."

"Dougie?" I ask.

"Yeah, Sabrina's boyfriend, Doug. They've been together since, like, before he hit puberty. We still call him Dougie to give him shit."

"I don't have any family," I say, "except my mom. I mean, we have family, but we're not really in touch, you know?"

TJ stops paddling and looks back at me. "No," he says, "I don't have any idea what that's like. Pretty much every person you saw working at that restaurant tonight is related to me." He pauses and turns around, and we start to paddle. "And we are all there every night. Believe me. Most days I wish I had a small family—or maybe no family at all."

I'm not sure how to respond to that, so I don't.

I steer us toward the scrub oaks and palmettos lining the edge of the lake. We paddle in silence, weaving through the dense marsh grasses. The other boats have rounded a curve, leaving us in a stillness so profound that I can hear droplets of water lifting from my paddle every time I complete a stroke. Each one catches the pale blue light of the moon as it falls from the tip of the paddle, and when a stray drop lands on the bare skin of my thigh, it feels warm, like it's gathered the light and heat of the sun and hoarded it for the night.

And then I hear it: *"Who cooks for you? Who cooks for you?"*

"Look," TJ whispers, pointing toward the bare branch of a pine.

A barred owl stares down at us, black eyes wide, face almost glowing in the light of the moon. We both stop paddling and glide in silence, watching that owl watch us.

"What kind is it?" he whispers.

"A common barred owl," I whisper back.

"It doesn't look common to me," he says.

He's right. The owl is mesmerizing.

*Who cooks for you? Who cooks for you?*

As we glide past the tree where the magnificent creature is perched, he spreads his wings and takes to the air. With two graceful pumps of his wide-open wings, he shifts into a soar, swooping down in front of us. His entire body glows in the light of the moon as he dives toward the water and skims across its surface. It's as if he's performing just for us.

He lifts into the air and turns, swoops down once more in front of our boat, and then pumps his wings and lifts off, heading across the treetops, in the direction of the other kayaks.

"That was—" TJ starts to say something, but stops himself. We are both sitting perfectly still, the boat still gliding slowly across the surface of the lake.

"What?" I ask.

"Strange," he says, turning to look at me. "And kind of fantastic."

"Yeah," I tell him. I don't say the rest. I don't tell him how my heart is beating more slowly now, how a calm has descended over me. I don't tell him how I know that the owl came here to find me.

I know what the owl wants to tell me tonight. I am sure of it.

TJ could never understand that a barred owl in the middle of a swamp has made this so clear to me—clear and bright. He asked me, *Who cooks for you?* and I knew the answer. Tonight, I know who does. Tonight, this is where I'm meant to be. Despite all evidence to the contrary, TJ and his cousins are supposed to be here in my life tonight, and I am meant to be in this boat with TJ, taking in the gentle beauty of the marshland.

*All will be well.*

We paddle toward the bend in a beautiful, dense silence, until the lake narrows into a tributary.

"This way?" I ask, easing the nose of the kayak toward the left.

"Yeah," he replies. "This will take us out to the intercostal." He looks around and then back at me. "It's too quiet," he says. "They're up to something—"

Just like that, they appear around the bend, and all hell breaks loose. It's pandemonium, the loud splashing of paddles slamming into the water, water arcing toward us from both sides, voices yelling and laughing. I am immediately soaked entirely through. TJ's cousins, their kayaks somehow protected under the trees, still laugh and call out and pummel us with water.

"Don't just sit there!" TJ yells. "Fight back!"

If the briny water weren't stinging my eyes, I'd have a better chance of knowing which way to direct the splash of my paddle. I lift my tank top to wipe my eyes, but it's useless. The waves of water are still flying toward my face. So I squeeze my eyes shut, grasp my paddle, and start to fling water back at them—at least, I assume it's moving toward them. I still can't open my eyes.

"Race to the point!" someone calls out.

And then, just as quickly as it began, the splashing stops. I wipe my eyes one more time with the bottom of my shirt. By the time I can see, all three boats have pulled out in front of us, and everyone's paddling like mad.

"C'mon, Viv!" TJ says. "Let's get this started!"

So I grasp my paddle and dig in. We hit our stride almost immediately. TJ's paddling sets the pace, and it's *fast*. We have one and only goal: to leave his cousins in the dust. Or, technically, in our wake.

We surge past Matheus and the short kid from the salad bar.

We are gaining fast on Sabrina and Doug, so I need to keep my focus sharp.

"Watch out, Dougie boy!" TJ yells, mocking. "We're about to smoke you."

Sabrina makes the critical mistake of stopping to splash us. Doug, still paddling with all his might, can't do it alone, so we ease past them, ignoring the shower of water that hits us as we go by Sabrina.

Carlitos and Demetrio, the brawniest (and presumably the oldest) cousins, are a boat length ahead. We race around a curve, closing the distance between us, and the intercostal waterway opens up ahead.

"See the point?" TJ asks.

I see it—a pebbled shoreline shimmering white in the moonlight, an ancient oak tree standing alone on the edge, its branches reaching out over the water. And, honest to God, that barred owl is perched in the highest branch, watching.

"I see it!" I call out, suddenly laughing. *Because what kind of owl sits perfectly still on the branch of an oak as utter chaos unfolds below him?* "We can take 'em!"

Carlitos glances back toward our boat. "We've got a little competition!" he yells, digging his paddle in deep.

TJ digs in deeper and picks up the pace of our strokes as we close the distance.

"We've got 'em," he says. "Dig!"

The bow of our kayak eases up beside them. Carlitos and Demetrio glance toward us quickly, but they won't be making any novice mistakes like stopping to splash us. They are completely focused on paddling, and—I gotta say—their biceps are enormous, daunting.

I dig hard, even though my shoulders are burning and my gut is clenched tight and my breath is coming in ragged, between bursts of uncontrollable laughter.

*Because I am not a quitter, and apparently neither is TJ.*

"Oh yeah!" one of the guys calls out from a boat behind us. "They're gonna take you!"

"You can do it, Vivi!" Sabrina yells. "Leave those boys in the dust!"

And that's all it takes. We dig deep and cruise by Carlitos and Demetrio.

"We gotta hit the tree to win," TJ says as the kayak careens onto the shore and lurches to a stop. "Run!"

I tumble out of the kayak behind TJ. I hear the other boat crashing onto the shore, but I don't dare look back as we race toward the trunk of that old oak tree. Instead I look up at the barred owl, lifting off a high branch. I pump my arms as the owl pumps his wings, and I ignore the sharp pain of the rocks under my bare feet.

As we approach the tree, TJ reaches back and grabs my hand. He tugs hard, launching me forward, and we both hit the tree at the same moment. He collapses to the ground, and I fall on top of him, both of us too busy sucking breath deep into our lungs to cheer. Carlitos and Demetrio slam hard against the bark and fall to the ground beside us.

I roll off TJ and hunch forward over my knees, breathing hard. TJ throws his arm around my shoulder and exhales.

"Damn," he says, between heavy breaths. "You're a lot stronger than you look."

I turn my head to see him shaking his head in disbelief. I bite my lip, and I nod, because *Yes, I think maybe I am a lot stronger than I look.*

# CHAPTER FOURTEEN

## *TJ*

**I CAN'T STOP** staring at her.

We're in the backseat of Sabrina's car, riding south toward St. Augustine Beach. It's almost six A.M., and everyone is asleep except for me and Sabrina, who's driving. Vivi has fallen asleep on my shoulder and I am wide-awake—buzzing with intense energy.

She's pressed against me, soft. No one else is watching, and the light from the streetlamps keeps floating across her skin, which is glowing and warm and still a little damp. She smells like salt and vanilla and—

I can't breathe. I also can't stop exploring Vivi with my eyes—the tip of her nose, the long, dark hair falling across her bare arms, the outline of that still-damp tank top against her shoulder, her shorts against her thighs. The curves of that red bikini through the white tank top that's clinging tight to her skin.

She shifts and burrows deeper into my chest.

*Jesus god. I have to stop.*

"Hey, Sabrina," I whisper.

She glances back.

"Throw me that towel."

Sabrina pulls a balled-up towel from the center console and hands it back. Trying not to wake Vivi, I reach my arm around her, spread the towel across her shoulders and chest and thighs, and then I sink down in the seat so that her neck isn't at a strange angle. She looks up at me with sleepy eyes and then they fall closed again.

Her head is resting softly on my chest and her wet hair is spread in waves across her face. She scratches her nose and sniffs, so I gently move her hair back from her face. And then I sit perfectly still, and when I know she's settled comfortably, I close my eyes and lean my head back and try not to move and try to stop imagining in excruciating detail every inch of what I just covered with that towel.

Ten long minutes later we are heading through Anastasia Island, nearing the beach.

"Her house is on A Street, right?" Sabrina asks, slowing as she rounds the bend.

"I think so," I tell her. I give Vivi's shoulder a gentle shake, wishing I didn't have to wake her. "Hey, Viv," I whisper. "We're in St. Augustine Beach. Where's your place?"

Her eyes blink open and she reaches out her arms to stretch, brushing her forearm across my lap. I sit up fast, and she jerks back into her seat.

"Oh God," she mumbles. "Oh my God, I'm sorry. Did I fall asleep on you?"

I shrug.

"Wow. That's embarrassing."

"It's cool," I say, wishing that were true, wishing she hadn't set off a thousand flaming torches under my skin.

*Because this is still a complication I do not need.*

Vivi leans forward. "It's the next left."

Sabrina turns toward the ocean.

"This one," Vivi says, pointing to a house on the right.

"The A-frame?" Sabrina asks.

Vivi nods.

"No way, Vivi! That's awesome. You live in the A-frame on A Street!" Sabrina calls out, nudging Doug hard. "This place is, like, legendary!" She nudges Doug again. "Look where we are!"

Sabrina has pulled up in front of the house, the car facing directly toward the dunes that separate A Street from the ocean.

"Whoa," Doug says, looking not at the weird A-frame house, but toward the ocean. "It's gonna be a perfect sunrise—let's go!"

Sabrina, Matheus, and Doug jump out of the car and head toward the path that cuts between the dunes. Vivi stands beside the car, the towel now wrapped around her shoulders.

"Well, uh, I guess, thanks for—"

She's glancing back and forth between her house (I mean, I guess it's her house) and the beach.

"Come on," I say, nodding toward the ocean. "You've made it this far through the night. You might as well come watch the sunrise, right?"

She nods, smiles, and heads out toward the beach.

"You people are, like, superhuman," she says, looking back toward me as she clambers over a dune.

My cousins and Doug are running, full sprint, toward the ocean.

"I mean, your family. You're all indefatigable."

"We're *what*?" I ask.

"SAT word. Sorry. I drilled hundreds into my head, and some of them refuse to go away." She drops down onto the sand. "Do you all ever get tired?"

I sit beside her as the others tumble into the ocean and dive through the waves. "I think maybe we're always tired, so we don't really know the difference."

"Maybe that's why you're so grumpy all the time at the hospital."

She looks at me and smiles a sort of mischievous smile that also happens to be incredibly sexy.

I run my hand through my hair, suddenly nervous. The sky is shifting from black to gray to orange, and I'm trying to figure out how to apologize to Vivi—again.

*Why am I always needing to apologize to this girl?*

"About that," I say. "I think I should explain."

"It's okay," she tells me. "I was just kidding around. You're fine."

"Why were you crying?" I blurt it out before I can give the words any thought. Because I need to know. "Why were you so upset?"

Her hazel eyes go wide. "What are you talking about?"

"That night at the restaurant—Thanksgiving? Why were you crying?"

She clutches her knees to her chest and lets her forehead fall forward. "Oh God." She groans. "You were there."

I don't say anything, since it seems obvious that I was and since she looks like she's about to puke or maybe cry.

"Were they?" she asks, looking out to the edge of the surf. "Were *all* of you there?"

"We're *always* all there."

"Oh God," she repeats. Then she turns to look right at me. "I don't know. I don't remember."

I started this, so I might as well finish it.

"Before it all happened, you were upstairs in the bathroom, crying really hard. I found you there. I tried to help, but—"

"You all must hate me," she whispers. "How can you have seen me like that and not hate me?"

I don't hate her. I know that now. But I hate what I hear in her voice—shame and regret.

"Hey." I nudge her shoulder. "You got drunk and did stupid shit. We see it all the time. It's no big deal, Viv."

She looks at the place I touched her and then back out to the ocean.

"It is to me." She sighs.

I do see the antics all the time, it's true. But there was something different about her—about that night. And now her lower lip's quivering and she looks like she's about to cry again.

"I get it now," she says.

"What do you mean?"

"Why you hated me from the start."

"Oh shit," I say. "Oh Jesus. I know I've been an asshole. I didn't know you. I mean, I thought you were somebody else. I mean, *God*, I mean—now that I know you, I mean, that wasn't even *you*."

*Jesus Christ, I am all over the place. What am I trying to say?*

"It was me," she whispers. "I promise."

"But you're not that girl—you're not like that."

"Like what?" she asks, looking right at me. Her eyes are shining and hard.

"You know," I say. "You get what I'm trying to say."

"Here's what I know." She's looking toward the orange horizon. "You and your family witnessed part of the worst twenty-four hours of my life. And the part you saw? I don't even remember it. All I know is that I woke up the next morning in a clean shirt from your restaurant and beer-stained jeans. My face was a wreck and I had no idea where my clothes or shoes had gone."

"My great-aunt washed them. We kept them at the restaurant for, like, months—in case you ever came back looking for them."

"Oh no." She groans again. "I'm so sorry."

"Sabrina tried to make those guys wait for her to get them, but they took off."

She shakes her head. "No surprise there."

"Those guys were assholes," I say. They were. Both of them.

"Yeah."

"Are those people your friends?"

"Luke and David?" Her voice goes high. "God, no. I haven't laid eyes on them since that night." She bites hard on her lip and closes her eyes. "But the girl, Gillian, she's my roommate—or she was."

I remember how weak and vulnerable Vivi looked, stumbling out of that room, holding on to the blonde in the short dress—Gillian, I guess. The asshole frat boys were watching them like vultures about to swoop in.

*I shouldn't have let her leave with them.*

I need to know. I need to ask her. "Did they hurt you? Is that why you were crying? Did they—"

She turns her head fast. "You mean *hurt* me? No. It wasn't like that. They were obnoxious, and they got me wasted and told the whole world about the stupid things I did." She studies her bare feet, dug halfway into the sand. "But they didn't, like, assault me or anything."

I feel this incredible relief swelling in my chest. I guess I hadn't realized how much I'd worried about that, about whether something terrible was happening, something I should have stopped.

"My dad was really sick," she whispers. "That's why I was crying—I guess." Then she looks up at me, so I look at her. "I came home for Thanksgiving, and I didn't know. They didn't tell me— I mean, I knew he was sick, but they didn't tell me how bad it was."

She leans back on her elbows and looks up to the sky.

"After three days of being suffocated by positive thinking, I had to get the hell out of that house. I mean, it *smelled like death*, but still, we couldn't talk about even the possibility. *God*, I couldn't breathe."

"And when you got the hell out of there, you came to our restaurant?"

She shakes her head. "First I let Luke and David feed me a six-pack of beer and a half bottle of tequila, *then* I stumbled into your restaurant.

All I remember is singing 'Low Rider' with Gillian and some bikers from Connecticut. And then, conveniently, I blacked out."

"Yeah." I smile, wanting so much to make her smile too. "We get a lot of those wannabe bikers. Were they, like, stock brokers or something?"

"Investment bankers." She grins, and I feel my lungs fill with air.

The sun emerges on the horizon. It's bright white, sending off yellow streaks across the orange sky. It's the kind of sunrise that you know you should look away from so that it won't burn your eyes, but you can't.

"Wow," she says. "It happens so fast."

I think she's referring to the sun, which is moving quickly away from the horizon, but I can't be sure.

We sit in silence, watching my cousins and Doug stand still in the surf, watching the sky fill with light.

"So you and your cousins don't ever drink?" she asks, sitting up taller.

"Nah," I say.

"Drugs?"

"Nope. Never."

"Any vices at all?"

I'm pondering how to give an honest answer to that one when I feel something shifting in my back pocket. It's my phone, set to vibrate. I pull it out.

It's 7:03 A.M. The hospital.

"I have the day off!" I bark at my phone. "Why are they calling me?"

Vivi leans over to look at my screen. "You should get that," she says. "Maybe there's an emergency or something."

*Yeah, I guess I should.*

Reluctantly, I hit the green button and pick up. "This is TJ."

"Waaaaaasssss uuuup, my *vato?*" I'm holding the phone away from my ear, because Ángel is screaming into it. "Where are you, dude? It's after seven and some old lady just came in to change my sheets and started singing songs about Jesus to me."

*Is that Ángel?* Vivi mouths, pointing at the very loud voice coming from my phone.

I nod.

"How did he get your number?"

I shrug, because it's a long story, which starts with me feeling incredibly sorry for the poor kid after he got that visit from the immigration officer.

"TJ? Are you there?"

"I'm here, Ángel. It's a holiday. It's my day off," I say, my face still a foot away from the phone.

"It's his birthday!" Vivi calls out. "Wish him a *feliz cumpleaños,* Ángel!"

"Oh, hold up!" Ángel says. "Is that you, Vivi! Are you with TJ?"

"Yeah!" she calls out.

*I am never, ever going to hear the end of this.*

"Where are you?" he asks.

"At the beach!" she calls out. "We're watching the sunrise."

At this point, I just give up and pass Vivi the phone. She starts talking to Ángel in rapid-fire Spanish, and I start trying not to freak out about all the shit Ángel is going to give me for being with Vivi at the beach at seven A.M—*watching the freaking sunrise.* He's gonna have a field day with this one.

After more animated conversation, she waves me toward the ocean and starts walking.

"He wants to hear the waves," she says. "He misses the ocean."

We walk down to the edge of the surf and stand there. She holds the phone out and we silently listen to the waves come and go.

"I wish you could see this sunrise," she says to him. "The sky is a hundred shades of yellow and orange. It's like fire, Ángel. You wouldn't believe it."

They talk for a little longer, and then she passes the phone back to me. He tells me he's bored, and why do I have to take the day off? I tell him to shut up and turn on the TV or something. Then he reminds me about the promise I made him—to bring reggaeton. I tell him I'll work on it.

When I hang up, we're still standing at the edge of the water.

"That was nice," she says. "I mean, for you to give him your number."

"Poor kid's bored out of his mind," I tell her. "He just needs someone to talk to sometimes, you know? No big deal."

"I bet it's a big deal to him," she says.

I shrug and watch the waves.

"He's going to die, isn't he?" she asks. "He's not going to get a heart, and he's going to die."

I can't look at her, but I know what I have to say.

"Yeah," I tell her. "I'm pretty sure he won't get the heart."

"And he'll die?"

"Yes, he'll die."

"Soon?"

"Probably."

"Okay," she says. "Thanks for telling me."

"I'm sorry," I say.

"Me too," she replies softly.

I know there's more I should tell her, but for now, this is enough.

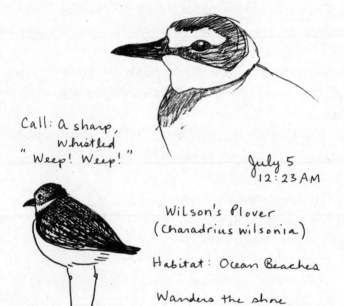

Call: A sharp,
whistled
" Weep! Weep! "

July 5
12:23 AM

Wilson's Plover
(Charadrius wilsonia)

Habitat: Ocean Beaches

Wanders the shore
for food
At risk of becoming
Endangered

# CHAPTER FIFTEEN

## *VIVI*

BIRD JOURNAL
July 5, 12:23 A.M.
Wilson's plover (*Charadrius wilsonia*)
Physical Description: medium-sized shorebird with brown
   back and white underbelly, pinkish-gray legs.
Habitat: ocean beaches. Lives year-round along much of
   Florida's coastline.
Diet: wanders the shore for fiddler crabs, worms, insects. It
   is a probing bird.
Call: a sharp whistled *weep, weep!*
*The Wilson's plover, a rare species, was named for the early*
   *ornithologist Alexander Wilson, who first observed this bird in*
   *a rare sighting in Cape May, New Jersey. It probes beaches,*
   *patiently searching for insects and crustaceans. This bird is*
   *very rarely seen, and it is at risk of becoming endangered.*

**"AND SO, THE THREE CHILDREN** plunged to a watery death!"
   I look out across the lawn, where the members of my tour group
have slowly dispersed.

"Awesome!" a teenage boy calls out.

Encouraged by his reaction, I decide to engage him in one of the follow-up questions I've prepared, about the elaborate pulley system the children were playing on when they met their untimely demise. But then I realize he is looking right past me.

I turn to follow his gaze, and I see that a younger boy has managed to bite the end off of his glow stick, sending iridescent green goo across his arm and chest.

The boy's mother lets out a yelp, and then she scoops him up and runs toward the bathroom.

Smart woman. That stuff is incredibly toxic.

"How'd it go?" Darren asks, coming to stand beside me.

He's trying to be nice, because it's clear, by the bored faces on my already dispersed group, that I bombed another ghost tour.

"I even went with kids this time," I say. "Innocent kids playing on construction equipment."

He shakes his head. "You've gotta make them *feel* it, Vivi," he says. "Give them something to *connect* with—tell them about the waterlogged footprints that you found in the keeper's house, that match the prints of the kids."

I look at him, puzzled. "What footprints?"

"Doesn't matter, Vivi." He's still shaking his head, and his voice has gone all soft. "You just gotta make stuff up sometimes. Give 'em what they want." It's like he's coaxing a child to try her spinach. "That's a great story you dug up, but you gotta find a way for these folks to *feel the presence* of those poor drowned kids."

At least he appreciates my archival research.

It's been a wild night on the ghost tour—something about national holidays makes people jumpy, I guess. First, a teenage girl came streaking out of the bathroom in the keeper's house, her cutoffs still unbuttoned. She insisted that rolls of toilet paper were being launched at her, even though no one else was in the room. Then an incredibly anxious mother scooped up her toddler and ran stumbling out of the basement when the guy next to her leaned against the wall with a water bottle in his back pocket, making a rather loud crunching sound. One of the little girls on the tour started to giggle. Before I could stop it, the entire group had joined in.

And now the exploding glow stick.

"Why don't you take a turn at the snack bar?" Darren says, his voice consoling.

*And so I am consigned to the snack bar, once again.*

Oh well, at least I can check my texts here.

TJ's been texting me all night, which is a bit disconcerting.

I head behind the snack bar and connect my phone to the speaker. That's another good thing about working the snack bar: we get to pick the music here.

I scroll back to the last text from TJ.

Okay. What about "El Taxi"?
*Give me a sec.*

It's TJ's birthday and his first night off in who knows how long, but I guess he's at home making that reggaeton mix for Ángel. He spent all day texting me and asking me to listen to songs to see if they have dirty words. He's convinced Prashanti would recognize vulgar words in any language. He's probably right—she's got that sixth sense. And neither one of us wants to risk getting in trouble with Prashanti. We're trying with all our might to make a "clean" reggaeton playlist for Ángel.

This is not an easy task.

So now I'm hanging out at the base of the lighthouse for the Fourth of July ghost tour, selling beer and candy bars, and listening to "El Taxi." Needless to say, I'm getting some strange looks from the patrons.

The song ends.

*It's okay. Not too bad. Mostly suggestive, not explicit.*

As soon as I send the text, I feel my cheeks turn pink. I still can't believe TJ and I are texting about anything besides what time I'm picking him up for work. It's like maybe we're friends or something. And here I am, texting him about explicit songs.

Done. What about "Toma"?
*Pitbull too?*
Lil Jon.
*Okay-gonna listen now.*

I find the song and press play, just as a little girl with blond pigtails steps up to the counter.

"Do you have apple juice?" she asks.

I reach into the cooler for a juice box. I'm standing there, handing this cherub-faced girl a juice box, and suddenly I'm hearing . . .

*"Let me see you get freaky, baby—"* In English.

The little girl's mom pulls her away and shoots me a dirty glance.

*"Si tu quieres que—"*

*Oh holy crap.* Is he actually saying that? My face turns bright red and I jump to grab my phone and hit the pause button, all the while praying that this little girl and her mom don't speak Spanish.

I furiously text TJ.

*Are you deaf???*
Huh?
*Jesus, TJ, I'm listening to this stuff with KIDS around.*
Oh, sorry. "Toma" is a no?
*NO!!!! And I'm gonna lose my job if you make me listen to
another one like that.*
K.

Darren calls out from a bench by the lighthouse. "Time to shut it
down, Vivi."

"Got it!" I reply, turning the sign that hangs in front of the snack
bar from OPEN to CLOSED.

"I'm heading up," he says.

Darren sets off for the top of the lighthouse to do the nightly
sweep. The green glow sticks around the tourists' necks all begin
floating toward the entrance, and I'm left alone in the snack bar—
finally.

"La Vuelta al Mundo." Calle 13.
*Okay. I'll listen.*

I search for the song and press play.

An airy mournful sound comes through the speaker, played on a
single flute. A simple guitar riff repeats behind it. I stop wiping the
counter and sit down on my stool. A man's voice joins the flute and
guitar, deep and longing.

The words wash over me, and I sit perfectly still, pulling my legs
to my chest and hugging myself tight.

When it ends, I listen again and again.

Are you still there?

TJ's text breaks in.

*It's poetry. It's beautiful.*
Ángel told me you'd like it.
*He was right.*
What's the best line?

And just like that, my heart is racing, because this all seems so intimate suddenly. Or maybe because I've been listening to a man telling a woman to give him her hand so that they can go around the world together. And I've been imagining TJ, and recalling how it felt to wake up in the back of that car this morning, pressed against his chest. I have no idea how to respond to him.

*Too many to choose from.*
Pick one.
. . .
Are you there?
*Thinking.*
. . .
Still thinking?

He's not going to let it go.

*Yo confío en el destino*
*Y en la marejada*
*Yo no creo en la iglesia*

*Pero creo en tu mirada*
*Tú eres el sol de me cara*
*Cuando me levanta*
*Yo soy la vida que ya tengo*
*Tú eres la vida que me falta*
Uh, translation please.

I stare at his text, knowing I can't do it. I can't write those words to him—not in a way that he'll understand. Because they express so perfectly my own emptiness and longing—a longing I didn't even know I had, really, until now. I want to go somewhere else, somewhere far away—somewhere I don't even know yet. And I think maybe I want to go there with him.

So I lie.

*G2G. Boss just showed.*

After I shut down the snack bar and clean up the spilled juice and beer, rearrange the candy and clean out the nacho cheese warmer, I clock out and change from my costume.

I'm standing in the parking lot, but I can't seem to get into my car. Those words in the chorus revolve around me, again and again.

*DAME LA MANO*
*Y VAMOS A DARLE LA VUELTA AL MUNDO*
*DARLE LA VUELTA AL MUNDO*
*DARLE LA VUELTA AL MUNDO*

I walk to the edge of one of the docks and look out over Salt Run. I stand perfectly still, watching the lights reflect on the water, when a small shorebird lands on the piling beside me.

It's a tough one to identify—a plover, I'm pretty sure.

Plovers are probing birds. They patiently pace through marshes, across beaches and dunes, seeking any little morsel they can find. They're amazing, and rarely spotted by humans, but it's hard to distinguish among the different plovers.

I pull out my phone to do the research. After a few misses, I finally land on it: the Wilson's plover. It's call? A sharp whistled *weep, weep!*

And just like that, I'm collapsing onto the dock, my heart flooding with pain.

Every night, I'm out here on the ghost tour with dozens of strangers who seem desperate to connect with the dead. But me? I'm killing myself to maintain the distance. *Why can't I weep? Why am I incapable of crying?*

My heart feels like it's being squeezed by a giant fist, and my chest is contracting, but still, I can't connect.

# CHAPTER SIXTEEN

## ÁNGEL

**IS THIS REALLY HAPPENING?**

My good-for-nothing uncle showed up a few minutes ago. He walked right into my room, Mrs. Rosales by his side. And you know what he said to me?

"*Ti' baj teya?*"

"*Mixti'.*"

Just like that, he wanders in and asks me, "What's up?" So I tell him, "Not much." Then he shoves a McDonald's bag at me.

"French fries," he says.

"*Chjonte,*" I say. "Thanks."

I haven't seen the man in a year, not since I went to work on the turkey farm, and he's talking to me like he just wandered in from work, and I'm sitting on that old beat-up couch in his apartment, watching music videos. He looks the same: bloated stomach, bloodshot eyes. He smells the same too. Like stale beer mixed with body odor.

I gotta tell you, though. I'm super excited about the French fries. I love McDonald's French fries. They're awesome.

I shove a handful of fries into my mouth, taking in the smell of grease and salt, loving the way the fry oil feels, slick against my fingers.

"Your uncle is here to talk about your case," Mrs. Rosales says.

"My case?" I ask. I don't know what that means.

*"Tu caso,"* she says in Spanish.

I'm gonna go ahead and admit to you that I don't really get it in Spanish, either.

"Some errors were made, and the consequences for you will be, uh, significant."

My uncle looks away—toward the wall where my goal for the day is written. Today's goal is to teach Vivi how to dance meringue. I like that one, I gotta say.

Vivi looks over at me from the corner where she's sitting. She doesn't need to be here. Mrs. Rosales speaks Spanish, and nobody speaks Mam except me and my uncle.

Anyway, Vivi smiles, just a little, watching my uncle read my goal for the day. Or maybe he's not reading it. I don't even know if my uncle can read. But I can, thanks to Mr. Willingham. He was my teacher when I got to Florida, before I had to quit school.

"Your uncle explained to me that he failed to take you to your attorney appointments. . . ." Mrs. Rosales says.

My uncle is still looking at the wall. I shove another handful of fries into my mouth.

*Dang. I'm loving this salt.*

They don't feed us any salt on the heart ward. I guess salt's supposed to make things worse for some of the patients' health. They don't seem all that worried about me and salt, though. I guess my heart's so messed up, a little salt won't really matter.

"And to your court dates." Mrs. Rosales is still talking about my uncle, but I'm up in my head, thinking about McDonald's fries.

My uncle shuffles from one foot to the other, but he doesn't say anything.

The first time I met him was when he came to pick me up at that shelter in Texas. The social worker found him, somehow. He was my dad's brother, but he came to work in Florida before I was born. I knew he existed, but that's about all I knew about him. When I was little, he used to send my grandmother money sometimes, but then he stopped.

Mrs. Rosales told me that I would go to live with my uncle, and that he would be my legal guardian. All we had to do was show up for a few appointments with lawyers, go to court a couple of times, and the government would likely give me permission to stay in the United States. She said it wasn't for sure, but since I had seen most of my family get killed, and since the people who killed them wanted me dead too, I probably had a good chance of staying.

Yeah, I know what you're thinking. You're thinking how terrible that is—that I watched my family get killed. And it was terrible, but I don't really think about it, so don't get all worried about me. I'm fine. I mean, my heart doesn't really work, so that's not fine. But you already knew that.

Back to my good-for-nothing uncle: he took me away from that shelter, away from the silver machines that had an endless supply of milk, away from the nice teachers and the grassy lawns. He drove me to Florida, bought me a McDonald's Happy Meal (I've been hooked on their fries ever since), took me to his piece-of-crap apartment, and said, *"Ilti'k tu'n taq'una."*

Yeah, he told me to get a job. Which, let me tell you, is not easy for a fifteen-year-old who speaks a language no one around here has ever even heard of.

I got a toy car in that first Happy Meal. I set it next to my bed—which was an air mattress on the floor. Every night, when I was trying to fall asleep in that apartment after wandering around the streets of Jupiter, looking for work, listening to all the noise and music and laughing and yelling from the apartments around us, I ran that toy car across the stained carpet and I imagined what it would be like to drive.

But here's the great part: when Mrs. Rosales found out my uncle wasn't sending me to school, she went completely crazy on him. I could hear her yelling through the phone, all the way from Texas.

The next day, he took me to a place called the international school. My teacher was named Mr. Willingham. He was nice, and somehow he managed to teach some English to a group of kids who didn't even know how to speak to one another. It was pretty cool, because there were people in my class from all around the world. Not just people who spoke Spanish—they spoke a whole bunch of weird languages, so it wasn't that big a deal there that I spoke Mam. That was cool.

I just did my thing. I got up every morning and got on the bus. They fed me breakfast and lunch at school, so I didn't have to worry all that much about when my uncle would go on a bender. He did that a lot. Sometimes he'd go a week without showing up. I liked it better when he wasn't around, to tell you the truth. Except the weekends. I got hungry on the weekends. I tried to ignore it by watching TV. Mostly videos. I like music.

We went to see a lawyer a couple of times—a nice lady named Mrs. Jessica. But then my uncle stopped taking me. I guess he forgot or something.

Anyway, since I'm being honest with you, I'm gonna tell you that my uncle is not a good person. He's what we call a *xjal taq'wix*. And I don't like him. He doesn't like me either. He's nothing like my dad was. . . .

*Enough about that.* I'm not gonna think about my dad. Because I don't have a dad.

My fries are gone already.

I lick my fingers, one by one. I'm not sure if Mrs. Rosales wants me to say anything, but I don't really know what to say.

"Ángel?" she asks. "Do you remember when the ICE officer came to visit? The man from Immigration and Customs Enforcement?"

*Yeah, I remember.*

"And he asked you if you were aware that you had an order of deportation?"

I nod. Vivi leans forward in her seat, straining to hear.

"Your uncle received the letter."

"I didn't know what it was," my uncle tells me, looking toward the door. He's dying to get out of this place—to get away from me. "And I wasn't sure where to find you, so, uh . . ."

You wanna know why he wasn't sure where to find me? Because when I turned seventeen, he made me get a job.

He woke me up on my birthday and he said it. *"Ilti'k tu'n taq'una,"* he told me again. And so I did.

The only job I could get was on that fancy turkey farm, which was great with me, because they told me I could live there. I'm telling you, I got away from my uncle as fast as I could.

I liked that place. It was peaceful, you know? I mean, until we had to slaughter all the turkeys.

"I spoke with the attorney who was trying to help you get special juvenile status. She said that you missed several appointments and key court dates. Were you aware of that?"

I shrug. "Yeah," I say. I'll tell you what I'm aware of: I had to be at all those things with my legal guardian, aka my good-for-nothing uncle. And he never took me, because he was too busy working or getting drunk. Probably getting drunk, mostly.

"When you turned eighteen, you lost eligibility for legal status through the juvenile program, and you were given an order of deportation."

I nod and look into the McDonald's bag. One more little piece of fry is stuck in the crease at the bottom. Score! I dig it out and pop it into my mouth.

"Excuse me, Mrs. Rosales." It's Vivi. She stands up and walks to my bedside. "Can you maybe explain to Ángel exactly what that means? In simple terms."

"We will keep you here at the hospital until you are in stable condition—until you are well enough to be transported safely back to Guatemala."

Wait, what? They're sending me back to Guatemala? What am I gonna do there?

I can't go home. They'll kill me. It's a fact. I'm telling you, people: I can't go back there. Plus, I don't have any family there anymore. Nobody.

"I can't go there," I say very quietly.

"Speak up, Ángel," Vivi says, coming to stand right by my bed. "Explain to Mrs. Rosales why you can't go there."

She puts her hand over mine and squeezes. I wonder if she feels the grease from the fries, the grit of the salt still on my fingers.

I'm looking at her hand on mine, and I'm trying to make some words come out—but I mean it; I can't make any come—not in any language. Not even Mam.

"His family is all gone," my uncle grumbles. "There's no one there to care for him."

"We are aware of that," Mrs. Rosales says. "We are working as fast as we can—doing everything we can to establish a relationship with a hospital, maybe in Guatemala City or Quetzaltenango— someplace that can take him and offer the care he needs."

"Will they have a transplant list?" Vivi asks, leaning forward, eyes bright. "Will he be eligible for a heart there?"

Oh, poor sweet Vivi. I'm telling you, when I look at that girl, I see hope. She doesn't know any better yet. I kinda love that about her, to tell you the truth. I love a lot of things about Vivi. I mean, I'm not *in love with her*. (That's TJ.) I just think she's amazing, for caring about me and my stupid, messed-up heart.

Mrs. Rosales shoots her a sort of mean look—like, *Shut up if you know what's good for you.*

"We don't know yet," she whispers. "But it's unlikely."

July 26
7:53 PM

"Junk Birds?"

Highly Social
Birds.
May experience
empathy

American Crow
(Corvus brachyrhynchos)

THEY'RE AMAZING! Two crows
nuzzled a third crow & we
watched them intertwine
their beaks.

# CHAPTER SEVENTEEN

## *VIVI*

BIRD JOURNAL

July 26, 7:53 P.M.

American crow (*Corvus brachyrhynchos*)

Social Behavior: highly social birds, generally live in small,
close-knit groups, but also congregate in large groups,
sometimes referred to as a "murder of crows." A large
grouping of crows can also be termed a "horde, hover,
muster, or parcel."

Crows and their cousins, rooks and ravens, have been
observed to regularly demonstrate consoling actions,
which suggest that they may experience empathy.

Habitat: so common throughout north America that birders
consider them "junk birds"—BUT they're AMAZING!

**"ONE! TWO! THREE! FOUR! FIVE!** Six! Seven! Stop. One!
Two! Three! Four! Five! Six! Seven! Stop."

Ángel is barking orders at me, and I'm stumbling around his hospital room.

Richard and I each have a hand around the other's waist. Our other hands are clasped in front of us, like we're going do the tango, and we're shuffling our feet as fast as we can, but apparently not fast enough, because Ángel keeps yelling, "Faster! Faster! *Rápido!*"

After Mrs. Rosales and Ángel's uncle left, Prashanti let TJ set up a little portable speaker in Ángel's room. He got the music going, and then he left to do his end-of-shift chores. Richard, Ángel, and I were alone in the room when Prashanti marched right in, put her hands on her hips, and announced, "Well, what are you all standing around for? It's time to get to work on Ángel's goal for the day."

Which is how I ended up standing in the middle of a hospital room with my arms around a gay fifty-year-old man who smells faintly of cigarette smoke, taking orders from Ángel.

"One! Two! Three! Four! Five! Six! Seven! Stop. One! Two! Three! Four! Five! Six! Seven! Stop."

Sharon comes around the corner and into the room, pushing Mrs. Blankenship in a wheelchair. Sharon's shaking her hips and shimmying her shoulders to the beat.

"What's going on in here?" she asks. "You throwin' a party and didn't invite us?"

"We didn't want to miss the fun!" Mrs. Blankenship calls out.

"I'm teaching Vivi how to dance merengue," Ángel says. And then:

"One! Two! Three! Four! Five! Six! Seven! Stop. One! Two! Three! Four! Five! Six! Seven! Stop."

"I love it!" Mrs. Blankenship says. She starts to snap her fingers to the rhythm as Sharon releases the wheelchair and begins dancing enthusiastically around the room.

"No move here!" Ángel calls out to Sharon, his voice filled with mirth. He's pointing at his upper body. "You move too much on top, Sharon. Top is no move. Move hips. Hips only!"

Sharon tries to adjust her moves, but she just can't seem to help herself. Her shoulders keep shimmying and shaking, and soon we are all shaking with laughter.

TJ shows up in the doorway, holding a huge stack of sheets in his arms. He peers in and shakes his head.

"How are the lessons going?" he asks. He's looking right at me, smiling.

I seem unable to produce an answer, maybe because I'm winded from all of the marching around. (Merengue is *fast*.) Or maybe it's because of that smile. I still can't get enough of that smile. Now that he's not withholding it from me, it's like a drug.

"Terrible!" Ángel says, throwing up his hands. "You show them, *vato*."

"What makes you think I can dance merengue?" TJ asks him, his eyebrows arching.

"Are you saying you can't?" Sharon asks.

TJ shrugs, still balancing the pile of sheets in his arm.

"I don't believe it for a minute," Mrs. Blankenship says. "A fit young man like yourself!"

A new song comes on. It starts with a single voice, repeating one line.

*"Algo en tu cara me fascina; algo en tu cara me da vida."*

When the horns start up, TJ shakes his head once and comes into the room. He drops the stack of sheets on the edge of Ángel's bed and grabs Sharon by the hand.

And just like that, the two of them are moving in perfect unison across the room.

"Keep still here," TJ demands, gently squeezing her shoulder. "Just move your feet and hips."

*"Eso!"* Ángel calls out, sitting up a bit in his bed. "See! *That's* how you dance merengue!"

Soon Prashanti is standing in the doorway with Bertrand, who must have just shown up for the night shift, and they're clapping and smiling while TJ spins Sharon around the room, their hips moving in perfect unison.

"One! Two! Three! Four! Five! Six! Seven! Stop. One! Two! Three! Four! Five! Six! Seven! Stop."

Ángel's still calling out the rhythm, but TJ doesn't need it. His rhythm is perfect.

*Dear God.* I feel a sinking in my gut, just watching him move.

I'm standing there, unable to take my eyes off him, my jaw probably hanging open, my cheeks turning pink, while everyone around me claps and calls out. And the singer repeats:

"*¿Será tu sonrisa? ¿Será tu sonrisa?*"

I drag my gaze away from TJ before he can catch me gawking. Mrs. Blankenship is shimmying her shoulders to the rhythm (sort of), and Bertrand takes Prashanti by the hand and leads her into the middle of the room. Prashanti is laughing and shaking her head, but Bertrand has his arm around her waist before she can say no. Bertrand is pretty good, but Prashanti is staring down at her feet as if she has no idea how to make them move to a rhythm. She's trying, though, which is super cute.

"Aye, yay, yay, yay!" Ángel calls out in a high voice. I love looking at him right now, because he's got an enormous, goofy grin plastered across his face. It's almost as good as watching TJ guide Sharon across the room.

*Almost.*

Richard abandoned me. He's sprawled out in the chair, panting. So I'm standing around, looking stupid, my arms crossed over my chest, tapping my feet.

When the song ends, Bertrand bows with a flourish and announces, "I have to get to work, friends." Prashanti follows Bertrand out of the room, and just like that it's over. TJ is scooping up the sheets. Sharon is pushing Mrs. Blankenship out of the room. (Richard is still panting in the armchair.)

"Not bad for your first time," Ángel says to me. "But you're gonna need a few lessons with TJ if you really wanna get it right."

TJ stops at that and turns to look back at me, shaking his head and grinning. "You're relentless," he says to Ángel.

"Sorry, my *vato*. I don't know what that word means," Ángel says. Then he grins really wide and says, "No speaka *inglés*, dude."

TJ shakes his head again. "See you at the car in ten?" he asks me.

"Yeah," I say.

And then TJ produces another one of his real smiles. For me.

"Hurricane Ronald is gaining strength in the western Atlantic. The storm, now nearing Category Four intensity, is expected to make landfall in Haiti in the early morning hours—"

I'm helping Ángel eat his Jell-O, and we're half watching the news on TV. Normally, I'd be annoyed that Ángel is asking me to feed him, but today's been a bad day, and I think he legitimately needs the help. TJ's in the room too. He's been changing bedpans, tidying, the usual stuff.

For two days we've all three been avoiding discussion of Ángel's visit from his asshole uncle, the unthinkable reality that he's going to be sent back to Guatemala in his condition, and—of course—the merengue lessons that TJ still owes me. I turned on the TV news, hoping for any distraction, only to hear more predictions of death and destruction.

"There they go again," TJ says.

"Who?" I ask.

"The weather people—every couple of years they get all hysterical about some hurricane, and then people scramble around and buy up all the water at Publix. The plywood flies off the shelves at Home Depot, schools close, and then there's, like, a little wind and some good surf and it's over."

He's got a point. If growing up in Florida teaches kids anything, it's that hurricane warnings are a big excuse for adults to skip work and drink excessively.

I try to scoop another spoonful of orange Jell-O into Ángel's mouth, but he holds up his hand, signaling for me to stop. He must be feeling terrible. He always inhales the Jell-O.

"Yeah, well, I hope it doesn't hit Haiti," I say. "They've been through enough already."

After I say it, a heavy silence fills the room. I'm thinking about Ángel, and about how much he's already been through. I think TJ must be too, because he darts a quick look at me, and his brows scrunch together. Then he turns back to cleaning out Ángel's water cup.

"It will be fine," TJ says after a long silence. "It's never as bad as they say it's gonna be."

Ángel's eyes fall closed, so I pull the tray of food away quietly, hoping not to disturb him if he's drifting off to sleep. He needs to rest today.

*"Tengo frío,"* Ángel mumbles.

"He's cold," I tell TJ. "Can you get him one of those heated blankets?"

TJ nods and leaves the room. I'm left alone with Ángel, studying his face. I remember when I first saw that face—pockmarked and skinny, black hair sticking up all around it. I think the expression— *a face that only a mother could love*—came to mind. It's strange, because Ángel's face hasn't changed at all, except that it might be a little skinnier now, but when I look at it, my heart fills up. I don't want to look away.

I'm still studying Ángel's face when TJ comes back in the room. We work together to spread the warm blanket across his thin body, tucking it around his toes and chin.

"*Chjonte,*" he whispers.

That's Mam for "thank you." He's been teaching me a little Mam, just to pass the time.

"You're welcome," I whisper.

We watch as he relaxes into sleep. Neither one of us seems able to leave his side.

"I keep forgetting to tell you," I whisper to TJ. "I can't drive you home on Friday. I have to go to Orlando after work." I hear my voice quavering, and TJ does too, because he looks right at me, studying my face.

"What's happening in Orlando?" he whispers.

"Mom and I need to get some things done at the house. We, uh, we're putting it on the market and I need to pack up boxes."

"You're selling your house?"

I nod, looking at Ángel's feet tucked under the covers.

"Where are you going to live?"

I shrug. I don't know where we're going to live. What I do know is that we can't afford the house anymore, and we need to find some source of income if there will be any chance at all of me going back to Yale in the fall. Even if I get a financial aid package that gives me a job on campus, I don't think I'm going to be able to sustain both of us with part-time work in the dining hall. Mom's not ready to go out and look for a job. For weeks, she was so out of it that she couldn't even pull together the forms I needed for those applications. Alice has been incredibly patient with us, but she finally called me on Monday and told me that if I didn't get the forms submitted this week, they wouldn't be processed by the start of the school year.

When I asked her, "What does that mean, exactly?" she replied,

"Well, Vivi, it means you and your mom will be expected to pay us $30,587 by August tenth."

"We have to pay for the whole year by August?"

"No, Vivi," she said, her voice patient and calm. "That's for the first semester. The second half will be due in December."

My very dignified response was, "Holy crap! You have got to be kidding me. Sixty-one thousand dollars?"

Alice was great about it. She laughed a high, tinkling laugh and then said, "It's $61,174, to be precise. I wouldn't kid about this, Vivi. Submit the forms."

I had no idea college was that expensive, but it certainly lit a fire under me.

Thank God, we finally managed to submit the paperwork yesterday. Now we wait. In the meantime, we need money, so Mom called an old friend who's a Realtor in Winter Park, and he put the house on the market.

"Anyway, we are going down to clear out some of the personal stuff and bring it back here—"

Ángel mumbles something, but his eyes are still closed. *Maybe he's dreaming?*

"Yeah, okay. I'll get Sabrina to pick me up," TJ says. "We're both off Friday night, so it's no big deal."

Ángel mumbles again.

"What? *¿Qué?*" I ask Ángel.

"TJ can help," he says quietly. "He's strong. He can pick things up."

I guess Ángel wasn't sleeping. And, once again, he's proving just how much he understands what's going on around him.

"Sure. Yes. I mean, yeah, if you and your mom need me—" TJ stammers.

*Did he really just say yes?*

"That's okay," I say. "You don't need to do that. It's your day off. You never get a day off."

"My *vato* has no life," Ángel mumbles. "He's got nothin' else to do."

TJ shrugs. "My homie has a point."

I look back and forth between Ángel and TJ, barely able to express the profound sense of gratitude I feel. "Thanks," I manage to whisper.

On the drive back to St. Augustine, we pull up to a four-way stop, just as a horde of crows takes to the air from a field across the intersection.

"Check it out!" TJ says, leaning forward to watch them alight. "What are they?"

I shake my head. "Did you really just ask me what kind of birds those are?"

"Yeah, why?"

"Do you know *absolutely nothing* about birds?"

TJ shrugs. "I know all about Rita. I hang out with her for, like, eight hours a day."

"Besides Rita?"

He shrugs again.

"They're crows, common American crows. They're quite literally *everywhere*. Birders call them 'junk birds.'"

"So you're not gonna pull out your binoculars?"

"For a murder of crows? I don't think so."

"A murder?"

"It's what you call a big group of crows."

"Okay, so what do you call a little group of crows? Cuz that one's posing for you." We both watch as dozens of crows lift off the field simultaneously, taking to the sky. Three remain together, perfectly still, in the middle of the abandoned field.

"You don't mind?" I ask.

"Be my guest."

I pull up onto the shoulder and roll down my window. TJ takes my binoculars and journal from the glove compartment and hands them to me.

We watch in silence. One crow stands erect, while the other two nuzzle into his neck. He turns toward one of the two, and they begin to twine their beaks, slowly spinning, their beaks pressed together.

"What are they doing?" he asks.

I shrug. "Not sure," I say. "But scientists think that these birds— crows, rooks, ravens—actually console each other after a fight. Maybe that guy in the middle was attacked, and the other two are his friends. They're just trying to make him feel better, repair his bruised ego."

"Really?" TJ asks. "Birds do that?"

"Not all of them," I say as I turn to a blank page in my journal and start to sketch. "But some of the smart ones do."

TJ watches as my pencil forms the shape of three crows. He sits in patient silence while I color each crow a deep, solid black.

For this, I am so deeply grateful.

Back in January I finally returned to Yale after almost two months away. I went home for Thanksgiving and never came back for exams, so my friends had started to wonder. Gillian didn't hesitate to share the tragic news, and I guess she took it upon herself to describe to everyone what a spectacular mess I had been over Thanksgiving.

Everyone knew about that night at Sabor do Brasil, too.

It was as if I had some sort of communicable disease. I walked into my first class of the semester—a first-year writing seminar, and every single person averted their gaze, even the teacher. I wanted to yell at them, tell them they were all a bunch of idiots and cowards, to remind them that a deceased father is not contagious. I didn't, though. I slumped into my seat and rested my head on the desk, where it stayed for the entire hour-and-fifteen-minute class session (and most of the subsequent class sessions too).

But those very same people, if I saw them out on a Saturday night, their cheeks flushed from too many beers, suddenly got all emotional and sympathetic. I can't tell you how many times Gillian cried on my shoulder. I sat squeezed onto a dingy couch in some crowded dorm room, comforting her, trying to figure out what the hell was wrong with this picture—shouldn't Gillian be trying to make *me* feel better? Shouldn't I be crying on *her* shoulder?

I quit going out on weekends. I also gave up on social media. I needed less connection, not more.

I don't blame her. Here's what I've figured out about people like Gillian: they have no idea how to deal with the searing, terrible pain of death, because their lives are good and they're just beginning to live. So they started avoiding me, and I started avoiding them, because I couldn't bear how much they were *living*. And they couldn't bear seeing how I was dying inside.

Over the past eight months, I've grown accustomed to this strange isolation. Now, sitting on a roadside in North Central Florida, I'm feeling a little overwhelmed, because a surly nurse's aid who doubles as a *churrasqueiro* and a scrawny sick kid who doubles as a pain in the ass are, against all the odds, friends to me.

I think maybe they're my only real friends.

# CHAPTER EIGHTEEN

## *TJ*

**"HOW'S MEDICAL SCHOOL GOING?"**

Alisha, one of the belly dancers turned samba dancers is taking off her wings a few feet away from where I clean the grill.

"You mean nursing school?" I ask. "I'm in nursing school."

My voice probably sounds more annoyed than it should. Alisha's nice, and I know she's just trying to make small talk, but it's been an incredibly long night at the restaurant and—to be honest—she flirts with me a lot.

The Saturday Samba has been so popular that Uncle Jay decided to expand it to Thursdays. As a result, it's two A.M. on Friday and I still haven't finished cleaning the grill.

Dad and Uncle Jay are in the kitchen, screaming obscenities at each other, and we are all doing our best to pretend it's not happening. It started around ten P.M., when we ran out of lamb. Or, at least that's what my dad told all the meat runners. As it turns out, we have plenty of lamb—shitty freezer-burned lamb that Uncle Jay bought off of a shady distributor and that Dad refuses to use.

I wasn't really paying much attention to whether or not we had lamb, since I spent the entire night managing stupid-drunk frat boys who seem to think that randomly groping samba dancers is perfectly acceptable behavior.

So, yeah, I guess I'm a little past using my manners tonight.

"Oh, sorry," Alisha says. "Nursing school, that's really great." She nods and I shrug. "Thanks for looking out for me tonight," she adds.

"Those guys were idiots," I respond, feeling my chest tighten with anger. "I'm sorry they treated you like that."

My mind flashes to the night that Vivi fell off the bar, and to the two assholes we let her leave with. Since that night, I've had what you might call a zero-tolerance policy for groping drunks. So it felt pretty good, actually, when I got to throw the frat boys out tonight, after they used their fancy new iPhones to take pictures of their offensive behavior.

I made sure that one of them dropped his phone on the cobblestones when I shoved him out onto the street.

*I hope the screen shattered into a hundred pieces.*

"No biggie," she says, cheerful. "I've gotten used to it."

I glance up from the metal brush I'm using to scour the grill. Her arms are folded across her chest and she's a little slumped. She's frowning, like she's feeling nauseous.

My eyes narrow. "You shouldn't have to get used to it," I say.

We both listen in silence as Demetrio breaks into the fight unfolding in the kitchen and tries to play peacemaker.

"What's going on back there?" Alisha asks.

"Let's just say you should be feeling very grateful that you don't understand Portuguese." I finish with the grill and wash my hands. Then I grab a big pile of clean tablecloths and start to fold them.

*"Filho da puta!"* Uncle Jay yells, while apparently throwing a metal object across the kitchen.

"I guess if you wanna learn how to tell somebody off in Brazilian Portuguese, now's your chance."

She laughs. "Good to know."

Alisha does the whole sequined-bikini thing incredibly well, I gotta admit. Hers is gold, and it looks amazing against her dark skin. I like her hair, too. She's got one of those natural, loose Afros that are trendy these days.

"So, how much longer till you're a nurse?" she asks.

"I've just got a couple of credit hours left—this is my last semester of clinical." If I take the classes online, I should be able to pull together the cash next semester—depending on how much it costs to replace my transmission.

"Are you at Santa Fe?" she asks.

"Yeah," I tell her, "but I'm gonna take the rest of my classes online. It's cheaper."

She carefully pulls at a loose string on her wings, tightening a gold sequin.

"I went to Santa Fe. I'm starting at University of Florida in the fall—mechanical engineering or maybe aerospace. I haven't decided."

"That's awesome!" I tell her. I mean it too. I guess I didn't expect a belly/samba dancer to be an engineer, too. *My bad.* I love it when people surprise me.

Uncle Jay comes storming out of the kitchen, red-faced and sweaty. He's got his suit jacket off, and his sleeves are pushed up to his elbows, like he's ready for a fight. When he sees Alisha watching, he pauses and produces a big fake smile. "Nice work tonight!" he says too enthusiastically. "Beautiful! Beautiful!" Then he glares at me and spits out, *"Seu pai é um cuzão."*

He takes three more steps and then turns back. *"E um imbecil!"*

"What did he say?" Alisha whispers.

"My dad's an asshole and an idiot," I tell her, shaking my head.

"For what it's worth," she says, putting a hand on her hip, "I think your dad's a sweetheart."

I grab another pile of clean tablecloths. "I'm not getting in the middle of it, that's for sure."

"Need some help?" she asks, reaching for one of a dozen white tablecloths.

"Sure."

We stand together in silence, trying to ignore the loud voices in the kitchen—Demetrio is trying to console my dad, make him calm down.

*That's not gonna happen.*

"Hey," she says, shifting from one foot to the other. "Are you working tomorrow night? There's this party at the beach, and I thought maybe . . ."

"I gotta go to Orlando tomorrow." I glance up quickly to catch her gaze. "I'm helping a friend move."

"Another time?" she asks.

"Yeah, sure." I focus on the tablecloth, bringing the edges together in an even line. "I mean, I don't really party, but we could hang out."

She thrusts her hand out. "Give me your phone," she says.

I'm not sure I like where this is going, but I'd feel kinda bad saying no, so I put the folded cloth on a stack and pull my phone from my back pocket.

Alisha grabs it and turns sideways. She puts a hand on her hip and puckers her red-tinted lips. She holds the phone up high and takes a selfie. Then she starts typing her contact info into my phone.

"Okay, done. I sent myself a text," she says, handing back my phone. "Hope that's okay."

"Yeah," I say, picking up another tablecloth. "That's cool."

And it *is* cool. It's fine. But I guess I'm also realizing that I'd much rather be moving boxes with Vivi and her mom than hanging out at a beach party with Alisha. And that's a little weird.

It's getting near the end of my Friday shift, and I'm trying to get through a long list of boring chores I have to do before I can leave for Orlando with Vivi and her mom, who has been hanging around the hospital all day, since she doesn't have a car to drive herself to Orlando. So I'm a little annoyed when Vivi's weird texts come in.

Hey. Are you a lot taller than me?

*Yeah I think. Why?*

Come to Ángel's room-ASAP!

??

Need help. Now.

I'm also a little embarrassed that I know exactly how much taller I am than Vivi.

If she were to stand face-to-face with me, her forehead would be at my lips.

It seems kinda urgent, though, so I quit restocking and I quit stressing about why I know where my lips would find her skin, and I jog over to Ángel's room.

The door is closed, and a bunch of people are inside, laughing. I throw the door open to find Vivi jumping at the end of Ángel's bed, apparently trying to push the ceiling tiles loose. Her mom is encouraging her from the edge of Ángel's chair, where she is perched, holding a bunch of thin strings with paper attached to them.

"*Salta!*" Ángel yells.

"I'm trying," Vivi says, laughing.

When I walk in, all three of them turn to look at me.

"What the hell?"

"Ángel wanted to see sky today," Vivi's mom says, pointing toward the whiteboard. I know what's there, since I wrote it eight hours ago. Ángel's goal for today: to lie on his back and look up at the sky.

"So Mom's giving him a sky full of birds!" Vivi says.

"Origami birds!" her mom proclaims, smiling wide. "We made them out of his prescriptions!"

*His prescriptions.* Every morning, during rounds, the resident brings in a stack of those things and leaves them, as if Ángel has any intention of reading through the drug interaction warnings or checking to see if the nurse is administering the right doses. It's absurd. They keep piling up on his bedside table, but no one has the courage to move them.

"Let me see one," I say. Vivi's mom hands me one—it's folded to resemble a bird taking flight, and someone has used the blue dry-erase marker to draw elaborate doodles all over it. Truth be told, it looks pretty cool.

"How many of these did you make?" I ask.

"Twenty-six?" Vivi says, looking to Ángel for confirmation. "Ángel got good at it."

"And where are you planning to put them?"

"We can tuck them into the edges of the ceiling tiles," Vivi says. "Which is why I need you."

I squint, entirely skeptical of their plan. "I can't reach," she says, explaining the obvious.

"It works!" her mom calls out. "I promise!"

"C'mon, my *vato*," Ángel says. "We 'bout killed ourselves makin' those. Give your homeboy a hand, a'right?"

I sigh and motion for Vivi to get off the bed. "Hand me one at a time," I say, climbing up to stand on the bed.

It's pretty easy to pop out the ceiling tiles. "I need some tape—there's medical tape in that drawer," I tell Vivi, motioning to the supply cabinet.

She gets the tape and breaks off a small piece. And then she starts handing pieces to me, one by one.

That's how I end up climbing around Ángel's bed, taking commands from Vivi and her mom ("Higher!" "No, lower!" "Just an inch to the left!" "A little more, a little more, STOP!"). I'm filling the ceiling with origami prescription birds, dangling from dental floss at varying heights over Ángel's head. And I'm praying that Prashanti doesn't walk in.

When I'm done, I climb back off the bed to check out my handiwork.

Ángel adjusts his bed so that he's lying completely flat. Then he looks straight up at those birds and says, "Boss."

"Does that mean 'good'?" Vivi's mom asks.

"Yup," Ángel says. "The ballz. G'on now! Y'all people better bust on outta here before Bertrand shows!"

Vivi and her mom lean down to hug Ángel while I give his fluids and oxygen a quick check.

"We're gone," I say.

The three of us head through the door and hurry past Bertrand, smiling and waving and using every ounce of our willpower to keep from busting out laughing.


Twenty minutes later we're cruising down I-4 toward Orlando. I'm in the backseat, listening to Vivi and her mom tell stories about some insane trips they took. It's amazing, listening to the two of them. They tell a story as if they're one person—where Vivi leaves off, her mom picks up without missing a beat. Listening to them, I get the feeling that they have told these stories together many, many times before. I also get the sense that they have engaged in some sick travel. I mean, off the rails.

"Remember that time we went canyoning in Borneo?"

*I don't even know where Borneo is—not even which continent it's on.*

"And the adventure guide—what was his name? Oh yeah. King Charles."

*King Charles? Maybe Borneo is a tiny island in Britain or something.*

"Dad kept calling him 'King Charles,' remember? He was, like, an expat from Australia or something? And we were in that cave filling with water, and Charles was just cruising along like it was no big deal, and Dad was like, 'Uh, King Charles, Your Majesty, I'm in need of some sort of royal decree right about now.' And I was laughing so hard that I started gulping in water."

*A cave filling with water? Is that even safe?*

"And then King Charles almost forgot to attach your second crampon?"

*What the hell is a crampon? Is that like a tampon? Are they talking about feminine products?*

"And I was about to drop three hundred feet and I was looking at him like, 'You can't weigh more than a hundred pounds—how are you going to hold me up?'"

*Three hundred feet? Isn't that almost as long as a football field?*

Vivi's mom turns to look back at me. "I'm telling you, TJ, Charles was smaller than Ángel, even."

I smile and say, "Wow," because . . . *wow.* Who *are* these people?

Vivi pulls off the interstate at a downtown exit.

"I have a meeting," Vivi's mom says, turning to look at me. "It won't take too long."

*At seven on a Friday evening?*

"Lawyers," Vivi says. "They work around the clock."

Her mom laughs. "We're meeting over a quick dinner," she says. "I'll take a cab home."

Vivi shoots her a threatening look. "It's a long way, Mom. I'll come back for you."

"No need," her mom says.

"You can't take a cab, Mom," Vivi says, her voice stern.

Her mom shrugs. "Oh, fine. John will be at the meeting. I'm sure he can give me a ride to Winter Park."

Vivi nods and pulls up to a curb in front of a fancy high-rise office tower. Her mom jumps out and waves. "See you kids soon!"

Vivi turns back to look at me as I sit dumb and silent in the backseat.

"Climb through," she commands. "I refuse to be your chauffeur."

I jump into the front seat. "Your mom doesn't really get the whole *flat broke* thing, does she?"

"So you caught that?" Vivi says through a smile. "It's not really her fault. She's never been broke before."

"Neither have you," I tell her, "but you're figuring it out."

She stops at a red light and turns to look at me. "Really?" she asks. "I mean, that's a huge compliment. Do you really mean it?"

"Yeah," I tell her. "You're doing your best, Viv."

She smiles and her cheeks turn a little pink, which makes me want to reach out and put my hand against her face, which freaks me out.

*This is still a complication I do not need.*

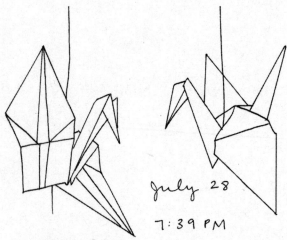

July 28

7:39 PM

NO BIRD
SIGHTINGS!
NONE!

unless you count
Mom's oragami...

# CHAPTER NINETEEN

## *VIVI*

BIRD JOURNAL
July 28, 7:39 P.M.
*No birds seen today, unless I count Mom's paper cranes.*
*Highly unusual.*

**THE CAR GROWS VERY QUIET** around the time we turn onto Park Avenue. I glance at TJ, intently watching as we pass through the picture-perfect town center. Pottery Barn, Starbucks—nothing unique, but everything is impeccably maintained.

"We're almost there," I say. My voice sounds anxious.

I turn onto our street, which dead-ends at the lakefront. I can see the still, blue water in front of us.

"Nice lake," TJ says.

I don't respond, because my house comes into view. I take in a sharp breath. Suddenly it all makes sense—why Mom wanted to be in St. Augustine this summer.

I don't think I can do this.

I pull into the driveway and look out across the lake. Afternoon clouds have gathered—they always do. But it's not going to storm.

Still, it feels like sheets of rain suddenly pour down around me. I can barely see through the windshield because I'm drowning.

I'm drowning in memories that I don't want to have.

The car has stopped, but I seem unable to move. I'm not sure I can breathe. I rest my elbow on the steering wheel and let my forehead drop onto it. It feels so heavy.

My entire body is heavy. I think maybe I am going to drop into the earth, right here. I think maybe it will swallow me whole and the rain will keep hitting me and I will curl into a tight ball and stay there.

*Oh God. This hurts.*

"Um," TJ whispers. "Uh, I'll get the bags."

He steps out of the car and closes the door quietly, like he's trying not to wake someone.

But *oh my god*, it's too late. Every single aching part of me has woken up.

*I can't do this.*

"I can't do this."

*I can't do this.*

I think I said it out loud. I didn't mean to say it out loud.

The trunk pops open. I sit perfectly still while TJ pulls bags from the car. I watch as he carries them to the door, grateful for this, at least. I can watch TJ move through this space, and maybe I can avoid seeing my father.

*No, he's everywhere. My father is everywhere.*

*He's stepping out of the car holding a bag filled with vegetables from the farmer's market.*

*He's standing in the middle of the driveway, waving his arms around wildly as he argues on the phone with opposing counsel.*

*He's shuffling across the lawn in his slippers for the Sunday* Times.

TJ places the bags under the awning and then he looks back at the car, where I sit, paralyzed. He catches my gaze and nods once, then he walks around toward the back of the house, toward the lake.

*My father, he's crouched at the end of the dock, tying his boat to the cleat.*

*He's standing at the edge of the water, morning coffee in hand, looking out toward the horizon.*

*He's sitting beside me on the swing, telling me that he refuses to die.*

*He's stuffed into a bright blue urn, perched on a table beside the water.*

*And hundreds of people are rising from their seats to sing, and that stupid songbird refuses to shut up.*

Cheerily cheer up! Cheer, cheer, cheerily cheer up!

*I will not cheer up. I cannot cheer up. I can't even feel myself standing up.*

*I am moving through crowds of people dressed in black, under a blinding blue sky, and I am nothing. I am disappearing.*

*I can't do this. I can't even* be. *How can I be without him?*

I should go inside. I should lift my head from this steering wheel and look toward the front door. My mind is telling me what to do, but my body won't move.

I don't know how to be here. Because to feel my father's absence was easy compared to this. The hard part is feeling his presence—I can't stop loving him. I can't keep him away any longer. Not here.

After I don't know how long, TJ's back at the car door, tapping lightly on the window.

"Vivi," he says. "Let's go inside now."


"What's the hardest part?" TJ asks.

He's standing by a stack of empty boxes in my entryway, holding a roll of tape. I look from his face to the boxes, wondering what sort of question he's trying to ask. Is this an existential sort of question?

Does he really want to know the hardest part of losing my dad at eighteen? Or is he talking about the disaster that is my family home?

Every piece of furniture in the house has a blue tag attached to it, a dollar amount written on it.

The sofa where my parents and I snuggled for Friday movie nights? $1,350

The wooden side table where I always dumped my backpack? $830

The small silver bowl that held my father's keys? $320

*Jesus*, why is all of this stuff worth so much money? And who is going to buy it? And who did all of this?

Last week John—the estate-planning lawyer who Mom is currently having dinner with—told me he had hired someone to run an estate sale, which seemed like a good idea at the time.

*But now?* All I can think is that estate sales are for dead people, and Mom and I are still alive.

We're still here.

"Viv?" TJ asks.

I scan the living room. Mom said that she'd almost finished packing our personal items last week, when she came over to meet with the Realtor.

She lied. Our stuff is everywhere.

"Tell me what to do, Viv." TJ looks through the hallway toward the living room, where half-full boxes litter the floor. "I want to help."

"The hard part?" I ask.

"Yeah," he says.

"I don't even . . ."

I feel myself sinking to the floor.

"Maybe his closet?" TJ asks. "Has anyone done his closet?"

*His closet.*

I shake my head, and then I feel my arms wrap around my knees.

"Upstairs?"

I nod, pulling myself into a tight ball.

TJ picks up two boxes and tucks them under his arm. "I'm gonna leave you alone, okay? I mean, I think maybe you need to be alone. But, uh, if you need me . . ." He tilts his head toward the stairs.

I take one long look at the stairs, and then I tuck my forehead between my knees and close my eyes.

On the terrible morning after my spectacular drunken idiocy, I woke up in a lawn chair outside of Gillian's condo. My face hurt. My hair smelled like puke. My stomach gurgled and I felt like I might vomit (again? I don't know. I don't remember). I called a car before I could even figure out where the others were or what had happened to my clothes and my sandals.

The ride from Ponte Vedra was long—long enough for me to try, a hundred times, to piece together all the things I couldn't remember about the night before. Long enough for me to study my face in the car's side mirror, wondering about the deep purple bruise and the small scratches on my cheek.

When the driver pulled up to my house, an ambulance was there. Lights flashing, sound off.

I threw the door open and I ran into the house. I only made it as far as this entryway. I leaned against this very wall and watched two paramedics rush ahead of me, up the stairs. I heard them moving quickly, talking loudly. Too loud. Too fast. My mind couldn't catch up.

I slumped to the floor, and the paramedics arrived at the top of the staircase. They carried a stretcher down the stairs. My father, unconscious on that stretcher.

They swung the door open to a too-blue sky. The sunlight was too crisp, the grass looked too green, and the lake behind us was too calm.

My mother followed behind them. The paramedic—a woman with long braids and a kind smile—whispered to her, almost cooed. She coaxed my mother along. Mom stayed close to that woman, and I don't know what the woman said, but whatever it was must have kept my mother from collapsing—kept her walking forward, stepping up into the ambulance.

Looking back on that moment, the only thing I'm grateful for is this: through her anguish, my mother couldn't see me.

Dad lived another day, but he never woke up. I spent every one of those twenty-four hours in his hospital room. I sat beside him, holding his hand, leaning forward occasionally to rest my head on his chest, listening to his heartbeat and talking to him about my favorite memories from our travels. I told him how sorry I was for leaving him that night. I told him I never should have left at all—I never should have gone away to Yale, when he was at home, dying.

I told him so many things, but I will never know whether he heard them.

*God, I hope he heard me.*

# CHAPTER TWENTY

## ÁNGEL

**"HELLO?"**

"Hey, man. It's TJ."

"TJ? You're calling *me?*"

*This is a first.*

"Yeah, so what?"

"So, what's up, my *vato?* You sound kinda messed up or somethin'."

"I don't know, man. It's like—"

"Where are you?"

"At Vivi's. I'm in her dad's closet, actually. I think maybe I'm, like, hiding up here or something."

"Where's Vivi?"

"She's downstairs."

"Doing what?"

"I dunno, man. She's, like, really sad. And I mean—oh Jesus—it's killing me, Ángel. She's so sad."

"So you're hiding in the closet?"

"Not exactly. I'm packing up her dad's clothes. I wanted to do the hard part for her, you know?"

I wonder what that would be like, to be able to go back home, to walk into my house and see it all—the stool where my mom knelt over the fire, the wooden bed where my parents slept, the bright red blanket with black stripes. My dad didn't have a closet—houses over there are just like one big room. But he had a little table that he put his jeans on every night. He would sit down in his chair and fold them all neat, and then he would lay his plastic belt on top, and he'd put his boots under the table and hang his straw hat on a rusty nail. I watched him do that every night, until I didn't.

I'll be honest with you, I never even thought about that table, or the pants or the belt, Dad's work boots. They were pretty new, too. In good shape. I wonder what happened to all that stuff. *Is it still there?*

"Ángel? Are you there?"

"Yeah. Sorry."

"I don't know what to do, man. What should I do?"

"You're asking *me?*"

Can you people believe he's asking me for advice? How messed up is that?

"Yeah, I'm asking you. You're, like—I mean, it's like you two *know* each other or something, like you *get* her."

I'll go ahead and tell you, since you're up here in my head and I'm being honest: he's right. I knew it the first time I saw her eyes. We *do* know each other. We know what it's like to keep living when the memory of death is threatening to take us down. That's what we both know.

"It can't kill you," I say.

"What?"

"How sad she is. Death. I don't know. It's not like you're gonna catch it."

"Jesus, Ángel. I'm not worried about *me*. I'm not a total coward. I can handle it. I just don't know what she needs. I wish I knew—"

"Have y'all eaten?"

"What?"

"Have you eaten dinner?"

"What the hell, Ángel?"

"Just answer. Have you?"

"No, uh, I guess no. What time is it?"

"Like, eight. Go make the girl some dinner, *vato*. She's probably hungry."

He breathes really deep. "Okay, yeah. I can do that. I can make dinner."

"And then just hang out with her. Talk to her. Ask her about her dad."

"Really? You think she'll want to talk about him?"

"Yeah," I say. "It helps."

Back at that shelter, I loved it when Mrs. Ramirez asked me to tell stories about my family. I could sit there forever talking about how me and my sisters used to fight over who had to feed the chickens. One time I took the entire hour explaining how we'd walk with my mom to town when she sold corn and handwoven hair bands, and she sometimes gave us a few quetzales to buy chicles—the kind with all the bright colors. And when we got home, Dad would beg for one of those chicles, even though he knew he wasn't supposed to chew gum, because his teeth were so bad. And my sisters kept saying, "No way!" and I'd slide up behind him and put a couple in his hand. Which always made him smile. His smile was butt-ugly, I'm telling you. My dad definitely could have used some toothpaste.

But it always made me smile too, seeing his ugly, snaggletoothed smile.

And the weird thing is, as soon as I walked out of Mrs. Ramirez' office, with the yellow walls and the squishy blue chair, it was like I never had a family at all. I never talked about them. I never even *thought* about them. Never. Except in that room.

"So, okay. I just need to feed her and listen to her, yeah?"

"Yeah."

He takes another deep breath. "I can do that."

"How's her mom?"

"Her mom?" He sounds confused. "Oh, uh, I don't know. She's not here yet. She went out to dinner or something."

"So, you and Vivi are alone?"

"Mmhmm."

I start laughing. I mean, I feel bad for the guy and all, but how has he not even thought about all the things he could do to get Vivi's mind off her worries, alone in a big empty house with her? Nothing's better at pushing away death than working on creating new life, right? And it is 100 percent clear that she's into him. I'm telling you, even *I* almost felt embarrassed for her the other day, when she was watching TJ dance around my room, her face all blotchy and red. She definitely wants to make babies with him.

"Okay. Never mind. New plan."

"Ángel. Don't go there—" TJ's got that pissed-off voice back, the one we all know and love.

"Go where?" I ask, all innocent-like.

"You know where." He sounds really mad, which—for some weird reason—always makes me want to bust out the rhymes.

"Aw, man. In the words of my man LL Cool J, she just needs 'the warmth that is created between a girl and a boy.'" I rap that part, and it sounds pretty sick, if I do say so myself. I love that video, especially at the end, when he's standing by that window and he's all like, *"I'll be waitin'. I love you."* You *know* that one brings all the ladies to the house. Or I guess it *did*, back, like, thirty years ago.

TJ is not impressed with the rhymes I'm bustin'.

"I'm hanging up now," he growls.

"Okay, okay," I call out. "But go feed the girl, *vato*."

"I will," he says.

Neither one of us says anything for a while, and then he whispers, really quiet, "Thanks, man."

"Naw, man," I say. "You don't need to say nothin'—I'm your homie, remember?"

"Yeah," TJ says through a laugh. "You're my homie."

As soon as TJ hangs up, Bertrand walks into the room.

I like Bertrand. He's kind. I mean, everything about him is kind. You don't meet many people like that, you know? And he's really good at finding veins. The other nurses dig around under my skin like they're shoveling shit from a horse pasture, but not Bertrand. Even in my wasted, crumbling veins, Bertrand always finds a good spot for the needle. Always the first time.

"Need a warm blanket?" he asks.

I nod and let my eyes drift shut. I love those cozy blankets, I'm not gonna lie.

July 28
11:17 PM

Where have all
the birds gone?

# CHAPTER TWENTY-ONE

## *VIVI*

BIRD JOURNAL
July 28, 11:17 P.M.
*Where have all the birds gone?*

**I COME DOWNSTAIRS** after tucking my mom into bed.

Walking into the kitchen, I feel approximately 206 emotions at once. These include, but are not limited to: despair, anger, frustration, annoyance, grief, nervousness, and lust. *Is lust an emotion?* Maybe not. Whatever it is, I am feeling it in a big way. I know I shouldn't be feeling it, since I've been drowning in grief for the past couple of hours, and since my mom just collapsed into bed at nine, without even being able to remove her shoes (stone-cold sober, I should add).

Now she is sound asleep, and I am (sort of) alone in my kitchen with TJ and, for whatever reason, desire appears to be taking over.

TJ is standing at the sink with his back to me, washing dishes. I can't stop watching him, studying the contours of his body.

He made me spaghetti with meatballs. He sprinkled Parmesan cheese on top. He even found some frozen Brussels sprouts and sautéed them with balsamic vinegar and oil. He made a perfect meal from the dregs of our freezer and the back of our pantry. I sat at the kitchen bar and he put the food in front of me. I inhaled two plates of spaghetti.

I had no idea how hungry I was until TJ fed me.

The entire time I was inhaling pasta, TJ was asking me questions about my dad. I can't really explain it, not even to myself, but something I've noticed about having a dead person in your life is that everybody seems scared to death of talking about that person, like it's gonna make him die again or something. So it was weird, and incredible, that TJ and I sat at my breakfast bar and chatted about my dad.

He didn't seem freaked out at all. The more we talked, the more *normal* I felt. It was like each simple story I told about Dad's favorite vegetable (artichoke) or the best trip he ever took us on (Cambodia) lifted some of that heaviness off my chest. I could breathe again.

Then Mom came home. She walked in the door, dropped her purse on the $830 side table, sighed, and said she was going to bed.

Her eyes were all sunken in, her shoulders hunched. It was like one dinner with an estate lawyer had taken two decades off her life. I took her by the elbow, she leaned into me, and I led her up to her room. Honest to God, I think she was about an inch from collapsing onto the hardwood floor.

I stole a glance at TJ as I led her to the stairwell. He had this stunned look on his face the whole time, like he was thinking, *How the hell did I end up in the middle of this?*

Now he's got his sleeves pushed up and he's washing the dishes. Seeing him in my kitchen with bare arms and soapy hands takes my breath away.

"My mom isn't like this."

*There. I said it.*

He wipes his hands on a towel, and then he turns around and starts to walk toward me. This is a little unnerving.

"I think you should know, she's not usually a mess like this," I continue. "I mean, she's really a great mom, actually."

"I know," TJ says.

"She just got more really crappy news—about my dad's life insurance policy or something. She's overwhelmed, and—"

"You don't have to explain."

"But I want you to know—I need you to know that she's not like this." I'm babbling. "Or she wasn't, and she won't be. She'll be fine—"

He doesn't let me finish my thought. "Viv?" He stands too close to me and lifts a finger to my lips. "Let's stop talking about your mom, okay?"

My eyelids fall closed and I feel his finger run along my chin.

My heart is pounding in my chest and I'm light-headed, feeling his touch. I stumble backward.

He winces and squeezes his eyes shut. "Sorry," he says. "If you want me to leave—I mean, if you and your mom need some time alone, I can maybe get somebody to—"

"No. Stay with me."

I hear the words come out of my mouth before they even make it to my mind, but it's what I want. I know that.

"Please stay," I hear myself say again. "We have tons of room, and—"

"Sure." He's walking around me, circling me, like he's afraid to get any closer. "I can stay."

I swallow hard. "Thanks."

He puts the apron on the kitchen counter.

"Let's get packing," he says.

———

TJ and I work well together. By midnight we have finished the office, the living room, and the media room. I tape the last box and TJ piles it on top of the others.

"What's next?" he asks.

I don't know what to say. I don't want this to end. I want to keep working beside him, but everything else we need to pack is upstairs, and I'm afraid we'll wake my mom.

"I think we're done till tomorrow. Aren't you tired?"

He runs a hand through his hair. "Yeah, I guess it's kinda late for you mere mortals."

He's got a point. At the restaurant, things are just getting started at midnight on a Friday.

"Okay if I crash here?" he asks, pointing to the sofa in the media room.

Leather sectional: $1,800

"We have a guest suite above the garage," I say. "If you want an actual bed."

"A suite?" His eyebrows lift and a smile curves at the edges of his lips. "Why not? I've never stayed in a guest suite."

I deserved that. I should have called it an extra bedroom.

I lead him down the hall and to the stairwell. I can feel him watching me walk up the stairs, his eyes on my back. I open the door to let him in.

"Be right back," I say. "The bathroom's right there. I'll grab you a towel, in case you want to—"

I feel the red blotches spreading across my chest and neck.

*Jesus God. What is wrong with me?*

"Shower," I say forcefully. "In case you want to take a shower."

I turn around and rush down the stairs, determined to use the walk to the linen closet to pull myself together. I grab two towels and a washcloth and head back up to the guest suite.

When I open the door, he's standing in the dark, holding an object in both hands. He lifts it to show me.

"What's this?" he asks.

The rose quartz.

My chest caves in. "Oh." I release a surprised breath.

To most people, it would look like a hunk of pinkish rock, but to me, it's so much more.

He gently places it back on the bookshelf. "I'm sorry," he says. "I didn't mean to . . ."

I'm feeling a little dizzy, so I sit on the edge of the bed and place the towels beside me.

"It's okay," I say, pulling in a deep breath. "I didn't know it was in here. It's just a big quartz stone."

"It's more than that," he says.

"Yeah," I admit. "It is."

"Tell me," he says, stepping closer.

"It's a silly story."

"I can handle silly."

*I can do this.* I can tell this story. It's a simple story—a sweet childhood memory.

"One summer we went to this lake in North Carolina, with my dad's family. I was, like, eight. My boy cousins—they were all older and incredibly mean to me. They left me out of every game, every adventure. You know?"

"Yeah." He nods. "I have a dozen of them, remember?"

"So my cousins, they kept finding these amazing stones by the river—mica and quartz, stuff like that."

He's studying my face, looking for clues to the meaning of this story.

"I got so sad. I felt totally inadequate because I never found anything. And they kept coming back to the lake house we were renting, bringing these treasures and lining them up on the deck for all to see. Every time I went down to the lakeshore with them, I came back empty-handed. They were big and they were boys and they were amazing explorers and I was nothing. I was just a baby."

He sits down beside me on the bed, still watching me carefully.

"But then, on our last day at the lake, my dad told me to go down to the shore while he was packing the car—to try one more time to discover a treasure. I walked down the stairs and started to scan the sandy shore, and there it was." I reach out and take the quartz from TJ. It's still so heavy in my hands. "The biggest, best rock any of us had ever laid eyes on." I turn the rock to examine it. It almost glows pink in the dim light. "I took off running, screaming for my dad. I was holding it up over my head, and he took the quartz from me, examined it from every angle, and then said, 'Well, if that isn't the most extraordinary rose quartz I have ever laid eyes on. A perfect reward for my brave, strong explorer.'"

TJ smiles. "I bet your cousins were pissed."

I shake my head. "Not exactly. That was our last vacation with them. For my entire childhood, I thought I had found the perfect rose quartz."

"It *is* pretty amazing," TJ says, reaching out to touch the surface.

"The thing is, I didn't really find it. It wasn't until Dad's funeral that my cousins told me the real story—they thought I already knew." I rub my finger across the rough edge of the stone, avoiding TJ's hand.

"I don't get it—"

"After I went to bed on our last night, my dad went out to town and bought it at a gift shop. He planted it there for me to find." I shrug. "My cousins laughed like crazy about it that night, after the funeral. They couldn't believe I didn't know."

I look at TJ, and something about the way he sees me gives me courage to say what I need to say. "But here's the thing, for all these years, I thought I was brave. Extraordinary. I thought I could do amazing things."

I swallow hard and lift the stone to my cheek. It feels cold and rough.

"I'm not." I sigh. "I can't." My voice is rising. "It was all a huge lie. I can't do any of it. I can't do it without him."

And then—finally!—I start to cry. I am crying for my father.

*Oh thank God, I'm crying.*

I'm sobbing. TJ is next to me on the bed, his arms wrapped around me, and I burrow my face in his chest. My heart is so full of aching that it feels like it will be the end of me, this pain.

I want so much for this to go away. *How am I going to make it go away?*

I'm folding in on myself. My chest contracts, pulling me toward it, pushing the pain through my entire body.

Then I feel his hand on my hair, stroking my head, my neck, my back. He's whispering in my ear, and it doesn't even matter what he's whispering, because I feel his breath hot on my neck and his hands on my body and—

The crying stops.

I lift my head from his chest and let the stone roll from my hands. It drops to the floor with a thud.

I look at him and I see a precise reflection of what I suddenly feel. It's not an emotion; it's a need. An intense, overpowering, entirely physical need.

My lips find his, and they're searing hot. I feel his hands grip my sides. He pulls me firmly against him, and he falls back onto the bed. I have no idea how it happens, but my legs are straddling him. I'm on top of him. I'm all over him, my hands and my lips searching his chest and his neck and his face. I shove his shirt up around his shoulders, needing to feel his skin against me.

TJ knows. He gets exactly what I need. He rocks onto his elbows and pulls his shirt off, and then he nods and I pull my shirt over my head. He sits up and wraps his arms around me, our lips searching, my hands grasping.

He leans back and touches his hand to my face.

"Is this what you want?" he asks.

Unable to form a single word, I nod.

"Tell me," he says. "I need to hear you say it."

"Yes," I whisper.

He looks directly into my eyes, and his hand moves slowly from my face down my throat, across my collarbone, while his other hand expertly unhooks my bra. For a fleeting moment, I wonder how he knows how to do this all with such ease. But then his hand is moving across my chest, and I am transforming into pure sensation. Every place he touches comes alive again. No, that's not right. It's like I'm coming alive for the first time, piece by piece. Every part of me leans into him.

I am desperate for his touch.

"We have all night." He sighs into my ear. "Take it slow, Viv."

Some part of me knows he's right, but hearing his strained voice, feeling his hand against the soft skin of my stomach—I don't want to slow down. I want everything at once.

He moves his hand slowly, deliberately. He's beside me, and I'm arching into him, incredibly vulnerable and wanting so much to pull him closer.

And here's the miracle: all I see is this heat, all I feel is the place where his fingers stroke my body. All I know is this precise moment.

He's making it go away. TJ is making it go away.

He's touching me with his hand, and he's making it go away.

# CHAPTER TWENTY-TWO

## *TJ*

**WE HAVE TO STOP.**

*How are we going to stop?*

*I am going to stop.*

*I need to stop.*

*I will stop.*

I put my hand on her shoulder and push her away gently.

"Rest," I say. "Get some sleep."

"Are you sure?" she asks. "You don't want—"

*Yes, I want. I want very much.*

But there are about a hundred reasons why we can't take this any further. For starters, it's not like I went on this little trip prepared to hook up. Honestly, I never really go anywhere prepared to hook up. But even if I did, I wouldn't be packing condoms for a trip to help a friend and her mom move out of their house because her dad died. And, more important, the last thing I want from Vivi is a hookup. I'm not sure what we are to each other, but we definitely aren't hookup material.

So instead I whisper, "No. I'm good."

Her eyes drift closed and I pull her head into my chest. She curls against me, her hair spread across my shoulder, her body in deep stillness. I stare up at the ceiling and breathe, forcing myself not to remember her as I just saw her, felt her, heard her.

*The way that she responded to my touch.*

I think about cleaning the grill at the restaurant and how much I have to scrub to get the residue from behind the rotators; I think about folding towels in the ICU storage closet and how Prashanti always makes me line up the edges so precisely; I think about watching my great-aunt make *pão de queijo* and then wiping the cassava flour from the counters.

I think about anything, anything at all but the thing that my body so desperately wants. I know she said yes, and—in that moment— I am sure some part of her meant it. But this is too important to screw up. She's too important. And *God*, she's a mess. She's hurting so much. I want for her to be better.

She needs to be better, or at least getting better. It needs to be right.

After she's fallen asleep, I pull away from her as gently as I can. I cover her with the fancy blanket that's draped over the edge of the bed. I fold the blanket carefully over her so that the row of gold tassels won't brush against her face or her bare shoulders. I grab a pillow and head downstairs.

I stretch out on that big leather couch in the media room and try to stop my mind from racing.

I really hope I didn't mess this up.

Gray morning light comes through the blinds. I long ago realized that sleep was not going to happen for me. If I can't sleep, I might as well make myself useful. So I get up and head to the kitchen.

I don't know how old this house is, since the outside has that nondescript big-nice-house look. I think maybe it's stucco, vaguely Spanish Colonial. It's nothing like the old Colonial buildings in St. Augustine, though, with their squeaky doors, sloping wood floors, and windows swollen shut with humidity.

Vivi's house is a lot like her mother. When I saw this house from the outside, I thought I knew what to expect—one of those generically beautiful homes, the kind people call "stately." I expected fancy furniture and heavy drapes, lots of mirrors with those ornate gold frames. But once I followed Vivi through the front door, I knew I had thought wrong. It's nothing like I expected.

First of all, the house is wide open. It has virtually no interior walls, at least not on the main floor. And it barely has any color, either. Most of the walls are white, and the furniture is all natural colors, like the kinds of colors you find at the beach. There's tons of wood everywhere, but it's bleached natural too.

It's not boring, though. Vivi's house is anything but boring. Because everywhere I looked there were these perfectly placed objects, evidence of her family's insane travels—carved wooden masks, strange teak chairs with leg rests that swing out from the bottom, bright woven cloths draped across white walls. Most of them are gone now. Vivi and I spent hours wrapping them in paper and packing them into boxes.

So, yeah, this strange house is a lot like Vivi's mom. She looks like she's just gonna be your typical rich suburban mom, with her highlighted hair and manicured nails, but then she surprises you by making a couple dozen origami birds to hang from the ceiling of a hospital room.

This summer I've learned enough about Vivi and her mom to know that I'll never have any idea what to expect from either one of them.

A heat pulses through me, because I'm letting myself remember the amazing, beautiful, unexpected Vivi who I walked away from last night.

*I am in need of some serious distraction.*

I go into the pantry and flip the light switch. They have a second freezer in here, which is overflowing with food. I found it last night, after I decided to make dinner, and I almost had to laugh, thinking about Vivi at Costco, and about how she's subsisting on ramen, beans, and rice in St. Augustine, when there are forty-dollar porterhouse steaks getting freezer burn in the back of this thing.

I dig out a steak and put it in the microwave to thaw. I find an unopened box of Bisquick in the pantry and mix up some biscuit dough, reading the instructions on the back. I figure it can't be too hard to make biscuits from a mix. We don't have any milk, but Vivi did bring half-and-half for her precious coffee, so I use that instead.

I set the oven to preheat. While it's heating, I clean up some of the garbage left over from last night's packing, and take the bags outside to the garbage.

There's a door from the kitchen into the garage. I open it to find a huge white Cadillac that looks like it's probably forty years old. I put down the stack of boxes and walk over to inspect it. It's a convertible Eldorado, with a creamy white leather interior. The leather is in pristine condition. It's trimmed in red piping, and the entire dashboard is red too. I'm not, like, a huge car person, but I know enough to know that this thing is a work of art.

I mean, a red dashboard?

I let myself slide in behind the steering wheel, which is enormous. It's three times the size of a normal steering wheel, and it's also red. The car is like a freaking valentine. I feel like it should have heart cutouts along the windshield.

Of course, the key is in the ignition. I can't resist turning it. The engine starts right up, with no hesitation. The radio even comes on. It's set to a jazz station.

I cut the engine, close my eyes, and lean back in the seat.

After a few minutes I hear the garage door open behind me. I turn to see Vivi, standing in the doorway. Her face is flushed and her hair's sort of messy.

Seeing her fills me up—I can't even begin to make sense of the way I feel.

"Hey, Viv," I say, hoping she can't recognize all of these unexpected emotions creeping into my voice. I'm not ready to try explaining them. "Did I wake you?"

She shakes her head but doesn't say anything. She also doesn't look at me. I think she's having a hard time looking at me.

"This car is amazing," I say, hoping to change the subject. "Whose is it?"

"It was my grandmother's," she says. "I think, technically, it's mine now."

"She must have been one awesome lady to drive this thing around town."

"I was named after her."

"Her name was Vivian?"

"No, Viola."

"Viola Flannigan," I tell her. "That's quite a name."

*Jesus.* I barely know this girl. Until now, I didn't even know her real name. And still I feel more connected to her than I knew was possible. It's like I'm feeling the future before it arrives.

"She was quite a woman," Vivi says. "My grandfather gave her this car for her sixtieth birthday. I'll never forget coming out of their house and seeing it with a huge red bow on top."

"Good present." I climb out of the car and head toward her.

"He adored her." Vivi shrugs. "God, they were so embarrassing, kissing all the time in front of us, but it was nice to know that—"

Before I even know what I'm doing, I'm taking her hand and pulling her into me, wrapping my arms around her waist. I lean back against the car, pulling her with me. I kiss her forehead and then her lips. But her body feels wrong—it's not careening toward me like it did last night. It's not still and calm, like it was after—when she fell asleep. She seems stiff, awkward, unsure of where she should be in space.

"What's wrong?"

"Nothing," she says. "I'm really hungry, actually."

She steps back and puts her hand on the doorknob.

"I'm making steak biscuits," I tell her. "Give me, like, ten minutes."

That produces a smile. "Of course you are," she says, shaking her head.

I follow her in through the door.

"I'm gonna get cleaned up," she says, gesturing up the stairs, where her room is. I saw it yesterday. I guess maybe I shouldn't have gone in there, but I couldn't pass it without looking in. It has light blue walls and a white bedspread. I think the most prominent feature is the enormous desk, stacked with schoolbooks and jars of still-sharp pencils.

"Be right back," she says.

I season the steak with oil and a little garlic salt and pepper. While the biscuits are baking, I grill the steak. They have one of those gas grills on their cooktop. It's far from the best way to make a porterhouse steak, but there's no use wasting this expensive cut of meat. I have a feeling this is the last time they'll be here. I slice the steak thin and put it between the warm biscuits. I wrap each one individually in parchment paper and foil and put them in the oven to stay warm.

Vivi doesn't come downstairs for a long time. When she finally does, she's wearing a green sundress I've never seen, and her hair is damp against her bare shoulders. She's not even to the bottom of the stairway when she blurts out, "Do you know what a short sale is?"

"A what?"

"A short sale."

I nod. "Yeah, why?"

"The Realtor already sold our house," she says. "Mom just showed me the contract." She's shaking her head slowly.

"Oh Jesus, Viv," I say. Because I have no idea what to say. I know that Vivi thought selling this house would pay for another semester of college. I also know that a short sale means not a penny goes to the seller. It all goes straight to the bank. Vivi's parents were carrying some serious debt if they had to do a short sale.

"I know he had a second mortgage to pay for all of the alternative treatments, but—"

She lets out a long breath and sits on the bottom stair. I walk over and sit down beside her.

"You'll figure something out," I say. I'm desperate to help her come up with a solution, but I've got nothing. How does a person find $61,000? She told me that's how much she needs—for only one year of college. People buy houses with that kind of money—yachts, fancy cars. That's a shit-ton of money for one year of school.

*Wait. Fancy cars.*

"Hey, Viv," I say. "You could sell the car—the Cadillac."

"What? *No.* I can't do that."

"Do you own the Tesla—I mean, outright?"

"I think so," she tells me. "I know we don't have car payments on it."

"So sell it and drive the Caddy. It seems like it runs fine."

She squints a little, like she's thinking about the possibilities.

"It's so strange," she says. "I've spent the entire summer being mad—mad at my mom for not telling me how bad things were, mad at my dad for dying and leaving behind such a mess, mad at the world for not giving me what I needed."

I can't come up with anything to say.

"I'm not mad anymore." She's looking down at her hands, folded neatly in her lap. "I'm just so sad because I see it now; I get why all this happened. He was afraid to die. He couldn't face it—he pretended none of it was happening. He bought me a car; he went off and did all of those stupid meaningless treatments. He sunk us into the ground, trying to avoid the thought of it."

"Everyone's afraid to die," I tell her.

"Ángel's not afraid."

"Are you kidding me?" I ask, probably too loud. "He's scared out of his freakin' mind. He's totally terrified."

"He doesn't act like it." She stands up, her back turned away from me, and heads into the kitchen.

"It's you," I tell her. "He's different when you're around—more calm or something." She turns to study my face. "You two are, like, I don't know. You have this strange effect on each other."

She nods. "Yeah," she says. "I think maybe you're right."

I look at her, so beautiful and so vulnerable, so incredibly alive and so deeply sad. And I know I can't give her what she needs. I can't even begin to know what she needs. I thought I was some kind of goddamned hero last night because I didn't let myself take anything from her. I thought I gave her something. I thought maybe it would help. But she's not feeling any better this morning than she was yesterday. And her situation? It keeps on getting worse.

I take a biscuit from the oven and toss it to her.

"Let's get this shit done," I say, looking at the living room, which is filled with boxes. "I'll follow you and your mom back to St. Augustine in the Cadillac—my buddy Travis can check it out, see what kind of shape it's in."

July 29
9:48PM

Still no birds.
Did that offshore
hurricane send
            them off course?

# CHAPTER TWENTY-THREE

## VIVI

BIRD JOURNAL
July 29, 9:48 P.M.
*Still no bird sightings. Perhaps the offshore hurricane disrupted*
  *the birds' flight patterns? This is the only plausible*
  *explanation I can come up with.*

**DRIVING BACK TO ST. AUGUSTINE,** I can't stop thinking about a confused cardinal I watched one spring morning in the quad outside of my dorm at Yale. I was supposed to be on my way to chemistry, but I couldn't bring myself to go into that lecture hall. It had been weeks since I had completed a problem set, and I was incredibly lost. Every time I went to class, it was like one of those recurring nightmares, when you wake up and realize you have to take an exam for a class you never went to.

Most days, I was managing to get to class, but—still—I had no idea what was going on in there. By the time I stopped to watch the cardinal, I should have been paying close attention to Professor Lorenzo talking about reactive intermediates and the octet rule (another quiz I barely passed).

Instead, when I heard the thud, I stopped to investigate, and then I ended up sitting on a stone bench, watching a cardinal throw himself against a window for at least half an hour.

Birds sometimes behave this way in the spring, when they are busy coupling, establishing their territory, preparing to protect their young. They see their own reflection in the glass and think they're seeing a competitor, another bird who is out to steal their mate or damage one of their eggs or maybe just invade their territory. So those birds—usually males, but not always—start attacking their own reflection in the window.

Again and again, this bright red cardinal hurled himself from the tree where, apparently, he was building a nest, and threw his body against the glass. His partner, a dull brown thing with the tiniest bit of orange on her crown, perched on a nearby branch and watched the idiotic behavior unfold. Finally (and quite legitimately) she got exasperated and flew away.

When the battered cardinal realized his mate was gone, he flew to the top of a nearby tree and started calling out for her like crazy. She didn't respond.

I guess that cardinal throwing himself against a window is a good reminder to me: even the smartest animals can be stone-cold stupid sometimes.

"TJ was very kind to help us with all those boxes," Mom says from the passenger seat.

"Mmhmm," I mumble.

TJ is driving in front of me in the Eldorado. He has the top down, and his shaggy dark hair is whipping around in the wind.

I'm feeling incredibly confused about what happened last night. I've fooled around plenty of times. I've even had a couple of real boyfriends, nothing all that serious, but still. I can honestly say that my body has never reacted that way to any person's touch—not even my own. The whole thing was so overwhelming, especially the way TJ stopped so suddenly. And then this afternoon, when we were taping up the last of the boxes, I made the mistake of picking up his phone when it rang. I only meant to hand it to him. I held the phone for no more than five seconds—long enough to see a photo of a stunningly beautiful girl in a gold sequined bikini. He took one look at the phone and then walked outside to answer. Neither one of us said another word about it, but I couldn't help wondering if she was one of the girls on whom he'd honed his incredible skills. Clearly, last night was not his first time doing that.

I'm sure that, for TJ, last night was a pity hookup—without going through with the actual hookup. So now I have to figure out a way to let him know that it's okay—I don't need anyone's pity.

So, if Mom wants to sit in the passenger seat and talk about TJ, instead of addressing one of the many important issues we're facing—including but not limited to our overdue power bill, the fact that she has nowhere to live, and my looming Yale tuition—she's going to get no response from me.

Mom and I are beyond broke. Our only remaining possessions are packed into an eight-by-seven storage container, and they consist of such useful objects as Balinese shadow puppets and Norwegian drinking vessels.

I am entirely over her pretending that none of this is happening. I refuse to let her use TJ as a distraction. *And me?* I'm going to have to find a way to stop being distracted by him too. I need to pull myself together. I need to focus.

I was going to be a homing pigeon this summer! I was going to come home, do a kick-ass job at my internship, and return to Yale, victorious, glowing recommendations in hand, ready to jump on the premed track. What happened to that plan?

*What is happening to me?*

We pull off the interstate and head into the Old City. Mom agreed to help her friend Wendy hang a new show, so I drop her at Wendy's gallery, on San Marco. Then I follow TJ down US 1. TJ eases the Eldorado into an old gas station, with a shop around the back. It looks to be abandoned. He steps out of the Eldorado and I roll down the window.

"Is anyone here?" I ask.

"Not yet," he says. "Travis is on his way."

I park beside the Eldorado and get out. We sit beside each other on the hood of my grandmother's car and I look up at the sky.

No birds. Not a single bird since we left for Orlando. *Where have all the birds gone?*

"I'm sorry," I say.

He turns to look at me. His eyes searching my face. "What are you sorry for, Viv?" he asks carefully.

Hearing him call me Viv punches a little hole in my heart.

"I shouldn't have—"

"Attacked me?" He smiles a broad, heartbreakingly beautiful smile, and his eyes sparkle with light. "I didn't mind."

"It was a mistake." I bite down hard on my lip, and that taste of metal fills my mouth.

"What's this about?" he asks. "Are you embarrassed? You shouldn't be embarrassed. It was—"

"Grief," I say. "I think it must have been my grief or something. I mean, it was so intense and I've never had . . ."

"Had what?"

"You know. *That* reaction."

He turns his head and looks right at me. I can feel my cheeks turning bright red. "Never?"

"Not really. No."

"I think either you have or you haven't," he says.

"I haven't. I mean, not until—"

He sits forward and rests his elbows on his knees. He clenches his hands into a tight fist.

"I'm a little confused," he tells me. "Shouldn't that be a good thing?" He's not looking at me anymore. He's looking at his hands, clasped together.

"I was so sad," I explain. "And you made me forget, I guess. I think maybe I took advantage of you."

He lets out a low laugh. "You think you used me? If that was using me, you can use me anytime, Viv."

"But you didn't even want—"

"I wanted." He sighs. "Believe me, I wanted. You have no idea."

I watch him clench his jaw.

"Looks like Travis is here," he says, gesturing toward a pickup truck that has pulled into the drive. "I'll go talk to him. Be right back." He gets up and starts to walk toward the service station.

I look back up to the sky, scanning the treetops for birds.

Maybe it was that hurricane, out in the Atlantic. I've read about migrating birds that get thrown off course by natural events, even if they are occurring far away—pomarine jaegers, seabirds that belong in the Arctic, showing up by a river in Pennsylvania; Trindade petrels, birds that usually spend their time over the deep waters of the Atlantic Ocean, wandering around in the Appalachians.

But the amazing thing about those birds? Their mental maps are so incredible, so wide, that as soon as the storm passes, they're back on course, headed home.

Sometimes I wish I had bird brains.

TJ comes back to the Tesla and sits beside me on the hood.

"Caddy's in perfect condition—I thought it would be."

"That's good news," I tell him. "Thanks."

"And Travis finally got the part for my truck, so it looks like I won't be needing to bum rides anymore."

That makes my heart drop into my gut.

"I can drive *you* for a change." He nudges my thigh with his, playful.

"I think maybe we shouldn't." I bite down hard on my lip again.

"Shouldn't what?"

"Ride together."

"I don't get it." TJ stands up and turns to face me. "Is this about last night? Because you need to understand—I care about you, Viv, and I wanted it to be right. Last night was not right."

"Exactly," I say. "It was wrong, and I was wrong to take us there."

"I didn't say it was *wrong*. I said it would have been wrong for us to plow right into having sex. I mean, obviously the whole thing was incredibly intense for both of us, and with you so sad, and in the house you grew up in, and that you're selling, and your mom upstairs having some sort of breakdown—I mean, I understand. I get that this is all really hard, but . . ."

He's pacing in front of me, talking fast.

"Please stop," I break in, standing up. "I'm just really confused—about everything."

"Okay," he says.

"I need to figure things out." I head toward my car door, and he turns to walk away. "I'm sorry," I add.

He turns back toward me. "For the record," he says, "I'm not sorry—not about any of it."

———————

"I said Snickers, not M&M's."

I turn to look at Darren, my arms overflowing with peanut M&M's.

"Huh?"

"Snickers. The snack bar needs more Snickers. And take some glow sticks out there too while you're at it."

"Sorry," I say. I am all about the apologies these days, and the mistakes. I'm big into mistakes.

After I left TJ, I spent several days in the public library down the street from the A-frame, researching for the ghost tour. I guess you could say it was a needed distraction.

In 1970 the lighthouse keeper's residence went up in flames— suspected arson. I decided this would be a perfect new story for the tour. I also figured poring over newspapers from the 1970s might keep my mind off TJ and the mess I've made.

I crafted an awesome story filled with gory details. But tonight, when I tried it out on my tour group, my story bombed. I knew things were going downhill when, in the middle of my description of the charred, yellow flesh of the arsonist's ghost, a mother swept her toddler up and ran over to talk with Darren.

I finished my story—so proud that I (weak constitution and all) could conjure up such gory details. But when I got to the end, Darren was by my side.

"Vivi," he said, touching my arm lightly. "We need to talk."

"Another failed attempt?" I asked.

"What they want is *connection*! They want to feel the presence of a spirit they can relate to. These people aren't looking for horror flicks, sweetheart. This is a family tour."

And that's how I ended up consigned, once again, to the snack bar.

I just don't get it. I am trying so incredibly hard—I'm like that stupid cardinal slamming himself against the glass, and I can't seem to do anything right.

I hang a bunch of glow sticks around my neck, grab a few boxes of Snickers, and head for the lighthouse.

I'm restocking Snickers when a FaceTime comes in from Gillian. I'm not sure I have the energy to talk with her, but I also don't have much else to do. If I don't answer now, I'll have to muster the will to call her back.

*Ugh.*

"Hey, Gillian."

"Vivi!" she says brightly. "It's so good to see your face!"

"You too," I say, placing the phone at the edge of the register.

"What are you wearing?" she asks, her face scrunching up to look (legitimately) puzzled.

"Oh." I gesture toward the costume. "It's for work—I'm supposed to look nineteenth century."

"I thought you were interning at a hospital."

"I am, but I work here some nights—it's not bad." I lift the phone to show her the lighthouse.

"It's pretty," she says. "I'm sorry I didn't text or anything. We've been doing, like, three cities a week. I'm exhausted. How are you?"

"Yeah, we're fine," I say.

"How's your summer been? It's like you dropped off the planet down there."

"It's been—I don't know—hard."

"Well," she says, "things are about to get better."

As I expected, Gillian plows right past the part that might require discussion of such topics as dead fathers, mothers adrift, and deep sorrow.

"Adeline decided to spend a semester in Japan, so we have room in our quad. Are you in?"

The enormous number pops into my head: $30,587. That doesn't even include books.

I force a smile. "That's really great of you to ask, Gillian, but I think I need a single room this year."

She makes a little pout with her lips. "Are you sure? You'll be so lonely—"

"I'll hang out in your common room all the time, I'm sure."

"Okay," she says. "I guess I'll have to ask Hannah—she's great, but I can't stand William, and they're always all over each other."

"Maybe they broke up over the summer."

"Oh no, sweetheart. If you were on social media—which you still aren't—you'd know they have, like, a hundred-day streak of kissing for us all to see. It's vile."

"That *is* vile. I'm glad I missed it."

"Have you declared yet?"

"Declared *what?*"

"Your major?" She says it as if I should know exactly what she's talking about. I do, but I forgot. Or maybe I made myself not remember. I have to meet with my adviser in less than three weeks, and I have to tell her what I want to major in. After my experience at the hospital this summer, I haven't got a clue.

The evidence is mounting: I am not destined for the medical profession. I wanted to be a doctor because I wanted to keep people from dying. I wanted to save others from the fate my father faced.

I thought that if I left them to pursue that future—if I went off to Yale determined to become a doctor—it would make the decision to go more palatable. It would make me regret it less.

But I guess I'm finally realizing that I can't keep pursuing this future that I'm not meant for. People die. It completely sucks, but it's a simple fact of life. And I think that maybe, if my dad could communicate with me now, he'd tell me that there are a million choices I could make to honor his memory.

I think he'd tell me it's time to let go of this one.

Darren walks across the lawn toward me, which I see as the perfect opportunity to get out of this conversation with Gillian. "I gotta go," I say. "My boss—"

"Oh okay. Don't be a stranger! At least text me every once in a while. I can't wait to party with you during move-ins!"

I nod and hang up. Darren passes by, not paying any attention to me. I stare down at the tangled pile of glow sticks that I need to organize. As I sort them, my mind—finally!—produces a series of clear thoughts.

Here is what I know:

I don't want to be premed.

I don't want to party with Gillian and her friends anymore.

I want to do something that matters and that I actually have the skills and the heart to do.

Right now I am doing one—and only one—thing that actually matters. And it's not untangling glow sticks. I need to focus on doing that thing well. Starting now.

I stand up and walk slowly toward Darren, who is sorting through electromagnetic flow meters to be sure they all have batteries.

He looks up, flow meter in hand, and frowns. "Everything okay at the snack bar?"

"You don't need me here anymore," I say.

He shakes his head. "Nope."

"I suck at giving ghost tours."

He nods. "Yup."

"So . . . why am I here?"

"Because you need a job," he says. "And I'm a good person."

Darren *is* a good person, but I'm done with ghost tours. I'm not ready to help other people connect with dead strangers. I've got some work to do first.

"I'm gonna quit," I say. "Save you the trouble of firing me."

He smiles big and lets out a chuckle. "Okay, sounds like a plan."

"Want me to help you with those flow meters before I go?"

"Nah," he says. "Why don't you go out and have some fun?"

Clearly, Darren has learned nothing about my life over the past couple of months. But that's okay, because even though I'm not sure why, I know exactly where I'm headed. I hang up my costume and punch my time card. Then I get into my car and drive west, toward the hospital.

I'm going to see Ángel, and I'm sure he'll be awake. Bertrand told me that he's been suffering from insomnia. It would be nice to see Bertrand, too. He's always such a calming presence.

I drive to the hospital on empty streets. I relish the feel of my car's leather seat beneath me. I turn up the incredible stereo and I open the enormous sunroof. I let myself accelerate a little too fast.

I love this car, but I also know that it's almost time to let it go.

# CHAPTER TWENTY-FOUR

## *ÁNGEL*

**YOU PEOPLE ARE NEVER** going to believe who just walked into this room.

Go ahead. Take a guess.

Oh. Oh yeah. That's right. I guess you would know, since you're already up here in my head.

It's midnight, and Vivi's here. She just walked right in and gave me a big hug. And then she told me she missed me. She climbed up onto the edge of the bed and she asked me, *"¿Qué pasa?"*

"What's up?" Like it's just another day. But for me, it feels like Christmas. Or like I'm a kid again and it's the feast day of Todos Santos. When she walked into the room, it was like I was standing in the plaza, in front of the church. Like the gun just went off, and the Skach Koyl started, and all these guys were riding by on their horses, and I almost couldn't handle the thrill of it, seeing those men fly past me, howling and kicking as their horses ran along the avenue, sending up clouds of dust.

I'm telling you, I can practically hear the marimba music still. Except I'm not in the town square, watching a horse race and listening to marimba. I'm sitting up in a hospital bed and Vivi is cross-legged on the end of the bed and we've got reggaeton playing soft so that we won't wake up Mrs. Blankenship next door.

Vivi came to see me—not because she *had* to, but because she missed me. She wanted to hang out with me.

Don't get me wrong, people. I'm not saying that Vivi has a thing for me. And between us, I don't have a thing for her, either. Not like that—not like TJ does. Honestly, I'm too tired for all that, and she's obviously in love with TJ, even though the two of them have been expertly avoiding each other since they got back from their little trip to Orlando.

Something happened, but nobody seems to want to let me in on it. I figure one of them will break down and tell me soon. Or maybe not. I'll figure it all out anyway.

I'm good at that, you know—figuring out how people are feeling, understanding what's going on between people. I don't know. It's like I always have been. Like, I knew when my brother fell for that girl—I knew it was for real. And I knew the first time I laid eyes on her father, who came from two villages over, to tell him to stay the hell away—I knew something horrible would happen. I knew that man was capable of doing terrible, unthinkable things.

And it happened. The unthinkable happened, but I survived it. I don't know why I survived, just to end up dying in a hospital room in Florida. All I know is that here I am with Vivi and she's got her eyes closed and she's swaying her shoulders to the rhythm of "Me Gustas Tú."

She seems different.

*"Que voy a hacer, yo no sepa."* She's singing along with Manu Chao, about not having any idea what to do, about being lost. And maybe that's what she's feeling, but—between you and me—the lost version of Vivi is much more calm and relaxed than the version I met

a couple of months ago. The "Vivi on a mission," I'll call her. She was frantic, desperate to keep moving, keep doing stuff. For almost two months, I never saw that girl sit still. Never. I think she was afraid to stop—she was afraid the sadness would catch up with her. I think maybe it finally did.

But now she's different. She's not exactly sad. She's calm. Being with her, I feel calm too.

Here's something that sucks about my piece-of-crap heart: sometimes it makes me feel like I'm drowning, like I can't breathe. Bertrand told me it was normal, to feel that way sometimes. He said it's better if I don't struggle against it, if I don't panic. When I panic, it makes my piece-of-crap heart work even harder. But no matter how hard it works, my heart's not getting much done anymore. I'm supposed to relax and let myself drown. Bertrand said it would be easier that way. He's teaching me things, trying to help me find ways to stay relaxed, even when I feel like I can't breathe.

I'm telling you people, that shit is not easy to do. But it's easier with Vivi here at the edge of my bed, singing about how lost she is.

The song ends, and Vivi opens her eyes.

"Do you need anything?" she asks. "Can I get you something?"

"Nah, I'm all good," I say.

"I guess I should go home and get some sleep. I have to be back here in five hours." She starts to stand up.

I shrug. "You could stay. I'll make room."

"*¿Seguro?*" Vivi asks. "Are you sure?"

I scoot over a little and pat the empty space beside me. "I'll even let you borrow my toothpaste tomorrow."

She smiles. "Yeah, that would be good."

"Can you make the bed go down?" I ask her.

"You want it flat?" she asks, climbing up into the empty space beside me.

I nod. "And maybe turn off the music?"

She levels the bed and turns off the music, and then she stretches out beside me, on her side. It's a big bed, and we are both small— we're not even touching. We look up at the origami birds that her mom made. She reaches up and runs her fingers across them so that they're moving, like flying around.

"Hey, Ángel?" she whispers.

"Hmmm," I mumble.

"Did you know that some birds grieve?"

I turn my head to look at her. "What does that mean?"

"*Afligirse*. You know, like, feel sad when another bird dies." Her hand runs across the birds again, sending them flying.

"No." I shake my head. "I never heard that."

"They even have funerals sometimes. When scrub jays come across a dead bird, they all gather around and cry—or who knows? Maybe it's more like an Irish wake. Maybe they're telling each other stories about what an ass he was. How he stole from them—scrub jays are notorious thieves."

I don't know what she's talking about. I think maybe it's a place near England. But I'm too tired to ask her to explain. I can feel my body getting heavy with sleep.

"It doesn't even have to be the same kind of bird—they mourn for all kinds of other birds. Robins, chickadees." She twirls one of the paper birds so that it starts to fly in small circles. "And crows, they sometimes bury the dead—they bring sticks and pile them on top of their dead friend."

"Like *funerales*?"

"Yeah," she says.

"I don't like funerals."

"Me neither," she whispers.

I close my eyes and listen to the sound her hand makes running against the paper birds, and we don't say anything else about *funerales*.

The quiet feels different with her here. It's not quiet, exactly. This place is never really quiet. But it's calm and I'm calm and I'm pretty sure Vivi feels calm too.

Bertrand opens the door slowly, and—as always—he glides into the room, quiet, careful not to disturb me. When he sees Vivi, he comes to stand beside us and whispers in his low, soothing voice.

"Oh my. It looks as if we're having a slumber party."

I watch Vivi smile up at him. "Yes," she says. "We decided we needed a slumber party."

"Well, then," Bertrand says through a smile, "I'll have to bring an extra blanket."

After he leaves, I ask Vivi, "What does that mean? Slumber party."

"It's when people sleep together in the same place—as friends."

"Oh," I say, letting my eyes close again. "I like slumber parties."

After Bertrand brings a blanket for Vivi and tucks us both in, I start to drift off, into the thoughts that help me stay calm. Bertrand taught me about that, too. When it hurts or when I'm having trouble breathing, I'm supposed to take myself to different places in my mind, to kind of separate from my body.

"Hey, Ángel," Vivi whispers.

"Hey, what?" I say.

"What are you thinking about?"

"*Arena*," I say. "How do you say?"

"Sand," she whispers.

"Sand on my feet," I tell her. "Watching the water come up and wash my feet."

"You're thinking about the beach?"

"Yeah, I think about the beach *todo el tiempo*."

"All the time," she repeats.

"It's my favorite thing. I'm gonna miss the beach."

"Hmm." She lets out a long sigh. "I missed it too, when I was away at college."

We lie next to each other in silence, listening to the steady gurgle of my IV drip. I guess we're both thinking about the beach and how much we'll miss it when we're gone.

"When do you go back?" I whisper. And then I sort of wish I hadn't asked, because I don't know how I'll survive if she leaves before me.

She doesn't answer at first. I'm thinking maybe she fell asleep. But then she murmurs very softly, "I don't know. Maybe I won't."

I wake up to a hand on my shoulder and the glorious scent of greasy French fries filling my senses. My eyes fly open, and there's TJ, standing beside me. He's not looking at me, though. His face is soft, vulnerable, even, and he's looking at the space beside me.

"Brought you breakfast," he says, nodding toward the bedside table.

Nothing beats a large fry from Mickey-D's for breakfast.

"Thanks," I say, reaching out to grab one. I turn onto my side before I remember that she's there. Vivi's asleep next to me, her hand thrown over her forehead.

She sighs and turns away from us, still sleeping. Her hand tucks under her chin and the covers have fallen off of her leg, still in cutoff shorts.

TJ sighs too. Poor kid. He's sort of a mess, now that Vivi's avoiding him.

"What's this?" he whispers.

"Slumber party," I say quietly, feeling proud that I remembered the new words.

He sighs again and reaches out to check my pulse. It's killing him, having his fingers so close to her body but not being able to touch her.

He holds my wrist and counts, but the entire time, he's watching her, studying her. It's like he wants to see every detail so that he can remember it later. When he rests my arm back by my side, he moves it a little too far to the right so that his fingers graze her back.

He's watching the place where his hand touched her.

Don't get the wrong idea. He's not acting creepy or anything. It's more like he wants to store up memories of her. I get that. I'm kinda feeling the same way.

But I think that the memories he wants are a little different, if you know what I mean.

"I'm gonna have to sit you up," he whispers, still watching her. "It'll wake her."

"S'okay, homie," I say. "Girl's been out cold for six hours."

He smiles a little and presses the button on the side of the bed. Just as he expected, she jolts awake the moment the bed begins to rise.

Her hands fly out and she pulls the blanket over her chest.

"Mornin', Viv," TJ says. "How'd you sleep?"

She darts her gaze back and forth between me and TJ. "Like the dead," she says. And then her face falls into her hands. "Oh God. Bad metaphor."

I have no idea what a bad metaphor is, just so you know. But that's what the girl said, or at least that's what I heard.

She rubs her face twice and swings her legs to the side of the bed.

"I'm gonna—" She scurries into the bathroom and slams the door shut.

"Go get her a toothbrush," I say, motioning like I'm brushing my teeth.

TJ rummages around in a drawer until he finds one still in the package. Then he grabs a pair of scrubs from the closet and goes to the bathroom.

"Hey, Viv." He knocks softly on the door. "Open up. I have a toothbrush for you, and some scrubs."

The door opens just far enough for her hand to fit through it. She takes the scrubs from him and then slams the door shut.

TJ starts to check my fluid levels, and we both listen to Vivi brushing her teeth.

"You love her," I say. "Admit it."

"So do you," he tells me.

"Yeah, but not like you do, *vato*." I nudge his shoulder and laugh.

"Shut up, homie," he says.

"Sorry," I say. And I mean it. I don't want TJ to be hurting, and he is. We hear the shower turn on, and both of us look toward the bathroom at the same time.

TJ sighs for, like, the fifteenth time since he came in here.

Poor kid. He's confused and hurting, and Vivi is making him crazy. I may not know much, but that I know.

Ten minutes later she comes out wearing clean scrubs, wet hair piled up on top of her head. She looks around fast, obviously to see if TJ is still in the room. He's not.

She salutes me, like a soldier. "Viola Flannigan, reporting for duty."

TJ walks back into the room, coming up behind her. "Just in time for our favorite part," he says, smiling.

He walks to the whiteboard and grabs the pen. He uncaps it and holds it just below those terrible, stupid words: "Goal for the day."

"I've got a great idea," Vivi says to me. "Let's not have a goal today."

"Sounds good," I say.

"A goal-free day!" Vivi exclaims. "Today we'll just *be*."

"Works for me," TJ says, putting the cap back on the pen.

"Write that!" I tell Vivi.

She takes the pen from TJ and turns to the whiteboard. I eat my fries and we both watch as she writes, in huge cursive script:

*just be*

She writes it so big that it covers some of the stupid pain chart, that row of faces grimacing, staring out at me all day. And then she starts to color over those faces, and she turns them into a bunch of birds taking flight. And a turtle with a goofy grin on his face, and a butterfly, and big, droopy flowers. And she draws a sun in the top corner, over the top of "Goal for the day."

TJ and I watch in awe as she transforms the most terrible thing in this room into a thing of beauty.

She's finishing the last ray of sunshine when Mrs. Rosales walks in with a bunch of doctors in white coats. TJ goes to the corner to gather up my dirty sheets, and then the crappy part begins.

I usually try not to pay attention when they're talking about me, and today is no different. They are huddled around a computer screen, looking at stuff about me, I guess. If Mrs. Rosales is here, I know it's important, but still I don't want to know.

I close my eyes and let the English words float past me. I keep hearing one over and over: "Stable."

I open my eyes and look for Vivi. I want to ask her what it means, because I thought it was a place that a horse lives. At least that's the word they used back at the farm where I worked.

I wish I hadn't opened my eyes, because I'm looking at Vivi and her face is crumpling up, like she's gonna cry.

I reach out to touch her arm. "What does it mean?" I ask.

"What?" she says. She seems startled by my touch.

"Stable?"

"*Estable*, like, um, you're not getting better and you're not getting worse."

"That's not too bad," I say. "Why do you look so—"

She places a finger over her lips. "Shh, let me listen, Ángel."

I close my eyes and think about sand on my feet, because I'm having trouble with my breath again and I need to calm down.

I don't open them until I hear Mrs. Rosales arguing with Vivi. The doctors are all gone, and Vivi and Mrs. Rosales are in a standoff in front of my bed.

"I can't discuss the details of his case with you, Vivi. You know that. You're not family."

"So how do you expect him to understand what's happening? You clearly aren't explaining it well. He doesn't know. He doesn't have family!"

"You're wrong, Vivi. He knows. He simply doesn't want to acknowledge it. He understands."

"Mrs. Rosales," I break in. "You tell her. Please explain. But please not here."

"You're giving me permission to speak to Vivi as family?"

"Yes."

Mrs. Rosales nods, her face all serious, and then she takes Vivi by the arm and leads her out of the room. Not far enough, though. Because I'm trying to think about the sand between my toes, but instead I'm hearing Vivi.

Vivi's talking loud, begging for Mrs. Rosales to find a way to keep me from getting deported. Mrs. Rosales is practically screaming at her, "You think I haven't tried everything I know to try? I have consulted with every attorney this hospital knows, with the ethics board. I have called two dozen people at the Department of Homeland Security, Vivi—maybe more! I have tried everything. *Everything!* This is happening, Vivi—we have to accept that this is happening."

"When?" Vivi asks.

"He's stable now, so they will transfer him to detention on Friday and—"

"Friday?" Vivi calls out. "Like, in five days?"

"Yes, Vivi. Friday. He'll be there for a couple of weeks, maybe three. They have a medical unit there, so they can take care of him. And then he'll be transported to Guatemala by plane."

"Where he has no family! Where there's no one to take care of him! What the hell? Do they expect him to go out and get a job? This is insane!"

"You need to calm down, Vivi. You need to speak more quietly."

"And what? What will he do when he lands? He can't even stand up on his own!" She's not speaking more quietly.

"I'm working on that. Please believe me. I am reaching out to every contact I have—the embassy, the consul general here, private hospitals—"

"But still nothing. You have no plan. You have nothing! How can you let them do this?" She starts to cry.

*Vivi is crying.*

I open my eyes. TJ stands perfectly still in the corner of my room, holding a stack of clean towels, listening.

"Go," I say. "Please go to her."

He nods, puts the towels down, and starts to walk out of the room.

"Tell her to remember the goal," I say.

He looks back at me, his eyes filling up. Then he walks out, and I hear him speaking softly, urging her away. I watch the doorway as he leads her down the hall, his hand resting on her back, his head down.

August 10
10=24 PM
Are the birds ever coming back?

# CHAPTER TWENTY-FIVE

## *VIVI*

BIRD JOURNAL
August 10, 10:24 P.M.
*Are the birds ever coming back?*

**"PLEASE, BERTRAND! I AM BEGGING** you. Please!"

Bertrand and I are in the hallway outside of Ángel's room, and I'm pleading in a loud whisper for him to let me take Ángel to the beach. I want to do something special for him before Friday, and the best thing I can come up with is to get him out of this hospital room for a few hours—take him to put his toes in the sand. I know Prashanti would never agree to help me sneak him out of here, so it will have to be a night trip.

"You know I want to help, but this is an insane plan, and it's also illegal."

"Illegal?"

"Yes, Vivi. Ángel is in our care. If we helped him to leave, and he didn't come back, we could be prosecuted—the hospital *and* any of us who aided in his escape. We would have huge trouble with the government."

"But you took a vow to care for him, not to lock him up. This is a hospital, not a jail. And hospitals are supposed to be in the business of healing, of promoting wellness." I glance back toward Ángel's door. "This is what he needs, Bertrand. You know it is. It's just for a night! A few hours! I'll be sure to get him back before morning."

Bertrand shakes his head and rests his hand on my shoulder. "I want to help, Vivi. But you have to come up with something else to do for Ángel, something reasonable."

I squeeze my eyes shut and nod, and then I go back into Ángel's room. His shoulders are hunched up around his neck and he looks uncomfortable.

"Hey," I say. "Need another pillow?"

He nods, and I head out into the hallway.

I've been spending the nights with Ángel. I don't really know why. Maybe it's because Bertrand told me that the nights were the hardest for Ángel—that he wasn't able to sleep much. Maybe it's because I know TJ won't be here at night, and it's too confusing to be around him right now. Or maybe I'm trying to avoid the A-frame and my mom and all the questions about our future that we haven't managed to come up with answers for.

Whatever the reason, being here feels right. After our first "slumber party," Bertrand set me up on the couch. It folds flat, and every night he brings me two pillows and some sheets. He even sneaks me one of those deliciously warm blankets.

Bertrand says Ángel sleeps better when I'm here. In truth, so do I.

I grab a pillow from an empty room down the hall. When I get back, Bertrand is standing beside Ángel's bed, holding a cup of pills. Ángel has water in his hand, but he can't bring it to his lips because his hand is shaking so much.

"Are you in pain?" Bertrand asks.

Ángel shakes his head. "Not much."

"On a scale of—"

"A three," Ángel breaks in.

How many times in the past months has he been asked that stupid question about the pain scale? I think about how many different ways there are to be in pain, and how utterly inadequate that stupid line of faces on the whiteboard is in helping a person to determine whether the pain is bearable.

I watch, neither of them noticing me there. I see the concern in Bertrand's eyes, the gentle love he has for Ángel—for every patient, no matter how demanding or mean they are. Bertrand even found a way to be kind to Mr. Jones—the man who notoriously announced that he didn't believe that the United States should accept immigrants—especially not from Africa. He said that immigrants took American jobs.

I wasn't there, but according to the stories I heard, Bertrand nodded, smiled a little, and said, "Well, Mr. Jones, I would say that you are fortunate to live in a nation that welcomes immigrants, since this ICU, where you receive such wonderful care, would be near empty without us." All the while, he was expertly locating Mr. Jones's artery, to replace the stint in his neck.

The nurses love telling that story. I've heard it several times. And it's true: almost every nurse and nurses' aide here is an immigrant or the child of an immigrant. Except Richard, and he would be lost without them.

"What is it?" Bertrand asks Ángel, his voice softly coaxing.

"I'm just thinking," Ángel says. "You know, about Friday and—"

Bertrand nods and takes the cup from Ángel.

"Open," he says.

Ángel opens his mouth and Bertrand places a pill on his tongue. Then he holds the cup to Ángel's lips so that he can take some water. They repeat this process five times, neither one of them saying a word.

"I'll help Vivi find you a pillow," he says, after Ángel has swallowed all of his pills. Bertrand is looking right at me, and I'm already holding a pillow. He doesn't want me to be in here, but I'm not sure why.

I back out of the room as quietly as possible. He comes into the hallway and leads me to the break room in silence. When he sees that we're alone, he closes the door behind him.

"One condition," he says, holding up a single finger. "I will help you on one condition."

"You will?" I ask, my face opening into a smile. "You'll let me take him to the beach?"

"TJ will come with you."

My smile falls. I don't think I can manage being with him, even if it is for a good cause. Every time I see him I feel like I'm melting inside.

"Why?" I ask.

"Ángel will need his oxygen tank, his IV drip. He needs a professional with him if he's going to leave this hospital. TJ knows how to care for him."

"I get that," I say, "but why not—I don't know—Richard? I'll ask Richard."

Bertrand lets out a huff. "Richard is a coward. He'll never agree to it. Plus, he deeply values his sleep." He looks at me and smiles a mischievous smile. "You could perhaps ask Prashanti?"

"Funny," I say, deadpan. "What about Sharon?"

"Sharon is a lovely woman. I adore her as if she were my own mother. But—on this little adventure you're planning—Ángel will not be needing someone to change his sheets and sing songs about Jesus; he'll be needing someone to check his fluids, replace his IV medicines, and carry his oxygen tank. That person is TJ. He knows better than anyone in this hospital how to care for Ángel." Bertrand leans against the door, crosses his arms, and smiles wide. "He's very skilled, your TJ."

With those words, a heat crawls up my throat and onto my cheeks. I'm certain that my face and neck are turning scarlet.

*My TJ?*

"And I'm certain he will do it, Vivi. He'd do anything for Ángel—and for you."

"Not for me," I say. "We're not really, um . . . We had sort of a—"

"Ask him," Bertrand breaks in as he opens the door to the hallway. "He may surprise you."


This morning, TJ surprised me.

"It's an insane idea, but I'll do it," he said.

It was that simple. Well, actually it wasn't simple, because the conversation went something like this:

"Really, you'll do it for Ángel?"

"And for you, Viv. I want to do it for you, too." He was standing in the linen closet, pulling washcloths from a pile. He turned to look right at me. "I'm trying to give you what you need. You know that, right?"

That statement took my breath away. It made me feel so weak, so dizzy, that I had to sit down, right on the floor of the linen closet.

"If you need me to stay away from you, I'll stay away. If you need me to help you steal a scrawny pain-in-the-ass kid from the hospital, I'll do that, too." He shrugged. "It'll be fun." Then he reached out his hand to help me up.

I didn't take his hand. I couldn't.

———

At one A.M. sharp, Bertrand gives us the signal. I take off down the back stairs, carrying an oxygen tank. I head straight to my car—the Cadillac, since I had to get the Tesla detailed, now that I'm trying to sell it. That thing is staying parked in the carport until it sells. I do not have forty more bucks to waste on cleaning it again.

*Okay, I'm delusional.* I didn't have it the first time.

I put the oxygen in the trunk and jump into the driver's seat of the convertible, not even opening the door. I crank the engine and pull a McDonald's bag from the floor of the passenger side. I balance the cup holder filled with Cokes on the front seat and toss the food bag onto the backseat.

I start the car and pull up to the cafeteria service entrance, just in time to see the big service door roll open.

TJ wheels Ángel onto the service ramp, one-handed, since he's balancing an IV stand with the other.

When the fresh night air hits Ángel, he pulls in a deep breath and starts to laugh.

TJ hits him hard. "Shut up, homie," he says. "We gotta stay quiet until we get out of here." He hits the parking brake on the wheelchair and turns to pull the service door down. I back up so that he can lift Ángel out of the wheelchair and into the passenger seat. He reclines the seat a little, then he folds the wheelchair and slides it into the backseat. He wedges Ángel's IV stand between the seats.

He does it all with such ease. Everything TJ does with his body, he makes look easy.

*I need to stop watching him move.*

The sound system in this car isn't bad, but our only options are the radio (which sucks in Central Florida) or cassette tapes. I can't seem to find any cassette tapes. It's fine, though. I use my portable speaker and play music off my phone.

"I guess I'm ridin' bitch seat," TJ says, wedging himself between the wheelchair and the IV pole, into the middle of the enormous backseat.

I honestly believe that someone could live in this thing, if necessary. The backseat is basically the size of a twin bed.

*Maybe I'll be living here soon. And Mom, too. Who knows?*

TJ opens the McDonald's bag and distributes extra-large fries. I pass out the supersized Cokes, and TJ gives me his phone.

"New playlist," he says. I connect his phone to the speaker, hit a playlist called "Reggaeton XX," and we hit the road.

Soon we're cruising down an empty highway, and Ángel's smiling so wide that I think his face is about to split in two. We're listening to "Reggaeton XX" at full volume. It doesn't take me long to figure out why TJ labeled it "XX." It's got all the explicit songs we rejected for the hospital mix.

*Oh sweet Jesus.* Once again, I'm feeling grateful that TJ doesn't know Spanish. I'm also trying very hard not to think about my feminism and popular culture class last semester. I'm absolutely certain that if Professor Austin-Jacoby knew I was listening to this particular song without launching into immediate protest, she would retroactively issue me a failing grade. As it is, I barely managed to pull off a C+.

When we get to the beach, TJ leans forward between the seats. "Go to Eighth," he says. "There's a beach access."

"We're actually driving onto the beach?" I ask.

I did not know this was part of the plan.

"Yeah, Viv!" TJ calls out over the music. "Wheelchairs don't do so well on the sand."

I stop when we get to the beach access kiosk. The gate is closed.

"Aww, damn!" Ángel exclaims, his arms flailing above his head.

Of course, there's no one working at the kiosk, since it's the wee hours of the morning on Friday. It's probably against the law to drive onto the beach this late, but I suppose we're already breaking a few laws by sneaking Ángel out of the hospital, so what's one more?

"No worries," TJ says. He hops out, pulls an already open padlock from a loop of chain, and lifts the chain from a post. He pushes the gate open. "One of my surfing buddies works this kiosk. He left it open for us."

TJ walks back to the car and puts his hand on the side, ready to jump back in.

"I think maybe you should take over," I tell him. "I don't think I can drive in sand."

I feel them both looking at me.

"Your girl wants the bitch seat!" Ángel calls out, reaching over to slap me on the back.

They both laugh like crazy while I'm climbing into the back. I'm not laughing. I'm thinking instead that I definitely just earned myself an F from Professor Austin-Jacoby.

But TJ was right. This *is* fun.

He pulls the car slowly onto the beach. It's a nice night, not perfect—the tide is half in; the sky is sort of cloudy, so that the light of the stars seems muted; and the moon is just a sliver, high in the sky. The air is warm and humid, heavy against the bare skin on my arms and legs. A light breeze from the east carries the scent of the ocean.

TJ drives fifty feet and cuts the engine.

"Stop the music," Ángel says. "I want to hear the . . ."

"Waves," I say.

"Yeah, the waves," he tells me, looking across the ocean.

TJ gets out of the car and goes around to the passenger side. He opens Ángel's door and lifts him from the car.

It strikes me, for the first time, that we must look incredibly strange. TJ's still in his scrubs, and Ángel's wearing a hospital gown.

I'm so used to seeing them in these clothes, I didn't even think—until we were all about to spread ourselves out at the edge of the ocean—about what they were wearing. It doesn't matter. We're the only people out on this stretch of beach at two in the morning.

TJ hoists Ángel onto his shoulder and adjusts his gown so that it's covering his backside. Then, cradling Ángel in his arms, he gently eases to his knees.

"Sit behind him," TJ says. "Let him rest against your legs."

I follow TJ's directions, and he shifts Ángel in his arms so that Ángel's back is against my shins, and his legs are stretched out toward the water. Then he fiddles with Ángel's oxygen tube and makes sure his IV isn't pulling at the skin on his arm.

Certain that everything is okay, he plops down beside me, resting his elbows on the sand.

Ángel is staring out at the horizon, silent, transfixed.

Since the wind is light and the ocean is calm, waves roll in at perfect intervals. Again and again, their foamy white peaks catch the light of the moon and bring it to our feet.

I turn to look at TJ and mouth, *Thanks*.

He nods, pressing his lips together in a tight line and looking right into my eyes.

Bertrand was right. He was so incredibly, unbearably right. I never could have pulled this off without TJ. I needed him.

I need him.

# CHAPTER TWENTY-SIX

## *TJ*

**"WHY AREN'T THERE ANY BIRDS?"**

Vivi is lying on her back in the sand, looking up at the sky. Her legs are still bent at an angle, and Ángel's still resting against her. I don't know how long we've been here. I don't really wanna know. This is all going to have to end soon. I know that much. Ángel has an appointment with the US government at eight A.M., and it's the kind of appointment you'd be an idiot to miss.

"I mean," Vivi says, placing her arm under her head, "this is the beach, for God's sake. Where are all the migratory waterfowl? The pelicans? Where are the terns and the plovers?" She turns her head to look down the beach, away from me. "Not even a sandpiper. Not a single seagull. Seagulls are *everywhere.*"

"Hey, Vivi," Ángel says. He's not looking at her. He can't seem to look anywhere but at the horizon. "What is it with you and the birds?"

"What do you mean?" Vivi asks, defensive. She props up on her elbow. "So I like birds. Is that a problem?"

"No." Ángel shrugs. "Birds are cool. But you *love* them. It's like you're—"

"Obsessed," I finish his thought. "Admit it, Viv. You have an unhealthy bird obsession."

"Shut up," she says.

"When did this start?" Ángel asks. "This, um, bird—"

"Obsession," I say.

"Don't make fun of me," Vivi says, and then she bites the edge of her lip.

*Damn*, she's cute. She's got this little flowery sundress tucked between her thighs, and her bare arms are stretched over her head. The only thing covering her shoulders is those skinny straps.

I jump up. "We need to adjust your position," I tell Ángel. "Grab my arms."

Ángel takes ahold of my arms—he's probably done it a hundred times before—and I pull him forward until he's sitting straight up.

"Where?" I ask.

"Back," he says.

We've done this so often that we barely even need to talk for me to understand him. I ease him away from Vivi and lie him flat on his back, parallel to the ocean. Vivi stretches her legs out into the sand and turns onto her side, letting her arm rest along her hip.

"So, the birds," Ángel says. "What's so great about them?"

"It's stupid," Vivi says. "You'll think I'm crazy."

I roll up my scrubs and stand with my feet in the water.

"We *know* you're crazy, Vivi. This was all your idea, remember?" I use my foot to splash a little water toward her.

A few droplets land on her shoulder, and she leans forward to wipe them with her hand.

"Tell us," Ángel says.

"It's my dad," she says. "I know this is completely nuts, but I think he sometimes comes to me in the form of different birds." She rolls onto her stomach and rests her chin in her hands. "It started right after he died. At his memorial service, there was this robin in the tree, and it wouldn't stop singing." She starts to trace shapes in the sand. "Since he died, it's like—it's like every time I'm confused or hurting or I have some problem I need to figure out—every time, a bird shows up. I research the bird, and something about it always helps me make sense of things. You know?"

Ángel rolls onto his side and grasps his stomach—because he's laughing like a maniac. It's a completely inappropriate response, I know, but I can't help joining him. It's infectious, that laugh.

"You think that your dad is *in* the birds?" Ángel asks through bursts of laughter. "The birds tell you what to do?"

"Shut up, Ángel," Vivi says, picking up a handful of sand and throwing it at his feet. "I told you it was—"

"It's not *crazy*," I say. "But it's not very *Vivi*. I think maybe that's what he's trying to say."

"What do you mean?"

"You're just so practical, so organized, so—I don't know—you don't seem like a person who would think that people's souls are floating around in birds."

"Well," she says, sitting up and tucking her legs underneath her, "maybe I'm not who you thought I was."

"Oh, you're right about that," I say. "I also never thought you'd come up with an elaborate plan to bust this kid out of the hospital and break the law, but here we are."

I don't say what I want to say, which is that eight months ago, when I was holding a dishrag to her bloodied nose, I never, ever would have thought she could be the one I can't get out of my head, the one I'd do damn near anything for.

But here we are.

"Here we are," Ángel says. "But where are the birds?" He starts laughing again, so much that I'm starting to worry about his heart.

"Shut up!" Vivi says, kicking him. Her voice isn't angry, though.

I don't think she's capable of getting mad at Ángel. "I haven't seen any birds since before we went to Orlando—honestly, none."

"That's impossible," I say.

"I know," she says. "What I mean is that—sure—there have been a few birds around, flying high in the sky or perched at the top of some tree. But they're not coming near—they're all so far away, I can barely even identify them. And they're not . . ." She hesitates, looking out to the horizon. "They're not paying any attention to me."

"The birds usually pay attention to you?" I ask, trying not to look at her like she's batshit crazy.

"You've seen it, TJ! Remember that barred owl when we were kayaking?"

I nod. The girl's got a point. That owl was acting very strange.

"That stuff happens all the time! Or it *did* happen. And I don't know how to explain it to you. But it *helped*. The birds were helping me, and now they're gone. I'm totally confused about every single thing in my life, I have a hundred huge decisions to make, and all the birds have flown away. I'm not making this up!"

Ángel grabs her foot and squeezes it gently. "Don't worry, Vivi. The birds will be back."

I grab my phone from the pocket of my scrubs and check the time. "Speaking of being back, we've gotta . . ."

"No! Already?" Vivi says.

I nod and reach down. Miraculously, she puts her hand in mine and lets me pull her up.


Twenty minutes later I'm sweating like a sinner in church, every inch of my body is covered in sand, and I'm starting to stress, for real.

The car is stuck—really stuck. I have tried to push it out many times, with Vivi flooring the gas. It just keeps digging in deeper.

This Cadillac does not want to go anywhere. I get that. We don't want to leave either. But the problem is, we have to be back to the hospital before the end of Bertrand's shift. The hospital is an hour away, and we absolutely have to have Ángel back in that bed before immigration comes to pick him up later this morning, or else all hell will break loose.

I can't even think about that.

The clock is ticking loud and fast.

"Ángel!" I call out, wiping my forehead. "Have you ever driven a car?"

He smiles big. "Nah, but a tractor, yes. Very many times. And a mower. I drive a mower. And one time a golf cart."

"Close enough," I say. "Viv, you need to help me push."

She gets out of the car and comes around to help me. We move Ángel, his IV, and his oxygen into the driver's seat.

*This is such a bad idea.*

He sits up in the seat and grasps the steering wheel. I adjust the seat all the way forward and tell him, "On the count of three, floor the gas. All the way to the ground."

He nods.

Vivi and I both go around to the back of the car. We lean into the bumper.

"Ready?" I ask.

"Yeah," she says.

"Close your eyes," I say. "The sand is gonna fly everywhere."

She squeezes her eyes shut.

"One! Two! Three!"

Ángel floors the accelerator and we both push with all our might.

We are straining and pushing and sand is pelting our faces, our arms and legs.

Nothing.

"Stop!" I call out.

Vivi and I both hunch over and suck in deep breaths.

"Okay," I say. "Again."

Ángel presses the gas and Vivi and I lean in hard. The sand flies up, and then I feel the easing of pressure on my arms. "Push!" I call out to Vivi. "Harder!"

The Cadillac launches forward.

"Woo-hoo!" Ángel calls out, still flooring the gas, heading straight for the gate.

"Oh, thank God." Vivi sighs. I reach out for a high five, smiling at her red cheeks, at her arms and legs covered in sand. "He's not stopping," she says, looking past me. "TJ! He's not stopping!"

I drag my gaze away from her face to see Ángel slow down, just enough to turn around and wave.

"Bye, suckers!" he calls out, still waving big as the car pulls onto Eighth Street. "See ya' on the flip side!"

"Oh shiiiit!" I hear myself scream.

"He wouldn't!" she calls out.

We both stand, frozen, watching the taillights fade. And then we simultaneously break into a full-on sprint.

The car takes a corner fast. We're running with all our might toward the turn, and Vivi finds enough breath to scream, "Ángel, don't you dare! You little prick! I'm going to kill you!"

I'm turning the corner, my legs moving as fast as they can, and I'm thinking: *Is he really gonna take off? Is he planning to run from the law? Is this kid that smart—could he be punking us? Could he have planned this entire thing?*

All these thoughts are moving fast through my head, and then I see it. The Cadillac pulled carefully beside the curb, idling.

I stop running and let my hands and chest fall toward the ground. I'm sucking in breaths, but Vivi is running right past me. "You are such a little douchebag!" she calls out. "You little prick! If you weren't already dying, I'd kill you myself!" She's hitting him over and over, but soft, not hard.

That makes Ángel laugh like a maniac. I'm laughing too, watching him laugh like crazy and fight off her slaps. At least, I'm laughing between the breaths of air I'm still trying to suck back into my lungs.

All the way back to the hospital, we keep laughing. The wind blows warm and damp around us, and we've got the reggaeton turned up to full blast. Ángel can't stop describing how crazy our faces looked when he pulled away, and Viv and I keep telling him what an asshole move that was.

I'd be feeling pretty good if I didn't smell like a locker room and have sand stuck in every crevice of my body. I'm thinking about the twelve-hour shift I'm about to work. I really hope I have time for a shower.

Vivi's still covered in sand too. I keep studying her arms and her face from the backseat. I'm tempted to reach out and run my hand across her skin—to wipe the sand away, to feel it rough under my fingertips, but I don't.

By the time Vivi pulls up to the service entrance, light is coming up in the sky. She turns off the music. I text Bertrand, and he sends one of the custodial workers from the fifth floor to open the service door. I think maybe the guy is a cousin of his or something. Whoever he is, it's very brave of him to risk his job helping us sneak a fugitive back into the hospital.

As the door rolls open, Ángel reaches over and puts his hand on top of Vivi's.

"Stay here," he says.

"I'm coming up," she tells him. "I'll be with you until they get here, okay?"

"Please, no," he says "I want to remember you here, like this—with the sand and the car and the light in the sky."

"But—"

"Please," he says. "TJ will take me back. He will stay. You will go. Please."

She nods, her eyes filling with tears.

"This is what we remember," he tells her, squeezing her hand. "This. Not that."

She nods again and watches as Ángel lets go of her hand, leans back in the seat, and lets his eyes fall shut.

"Let's go, *vato*," he says to me.

I want to say, *Okay, homie*, because I know that's what I'm supposed to say. It's what I always say. We have done it a hundred times before, right? But I can't make the words come. So I unfold the wheelchair in silence, open his door, and lift him out. Bertrand's cousin comes to take the oxygen tank, and I start to push Ángel up the ramp.

Vivi doesn't say a word, and neither one of us looks back.

We make it to the heart ward forty-eight minutes before the end of Bertrand's shift—with time to spare.

I take a quick shower and put on scrubs.

"Let's get him cleaned up," Bertrand says when I come back into Ángel's room.

Bertrand and I work quietly and carefully.

We start by giving Ángel the best goddamned sponge bath anyone has ever had. We clean off every last grain of sand; we use Q-tips to clean out his ears. We trim his toenails. We fill his hair with shampoo and then release the bubbles with warm water. We don't say a word, because we want to let him rest. Ángel, clearly exhausted, keeps his eyes closed and his body limp.

When he's clean and dry, Bertrand steps back.

"Let's get him a fresh line," he whispers. "Who knows what kind of nurses they have in that place they're taking him. I don't want them digging around under his skin, causing him pain."

I nod and head over to the supply drawer.

"I want you to do it," Bertrand says. "I'll show you."

"I can't," I whisper. "You know I'm not a nurse yet. I'm not supposed to—"

"You're a better nurse than nine-tenths of the nurses in this hospital," he says. "You can and you will. Come on."

I nod and follow Bertrand to Ángel's bed. He takes Ángel's arm lightly in his hands and he starts to explain, quietly, the unique contours of his arm, the strange patterns of his veins and arteries. He points out which ones are shot, and which ones are still good. Then he makes me take Ángel's arm. "Go on," he urges. Ángel opens his eyes, looks at me, and nods once. I take the needle and I plunge it deep into Ángel's arm. I feel resistance, and then I press gently so that the needle will move through the walls of the vein. I feel it stop in precisely the right place.

"Good," Bertrand says. "Very good."

We connect the new stint, administer his meds, check his oxygen and fluid levels. We prepare Ángel in the only way that we know how, and then we wait.

When they come for him, the bastards put him in handcuffs.

Prashanti has arrived by then. She pleads with them not to. They tell her it's protocol. Bertrand and I lift him out of the bed and into a wheelchair. The two cops, in bulletproof vests with ICE written in huge letters across their backs, stand on either side of the wheelchair, their hands resting on their guns. They tell me to push Ángel out into the hall, and so I do.

It feels like the entire hospital has come out to say good-bye. Most of them don't speak. They line the walls of the hallways, watching. Doctors, nurses, techs. Mrs. Blankenship and Mr. Blackstone. Custodial workers with their mop buckets and white-jacketed interns. They all stand side by side and watch.

We move out of the ICU and into the central atrium. A couple of people are behaving really strangely, trying to stop the police from taking him, and I hear some people singing. I think maybe it's Sharon leading a small impromptu choir—one of her Jesus songs, but I can't place which one.

A few people reach out to hug him or to slap him high five, but most do nothing but watch and bear quiet witness.

When we reach the other side of the atrium, Deshawn, the cafeteria worker who brings Ángel's food, gives him a fist bump, which isn't all that easy to do in handcuffs. Ángel smiles and lets his cuffed hands drop to his lap. And then we're heading through the glass doors, toward the cop car that will take him to some detention center in Georgia.

Bertrand and I lift him into the car, and then Bertrand wraps him up in one of those warm blankets he likes so much.

"Thank you," Ángel murmurs, his eyes closed.

We step back and the cop shuts the door.

The whole thing is so pointless and terrible that I want to punch the side of this stupid black car. I want to kick the shit out if it. I want to scream and yell and destroy something—or someone.

But I don't, because Ángel has opened his eyes. He's looking at me through the car window. So instead I put my hand up to the glass, and he puts his hands up on the other side of the glass, one handprint against mine.

We stay like that, looking at our hands, until the cop car starts to pull away.

Ángel was right to make Vivi stay away. It's fucking heartbreaking.

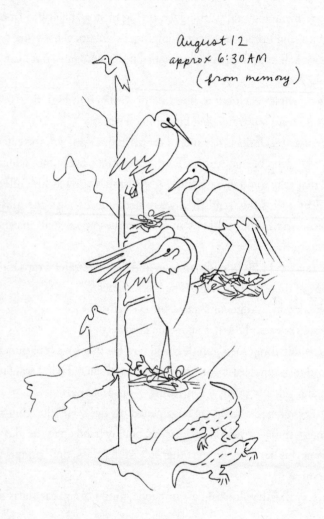

August 12
approx 6:30AM
(from memory)

# CHAPTER TWENTY-SEVEN

## *VIVI*

BIRD JOURNAL
August 12, approximately 6:30 A.M. (from memory)
*I have no words to describe this abundance. None at all.*


Hey. You okay?
*Not really. You?*
Same.


When the text came in from TJ, I was stretched out on my bed in the A-frame's loft, staring up at the ceiling, listening to the awful silence.

No *wheep, wheep* of the American oystercatchers, no *kyah-yah* of the willet, no semipalmated plover's *chu-wee* or sandpiper's *spink*. Not even the rasping *squawk* of the brown pelican.

Nothing.


*How did Ángel do?*
Fine.


I stare for a long time at TJ's response. *Fine.* Such a pointless word. Does it mean anything? Or is it just filler, one of those words that waits around to be used when there's absolutely no way to say what needs to be said?

When I don't respond, TJ sends me another text:

But Richard was a hot mess.
*No surprise there.*
Crying like a baby. And that resident from California, Dr. Santana, she practically threw her body across the hall to keep them from taking him. Prashanti had to hold her back.

I sit up in my bed to respond.

*Would have been worth seeing.*
And the whole time Sharon was singing really loud—some Jesus song about a rugged cross or something.
*Of course. Was Bertrand there?*
Yeah, he stayed. Helped me get Ángel into the cop car.

*The cop car.* I was almost smiling, thinking about Prashanti and Dr. Santana, Sharon and the Jesus songs. But I'm not anymore.

Did they treat him like a criminal? Did they make him sit in the back? All of these questions rush to my mind, but I don't think I can handle the answers to them. Seconds tick by, and I know TJ is waiting for a response.

*That must have sucked.*
Yeah.

TJ doesn't give me time to try forming a response to that one. Instead he sends another text immediately:

Can I come get you at five tomorrow? I wanna show you
something.
*Okay.*
Five a.m.
???

What in the world could TJ want to show me at five in the morning? And why would he be willing to lose precious sleep to do it?

Are you in?
*I guess. What's another sleepless night?*
See you at five.
*Okay.*
Sweet dreams.

I do not have sweet dreams. I stay up all night thinking about Ángel, wondering what it's like—the prison they took him to. I stare
up at the roof, missing the acoustic tile ceiling above the sofa in Ángel's hospital room, my mom's origami birds. I stress about whether
they have a bed that moves up and down, warm blankets—any blankets at all.

I stress about Alice, my financial aid counselor, and the email she
sent me this afternoon.

> *Dear Vivi,*
>
> *I hope that you are enjoying these final days of summer. Here
> in New Haven, we are all hard at work preparing for your return
> and the return of your fellow students. I contacted a colleague at
> the College Board about your CSS PROFILE form. Unfortu-
> nately, it's still in process, which means that you and your*

*mother will receive a bill for the full fall semester tuition early
next week.*

*Please don't despair! We are working with the bursar's office
to confirm that you will be granted a temporary waiver until we
determine your family's financial obligation, and you should
be allowed to register for classes.*

*More soon!*

*Alice*

I stress about my "family's financial obligation," trying to figure
out how Mom and I could possibly pay even a small portion of the
thirty-thousand-dollar bill, while also managing to get a roof over
Mom's head and food in her fridge. The Tesla money is all we have,
and it's not going to last forever.

And, of course, I also distract myself from all of this anxiety with
memories of TJ's touch, wondering where he wants to take me at five
in the morning and how my body is going to handle being alone with
him.

Which makes me stress.

Finally, at four fifteen, I drag myself out of bed and take a long,
hot shower. I make two coffees and sit outside on the stairs to wait
for TJ.

I know I shouldn't feel so relieved when I see him pull up in a beat-
up old SUV, his headlights shining in my face. But *God*, it feels good
to see him. Immediately my chest hurts less, and my breath comes
into my lungs more steadily.

He leans out of the driver's-side window. "Jump in."

I guess this is the "piece-of-shit truck" that threw us together. I
like it. It's sexy, actually, especially with him in the driver's seat, his
bare arm resting on the windowsill.

I climb into the seat. The fabric is torn, and foam bulges out from the rip. I reach across the gearshift to hand him the coffee I made for him.

"Looks like we have enough coffee." He gestures toward the backseat, where a thermos and two empty mugs are shoved between the cushions.

"Yours is better," I say. "Thanks."

"Where's the Tesla?"

"Sold it. They came to get it Thursday. A couple from Ormond Beach. They paid cash."

"That's great!" He pulls away from the house. "So you have the money to go back to Yale?"

"Technically, yes," I say. "But it seems a little irresponsible to spend all we have on a semester of college."

"Don't those schools have, like, fancy scholarships and financial aid and stuff?"

"Yeah," I say. "I should get financial aid. But I don't know how much yet, so it's kind of stressful. I'm just wondering whether it's really worth it—maybe I should look into state schools."

"Sounds good to me," he says. "But you're asking a guy who's about to graduate from community college, so—"

"You're about to graduate?"

"Yup. I'm finishing my practicum at the hospital next week. Then it's just two easy online classes until I'm Thomas Jefferson Carvalho, Registered Nurse."

"That's amazing," I say. "You know what you want to do with your life. And you're doing it!"

"It is." He smiles. "And it's especially cool that I've finally finished paying for it."

At a stoplight, TJ reaches past me into the glove compartment and pulls out a red bandana.

"We're almost there," he says. "I know this sounds creepy or perverted or something, but it would be really great if you would put this over your eyes."

I let out a laugh. "Not gonna happen."

"Please," he begs. "I promise this outing is one hundred percent G-rated."

I shoot a skeptical look at him, feeling the heat rise to my cheeks.

"Promise," he says. "Pinkie swear."

He holds out his pinkie toward me. Not sure I can handle even the touch of his finger, I grab the bandana from him instead and busy myself folding it.

"You'd better be telling the truth," I say as I wrap it around my head and pull it tight.

Three minutes later the SUV makes a right turn and then slows to a stop.

I hear him get out and close his door. I fumble to open mine, but he gets to it before I can find the handle.

"I'm going to hold on to your elbow now," he says as I step down from the SUV. "Just to guide you."

His touch is light on my elbow, but still it feels like his hand is tugging my entire body toward him. I want to climb into his touch and stay there. I want to feel his hand on my arm, my shoulder, my stomach. I want to feel that gentle touch across my chest. . . .

I decide to focus on my other senses. Sight is out, so I concentrate very hard on our footsteps on the asphalt. We stop and I hear keys in a door. I hear an alarm beeping.

"Wait here," he says, and his arm drops from my elbow. I listen as he punches in numbers and the alarm stops. I feel him by my side again, before he even takes my elbow. I focus on the sound, and the feel of the air on my skin. We are inside, walking through a cool room. But not for long.

I hear a door swing open, and the warm air hits me. We step out onto a boardwalk or a dock, something made of wood, and he leads me through the dark. It's impossible not to notice the smell—or rather, stench. It smells terrible, like some combination of a zoo and a swamp. I bring my hand up to my nose.

"Yeah," he says. "Sorry about the smell. It's pretty nasty."

"What is it?"

"You'll see."

We walk for a minute or two and then he stops. "Sit down. No, wait. Lie down. It will be better if you lie down."

I'm not feeling all that G-rated, hearing him say this, his voice anxious. I lie down on my back. Wood slats press against it. I start to notice a sound, soft at first.

"Yes!" he whispers, sounding proud of himself. "Perfect timing."

"For what?" I ask. The sound is growing louder. It's like the world is waking up. It's—

"Ready?" he asks, pulling the bandana from my eyes.

Birds. It's birds. *Oh my God*, so many birds in one place. I'm on my back, looking up into the trees and they're *everywhere*. The sun is coming up and the birds are waking up and *oh my God*, it's astounding!

"Is this enough birds for you?" TJ is sitting at my side, studying my expression, my utter delight.

White egrets, cattle egrets, snowy egrets, roseate spoonbills . . .

"Roseate spoonbills!" I call out. I can't help it. They're everywhere.

"Which ones are those?" he asks.

I point up to a tree, where there are six perfect specimens all huddled together—waking up, stretching their wings. "There," I say. "And there!" I point across the boardwalk to another tree. "And there, and—oh my God, TJ—look at that tricolor heron. It's amazing!"

Tricolor herons, blue herons, wood storks . . .

"You think maybe these guys will help with all those big decisions?" TJ asks.

I'm so overwhelmed that I don't know what to say. I don't even know where to look! There are birds everywhere, crammed into every tree that surrounds us.

"A great egret." I sigh. "Look at that great egret—oh no, wait! There are two of them. Look, TJ!"

"I'm looking!" he says, his voice rising to meet my excitement. "I see them. I mean, they're all just birds to me, but I see them!"

I had no idea there could be this many birds in one place.

"Why are they all *here?*" I ask, my voice filled with wonder. "What are they all doing?"

TJ lets out a laugh. "There are a couple hundred alligators swimming around below us," he says. "Scares away the predators."

"Alligators?" I jump up to a seated position and look around me. He's right. We are sitting on a boardwalk, and below us is a swamp in which alligators are, quite literally, packed so tight into the murky water that they're piled on top of each other. And most of them are huge. Enormous.

"Are we at the—"

"Alligator Farm." He nods and lifts a key to show me. "Sabrina gave me her key. So, yeah, we're breaking the law again—two nights in a row. Not bad."

I laugh, and it feels fantastic.

"We'll need to get out of here before it opens," he says.

"How long do we have?" I ask. "And why didn't you tell me to bring my journal? I can't believe I don't have my journal!"

"About a half hour," he says. "And I wanted you to watch them, not scribble in that book the whole time. Plus, it would have ruined the surprise."

"I was so incredibly wrong about the Alligator Farm," I say, easing onto my back again. "So, so wrong."

TJ stretches out on the boardwalk so that we are lying head to head. We don't speak. Instead we rest together above the predators, under a sky full of birds.

# CHAPTER TWENTY-EIGHT

## TJ

"I KNOW WHAT I'M GOING to do," Vivi says, sitting up on the boardwalk.

The morning light has turned from red to pink, so we don't have much longer out here, unless we want to get busted.

"Are you trying to keep me in suspense?" I sit up to face her.

"I think I need help," she says.

"I'm in."

She looks at me, hard. "I haven't even told you, and it's crazy—crazier than the beach bust-out."

"Doesn't matter," I say. "I'm in."

It's true. Vivi could tell me that she wants to hold hands and launch off the side of this boardwalk into a pile of hungry alligators, and I'd probably say yes to her.

"I'll take a semester off of school—maybe a year, if that's what it takes—and go to Guatemala. I think I can get Mom to come too."

I let out a nervous laugh. "Uh, okay. That's a little unexpected."

She glances out at the swamp. The gators are starting to wake up below us, sending out their low-throated croaks.

"Is it crazy?" she asks. "It's crazy, isn't it?"

I watch an alligator climb across the backs of three others, slow, hesitant, deliberate—everything that I don't want to be right now.

"You think they have decent internet over there?" I ask.

She darts a puzzled look in my direction. "Yeah, probably." She nods.

"Then I'm in," I say.

"Really? You would do that?"

"Why not?" I ask.

Because the crazy thing is that I can—I can leave this place.

I came home last night to a mandatory family meeting. I was so tired, and all I wanted to do was sleep, but once I figured out what the screaming was about, I felt nothing but gratitude.

"It finally happened. My dad and my uncle, they gave up working together. They're not even talking to each other. My uncle's getting a cousin to come down from New Jersey to run the kitchen—my dad quit."

"Seriously?" she asks.

"Mmhmm. Looks like Dad finally figured out how to say no to Uncle Jay. He and my mom and my great-aunt are gonna open a little coffee shop out here on the island."

I guess it's bad to *want* a nasty family quarrel, but the time had come for them to get this over with.

"And you'll have to work at the shop? Or will you stay at the restaurant?"

"Neither. That's the amazing thing. Uncle Jay said he can't let me work for the restaurant anymore—I need to show loyalty to my parents and all that crap—and Mom and Dad don't need my help. Their place is small and easy to run. Looks like I am out of a job."

"Sorry," she says.

"*Jesus*, don't be sorry!" I lean back on my elbows and look up toward the trees. "For the first time in my life, I'm free as a bird. My family doesn't need me at the restaurant, I've finished school—except for a couple of online classes—I don't have any bills hanging over my head."

A huge blue-gray bird swoops down over our heads. We both watch it pump its wings and then land in a tree above us.

"I want to be with him until . . ."

She doesn't finish her thought. I think she needs to say it. I'm pretty sure it would help.

"Until?" I ask, reaching out to touch her arm.

"Until . . . I want to help him die," Vivi says. She looks at my hand on her arm and then turns to watch the heron stretch his long neck.

"I know," I tell her. "So do I."

"Do you think he's going to survive that place?" She looks at me, eyes shining. "I mean, what if he doesn't get the treatment he needs. What if he *dies* there—alone?"

I squeeze my eyes shut and let out a long sigh. I have to tell her the truth, but I can't seem to make it louder than a whisper. "I don't know."

We sit together in silence, listening to the loud squawks and cries of the birds above us. I'll admit it, these birds are beautiful—but they sound like a traffic jam—like car horns and squealing tires.

"We'll go anyway—we have to hope, right? But I can't do it without you," she says. "You know that—I mean, I don't know how to take care of him."

"That's not true," I tell her. "You know better than anyone what Ángel needs. Sure, I know the technical parts, but anybody can do that, with training."

She lets out a burst of air through her nose. "Not anyone," she says. "Have you forgotten about my *weak constitution*?"

"Well, yeah, there's *that*." I lean forward and nudge her knee. "Hey, can I ask you something—you promise not to get mad?"

She shrugs. "Why not?"

"What in the hell made you think you wanted to be a doctor?"

"Dying dad and all that." She shrugs again. "I guess it made me feel better about leaving him, imagining that I was heading off to college to learn how to save lives."

"Makes sense—"

"Maybe for some people," she says, shaking her head, "but not for the girl who's always fainted at the sight of blood."

"Yeah, I handle the bodily fluids better," I tell her, "but you're still the person Ángel needs most. Plus, I'd never get by in Central America without you and your mom. You two were made for this stuff. It's like you've spent the past ten years traveling the world, getting ready for this moment."

"I like that," she says. "That's a good way of thinking about it all." She climbs onto her knees. "Do you really want to come with us?"

I slide my hand into hers and pull her closer. "Do you really want me there?"

She leans in to kiss me, her lips soft against mine. I rest my hands gently on her hips, feeling the thin cotton of her dress under my touch, feeling the enormous relief swelling in my chest.

Our kisses are different from the first time. We move together slowly, deliberately. We lie down together on the boardwalk, and I let my hand slip under her sundress. I run my fingers along her thighs, her waist, and she lifts my shirt gently to rest her open palm on the bare skin of my chest.

She wraps her arms around me and plants tiny kisses on my hair, my neck, my cheek, my ear.

And then, finally, she answers my question.

"I do," she whispers. "I really do."

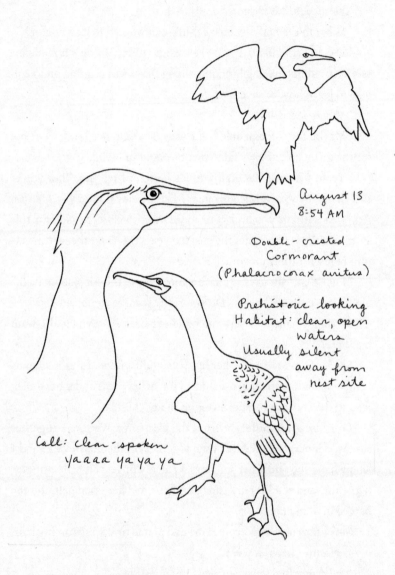

August 13
8:54 AM

Double - crested
Cormorant
(*Phalacrocorax auritus*)

Prehistoric looking
Habitat: clear, open
waters
Usually silent
away from
nest site

Call: clean-spoken
yaaaa ya ya ya

# CHAPTER TWENTY-NINE

## *VIVI*

BIRD JOURNAL

August 13, 8:54 A.M.

Double-crested cormorant (*Phalacrocorax auritus*)

Physical Description: gangly, prehistoric-looking
　　waterbird—matte black with yellow-orange face.

Habitat: common on clear, open waters.

Social Behavior: fly in V-shaped flocks. Float low on the
　　surface of the water; also dive deep to catch fish.

Call: usually silent away from nest site, their call is a clearly
　　spoken *yaaaa ya ya ya*.

Double-crested cormorants are highly unusual birds, since
　　they are as comfortable in the water as they are in the
　　sky. They both swim and fly with grace and endurance.

**WHEN I COME** into the kitchen the next morning, my mom is
making art.

*No surprise there.*

"Hey, Mom." I squeeze between her, two deep fryers filled with
melted wax, and a huge vat of orange dye, making my way carefully

toward the coffeepot. "Did you know there's a lake in Guatemala where the water rose seventeen feet in two years and no one knows why?"

"And?" she asks. Her back is turned to me, but I can feel her attention shifting toward me. She knows where this is going.

"It's a mystery. The lake is surrounded by three dormant volcanoes. It's the deepest lake in Central America, and scientists can't explain what is making the water rise. It's called Lake Atitlan," I tell her, closing the fridge.

"And?" She turns to look up at me. There's a smirk on her lips and a sparkle in her eyes.

"They call it the belly button of the world, but it's supposed to be a place of extraordinary beauty, quaint Mayan villages, ancient ruins dating back two thousand years."

"And?"

I pour cream into my coffee, scoop in some sugar, and lift the cup to my mouth. I try to breathe in the scent of it, but it smells like the inside of a European cathedral in here—probably all that melted wax.

"And there's a town there called Panajachel. A ton of expatriates live there—the kind of people who would really be into buying batik art."

"Interesting," she says, her face lighting up. "And?"

"And there's a clinic in the village that has a rotating staff of doctors and nurses from around the world."

She nods. "And?"

"It's incredibly cheap to live there. You can get a four-bedroom waterfront home for five hundred a month—with a papaya tree in the yard and bougainvillea blooming across the front entrance."

"Papaya for breakfast every morning." She nods again. "That sounds good."

I look outside the kitchen window, toward the brightly colored squares of cloth she has drying on a line.

"I want for us to go live there, with Ángel, and TJ—he wants to come too. He knows how to take care of Ángel. And we'll stay until . . ."

"Until . . ." She's standing beside me at the window, watching me.

"Until Ángel doesn't need us anymore, and then we'll come back and I will be ready for school." I turn to look at her. "I can take time to work out the financial aid situation at Yale, or maybe I'll apply for the honors program at University of Florida. Either way, it won't cost us everything."

"Are you sure?" she asks, studying my face. "You've worked so hard for all of this—I hate that my mistakes are keeping you from your dreams."

"What mistakes, Mom?"

"Vivi," she says, taking my hand in hers. "You need to understand this: I wouldn't trade a single moment of our lives together for some life insurance policy or that big empty house. I'd rather keep the memories. Does that make sense to you?"

I nod because, honestly, it does. My parents lived the life they wanted, and they did it with incredible gusto. That takes courage.

"But we should have set aside money for college—we shouldn't have assumed that your father would always be around to provide for that. I'm sorry, Vivi. I'm so sorry we did this to you. I'm so sorry our decisions in the past are keeping you from the future you dream of."

"I'm not even sure what my dreams are, Mom." I bite my lip and pull my hand away. "Do you think Dad would be disappointed? I mean, if I don't go back to Yale?"

She lets out a sigh. "How could your father be disappointed in you, Vivi? You are the bravest and most resilient woman I know. And your dad—he was wonderful. He was the love of my life. I'm adrift without him—but we both know he wasn't perfect."

"Yeah," I say. "He wasn't."

"And while I hid out in this house, making art, overwhelmed by our situation and trying to find a path out of my grief, *you*"—she steps over to inspect one of her anemones; she gently lifts the cloth—"*you*, Vivi, found a way to build us a new life—a life filled with meaning and purpose. How could your father not be proud of that?"

I stand in silence for a while, watching my mom work. It's strange, how she has spent the entire summer underwater, making art from sea creatures, while I've been obsessively focused on the sky. I think about the cormorant I saw early this morning, when I was walking on the beach, strategizing how I would present this plan to Mom. Cormorants dive deep into the ocean for food, and they are as comfortable underwater as they are in the sky.

"Pour me a cup?" Mom asks, gesturing toward my mug of coffee. She's wearing yellow rubber gloves, or at least they used to be yellow. Now they're stained with layer upon layer of color.

I get a chipped mug from the pantry and pour her coffee. When I turn to give it to her, she's wrist-deep in red dye.

I think maybe it's time for me to embrace my inner cormorant.

"Want me to . . ."

"Help?" Her voice sounds a little too enthusiastic. "Oh yes, Vivi, that would be so great! I'm trying to finish this sea anemone series for the show at Wendy's gallery, and I'm down to the wire."

"How does it work, exactly?" I ask, realizing that I have spent an entire summer seeing my mom make batik art, and I never took a moment to really watch. It's time for me to dive in and find my mom again.

"You start from a blank white canvas," she tells me. "An old sheet, any old rag, as long as it's white."

"Oh, that explains it!"

"Explains what?" she asks, all innocent.

"Why we are down to exactly two sheet sets this summer. Both of them pink."

She laughs. "You know what they say! You have to make sacrifices for your art."

"So, what does the wax do?" I ask, pointing toward the deep fryer turned wax-melting system.

"You cover whatever part of the canvas will stay white with wax, to protect it from the dye. You dip the canvas into the lightest color, and you let it dry. Then you cover any part of the canvas that will stay that color with wax, and you dip the whole thing into the next-lightest color."

She points to a canvas that's only partially finished. I can see the beginnings of a sea anemone, the jagged edges of its dark spine starting to emerge from the washed-out colors on the sheet.

"And you keep adding layers, darker and darker, until you have your finished product."

"Okay," I say. "I think I get it. Put me to work."

"Those are ready for the ocean." She hands me a thick brush. "Wax over every piece that you think should remain red—basically the entire anemone. That will protect the cloth from taking in more dye—and then we will dip it into the indigo."

I spread the sheet out onto the linoleum counter and start painting wax onto it. We work in silence, and after a while, I've fallen into a rhythm.

When the wax is dry, Mom puts her gloves back on and carries the sheet over to a vat of deep blue dye.

"What if you mess up?" I ask. "I mean, if you cover something with wax that you actually meant to dye? Or you dye something that you should have protected?"

"Happens all the time," she tells me. "See this one?" She traces her finger along the edge of an elaborately wound tentacle. "It was a spill! It's actually fun, figuring out how to work around the mistakes, how to incorporate them into the design. It's not like painting or sketching—there's no eraser, no ammonia. You just have to get creative and keep moving forward."

I guess it's moving forward, but it also seems to me like it's a process of working in reverse—you have to imagine something out of nothing. You have to keep that image in your mind and then slowly—piece by piece, dip by dip—build your way toward it. And if you make a mistake or two, you just keep going.

But the amazing thing? That mistake—no matter how big or how terrible—melts right into the pattern of the canvas; it becomes an integral part of the art.

# CHAPTER THIRTY

## ÁNGEL

**I REFUSE TO DIE HERE.**

This place sucks. *Atsalu taq'wixil.*

Does that expression work in your language? It seems like it would be a fairly universal way to get my point across.

Anyway, this place sucks, and I refuse to die here.

When I first showed up, I was in no shape to leave the infirmary. The ambulance ride from the hospital almost did me in. It felt like forever. By the time we got here, my head was a mess. I couldn't even hear myself think. All I remember is seeing a high fence with about four layers of razor wire on it, and looking through it at a big windowless prison spread out across a field surrounded by guard towers.

For a week I barely even ate. I was pretty psyched once I could sit up again and finally felt hungry.

The nurse with the Snoopy scrubs was working that day. For real, the lady is working in a freaking prison, and she chooses to wear powder-pink scrubs with a dog doing a little jig across them.

Anyway, she's okay, the Snoopy nurse. One night I told her I was hungry for actual food, and she got all excited. The next morning, she woke me up at four thirty in the morning, saying it was time for breakfast, her voice all chipper.

I rolled over and mumbled that breakfast happens when the sun comes up.

Snoopy Lady said, "Not here it doesn't wait for the sun to come up. Breakfast happens at five or it doesn't happen at all." She has a funny accent. I asked her about it, and she said that's how people in Georgia talk. I guess I'm in Georgia now. I dunno.

"You hungry, or what?" she said. "Cuz now's your only chance till noon."

I *was* hungry. She loaded me into a wheelchair and took me through about ten metal doors. I sat there and waited while she took out her keys and unlocked each one of those doors. By the time we got to the last one, my head was starting to hurt from hearing them all thud behind us.

When we rolled into "the mess"—that's what they call it—all I saw were the enormous, life-sized photographs that lined the freaking walls. Get this, people: tropical island paradise. That's what they show. Sandy beaches, blue waters, a lonely palm tree waving in the breeze.

WHAT. THE. LIVING. HELL.

Downright cruel, I'm telling you. Evil.

We turned a corner, and then I saw the rest. Guys in red jumpsuits sitting around plastic picnic tables, picking at the Styrofoam plates filled with something that I guess the people who run this place call food. On every plate, a blob of yellow, a blob of white. No Deshawn here to come and take our breakfast orders. Oh no. Snoopy Lady pushed me into line, behind a bunch of guys in prison jumpsuits shuffling along, grabbing their food from the counter. I'm telling you, people, it was so weird, because I got to that counter and all I saw was a big metal wall, with a thin slit at the bottom, and through that slit, hands pushed food at us. But we couldn't see who was feeding us. All those servers showed us were their hands, shoving full plates out for hungry people to grab. And the guys in line? They took their plates, looked down, and frowned. Some of them even sighed. Because the food in this prison is barely food.

I didn't know yet that the people on the other side, the guys working in the kitchen, in the commissary, in the barbershop, the janitors, the sweepers, the dishwashers—they were all detained immigrants like me—locked up in here, working as "volunteers." Yeah, that's what the guards call them—the immigrants who are held in this place. The ones who work to keep the place going, they're called "volunteers," and they might as well be volunteers, because they only get paid a dollar or two a day, and the only place they can spend that money is the commissary, where a packet of ramen noodles costs, like, five bucks.

I'll be honest with you, people: I'm desperate for some fries from Mickey-D's. I might be willing to wash dishes for five days to get my greasy hands on some of those.

Doesn't matter. I'm too sick to "volunteer."

Today Snoopy Nurse seems to be on a mission. She's standing at the foot of my bed, staring straight at me, her hands perched on her hips.

"Know what you need?" she asks. "Fresh air!"

I shake my head. I don't have the energy to get up today.

She nods vigorously, her expression stern. "Up we go!"

Sometimes I wish this lady would ignore me like all the rest of them do. Most of those nurses sit around and pick at their fingernails all day, or they eat potato chips and drink sodas and maybe every few hours stick their heads in the room to see if I've kicked it yet.

"You like soccer?" She's yanking on my arm, and it hurts like hell. Everything hurts. She drags my feet around to the side of the bed.

"C'mon, sugar. I'm gonna slide you right on into this wheelchair. You just relax."

She tugs and yanks, and every place she touches me aches deep in my bones, but I get there.

"All you people like soccer!" She's starting to wheel me toward the first of probably three hundred metal doors between the infirmary and the outside. My head already hurts. "I mean, you people from South America."

*Us people from South America?* I've gotta be honest—I don't even have the energy to answer that one.

We pass by the rooms where the not-sick prisoners sleep. They're big open spaces with tons of beds stacked on top of each other. They've got toilets and showers in there, right out in the open for everybody to see everybody else doing their business. Snoopy Nurse told me that sixty men share one of those rooms. She said I'm lucky. I guess maybe she's right. It would suck in here even worse if I had to take a dump in front of fifty-nine other guys every day. The only private rooms are in the infirmary and solitary confinement—and nobody's lucky to end up there.

By the time we get to the place they call the "yards," I have a brutal headache. If I were back in the ICU, I'd be telling TJ to circle the face with the squiggles for a mouth. I never did that, not even once. I always went with either the smile or the straight line.

Snoopy Nurse pushes open the door to outside and the sunlight hits my eyes. I squint and put my hand over them. It hurts. It's like a thousand knives stabbing into my brain and then twisting back and forth. I'm telling you, people, we are getting close to a ten on the pain scale.

"Let's go watch some of your *com-padres* play *fút-bol*!" She leans down to look at me. I can't open my eyes, but I can tell she's leaning over me because her shadow has blocked the sunlight, so I'm getting a moment's break from the stabbing knives of light.

"See!" Snoopy Lady is way too cheerful for my pounding head to take in. "I'm learnin' some Spanish, Ángel!"

And I thought TJ's Spanish was bad.

She wheels me along the sidewalk. I know I'm outside, even though I can't open my eyes. I smell the dirt. It smells good. Not like cleaning supplies. The infirmary always smells like bleach.

"*Pásalo! Pásalo!*" I hear the thud of the fútbol, a bunch of guys yelling and calling out.

I open my eyes to see twenty or so men all wearing blue jump-suits. They're running around on a deep-orange patch of dirt. There's no grass, no goal. Poor dudes don't even have cleats. They're running around in their socks, stained orange from the strange-colored dirt. Big clouds of orange dust surround them, and every time one of them kicks the ball, another cloud puffs up. They don't care, though. They're gonna play no matter what. They've tossed those weird plas-tic slip-on shoes to the side. Most have, at least. Some of them took off their socks and put them on over the plastic shoes.

Smart.

A couple of these guys are good, I'm not gonna lie. When one dude steals the ball and dribbles all the way across the field, I can't help letting out a yelp. I think I'm trying to say, "*GOOOOOLLLL!*" but it doesn't come out that way. Even the stupid yelp makes me suck in a deep breath. I feel the air, gritty against my nose. It's dusty out here and it makes me want to sneeze. I try to reach up and wipe my nose, but I can't get my arm to do anything. I double over and sneeze again.

*Oh damn, that hurts.*

I sneeze again.

I'm trying to suck in air, trying to fill up my lungs, trying to ig-nore the way my chest feels like it's collapsing in on me.

And then I'm coughing. My head is in my lap and my whole body is contracting in on itself. I'm about to cough up a lung. I'm hacking and wheezing and I can feel it: all those guys who were running around on the dirt stop to look at me.

*Please God, do not let me be dying.*

A couple of them jog over to see what's going on. One of the guys kneels down and touches my shoulder.

*"¿Qué te pasa, amigo? ¿Necesitas ayuda?"*

He talks like a Mexican, his words jumping up and down.

*"¿No hablas español? ¿Qué hablas, amigo? ¿Cómo te ayudo?"*

He wants to help me. Do what? I don't know. Not much he can do, unless he's got an extra heart he wants to loan me. By now I probably could use a new pair of lungs, too.

He stands up and calls across the dirt field. *"Oye! Pascual! Es indio! Ven! Rápido! Es indio!"*

Finally I stop coughing long enough to see the Mexican calling somebody else over—a small guy with long black hair jogs toward me. He's *indio*, like me, but I bet he doesn't speak Mam. We've got lots of *indios* in Guatemala. Most of them don't know how to speak my language.

*"Ma b'a'na?"*

Oh. He does speak Mam. He's asking me if I'm okay, and I don't know how to answer.

*"Min b'I'n wune',"* I whisper. "I don't know."

I turn my head sideways. It's still resting on my lap. Nurse Snoopy is running over to a guard, I guess maybe trying to get some extra help, or freaking out because her patient's about to drop dead out here in the yards.

He keeps talking. *"Ti tb'iya?"*

"Ángel," I whisper.

*"B'a'natsun. A nbiye' Pascual."*

"*Ma.*"

It's so simple. Pascual is sitting down beside me, resting his hand on my back. And he's asking me what my name is and telling me his own. That's all. But hearing the words, seeing his face, so familiar. The broad cheeks, clear skin and the wide eyes the color of my own mother's . . .

He keeps his hand on my back and murmurs, talking to me in Mam. I close my eyes and feel the words fill my mind, the familiar sounds. Tears run down my cheeks, warm and clean, pushing the dust from my face.

My lungs fill with air, and this stranger keeps talking, stringing together the syllables of my childhood. I'm crying, and he's piecing me back together, taking me home.

"Go on now!" a male voice barks. "Get on outta here. Nobody said you could come over here, boy!"

I open my eyes to see a guard jerking Pascual to his feet.

"*Kayixtiba, Ángel. Kayixtiba.*" Pascual whispers good-bye, holding my gaze as the guard drags him back inside that terrible place.

"Don't go bringin' this boy out here again, Gladys," the guard barks at Snoopy Nurse. "Ain't nobody gonna die on my watch!"

Gladys kicks the brakes on my wheelchair. She pulls the handles, and my chair starts to roll back.

"His name is Ángel!" she says. "He is a man, not a boy." She shoves the wheelchair forward a little too hard. "And I'd like for you to know, Officer Wills, that Ángel knows English. He understands every word you are saying." She starts to push me toward the big metal doors. "So you watch what you say! You hear me, Officer Wills? You watch what you say about this young man!"

She shoves the door open and we are back inside. And I'm grinning like an idiot, because Snoopy Lady just went all badass on the mean guard.

But I can't keep my smile, because my head is throbbing again. I close my eyes and let her push me through the halls.

"We're back, sugar," Nurse Snoopy whispers. She helps me back into the bed and eases my back onto the hard mattress. "Want me to read that nice letter from your friend again?"

I nod, still not able to open my eyes. I listen as she rummages in the bag under my bed.

Yeah, this place sucks. *Atsalu taq'wixil.*

It completely and totally sucks. But whenever I want to give up on my stupid, messed-up heart, all I have to do is ask Nurse Snoopy to pull the letter out from under my bed. She unfolds it, and I trace all those birds with my finger and listen while she reads it to me, over and over.

I refuse to die in this place.

Dear Ángel,
  Don't WORRY. We will be
in Guatemala when you get there.
  When you get off the plane,
Look for the car playing bad Reggaeton.
We will try to bring fries from
              McDonalds.
    Love,
    Vivi & TJ

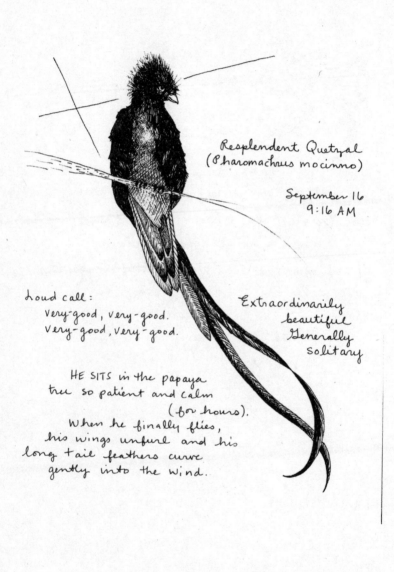

Resplendent Quetzal
(Pharomachrus mocinno)

September 16
9:16 AM

Loud call:
Very-good, very-good.
Very-good, very-good.

Extraordinarily
beautiful.
Generally
Solitary

HE SITS in the papaya
tree so patient and calm
        (for hours).
When he finally flies,
his wings unfurl and his
long tail feathers curve
gently into the wind.

# CHAPTER THIRTY-ONE

## *VIVI*

BIRD JOURNAL

September 16, 9:16 A.M.

Resplendent quetzal (*Pharomachrus mocinno*)

Physical Description: astoundingly beautiful member of the
*quetzal* genus. Iridescent green body; red belly; splendid,
multicolored tail coverts.

Social Behavior: generally solitary; remain for long periods
in one place, particularly in fruit trees.

Habitat: found in cloud forests throughout southern Mexico
and Central America

Call: *very-good, very-good.*

*This is, without a doubt, the most extraordinary bird I have ever
seen!*

**WE HAVE FOUND** the right home for Ángel.

How do I know? That papaya tree in the yard—the one I told
Mom about to convince her to come here with us—it's beautiful and
fragrant, with enormous spiky leaves that reach out over the water's
edge like a parasol. Its trunk overflows with ripe yellow fruit.

And that tree just happens to be the favorite resting place of one of the world's most glorious birds: a male resplendent quetzal.

*And oh, how resplendent he is!* His wings and crown feathers almost glow with iridescent green and blue and all the variations of colors between. His breast is a brilliant red, so bright that I almost feel the need to turn away. I don't, though. I watch.

On sunny mornings, the lake reflects the same colors as the resplendent quetzal—iridescent greens and blues—sunlight shimmering on its still surface. It's ringed with volcanos, bright green mountains with soft curves and flattened peaks. This place is an oasis, a refuge for those who have the luxury to travel the globe and then choose the perfect place to settle. I know that now. I know how incredibly fortunate we are.

To get here, I maneuvered a borrowed truck through crowded city streets tagged with graffiti. On the outskirts of the city, we passed entire towns built from scraps of corrugated metal, houses clinging to sloping hillsides, patched together with colored tarps. We moved through nearly deserted villages, where it seemed the population of stray dogs might have been greater than that of humans. We followed a brightly painted bus overflowing with people along the curving road to Sololá. And then the horizon opened in front of us, and the lake glowed blue in the distance. We maneuvered through the cobblestone streets of Panajachel, passing fruit stands and markets filled with colorful woven textiles. We passed quaint restaurants and loud T-shirt vendors calling out to us in English. We continued toward the lake, toward the great volcanoes, their peaks covered in wispy clouds.

We traveled rutted dirt roads. I gunned the engine and we climbed steep hills. I looked back and saw TJ gripping the edge of the truck, holding on tight, his face filled with wonder. And then we arrived at our home on the edge of the lake. I pulled onto the gravel parking pad and TJ hopped out of the truck. He rushed toward the lake, not looking back. He pulled off his shirt, tossed his flip-flops aside, and dove deep into the blue water.

Mom and I sat, silent.

We have traveled the world, but never have we seen such a place. It's extraordinary, just like my resplendent quetzal.

And, just as I've always been, I am grateful for the Tesla my father gifted me. I am grateful because it gave us this. And this is beautiful.

Every morning TJ and I both get up at dawn. We go outside while Mom is still sleeping. He swims and I watch. I watch TJ glide through the still water, and I wonder how this all happened. I think about the first time we met—the one I can't remember—and the second time, which made me desperate to avoid him. I think about how natural it feels that we are here together, and I imagine our future with such ease. I still have no idea what's coming next, but I know it will include TJ.

I also watch that quetzal, perched on the edge of the papaya leaf in all of his colorful glory. That bird can sit so still for hours on end. So patient, so calm. When he finally takes flight, his wings powerfully unfurl red and yellow and black, and his long blue tail feathers curve gently into the wind.

As my quetzal flies away, he calls out in a loud, melodious voice: *very-good, very-good. Very-good, very-good.*

He goes off to find fruit or lizards, to fill his belly with good things.

I don't worry when he leaves. I have learned, over these few short days, that he always comes back to me.

TJ climbs onto the dock, shakes the water out of his hair, and wraps a frayed towel around his waist. He leans down to kiss me, his damp hand cool against my cheek.

His kiss, though. After all this time, it still sends heat through me. I'm not afraid of that anymore either.

He pulls me to my feet and we head inside. The house is simple—bright ochre walls and tile floors. Rattan furniture covered in woven fabric. It's nothing special, but it's warm and homey. The sofa is a bit worn at the edges, and the bedspreads are thin and frayed. But it is our house for now, and it is ready—we've been here for five days, unloading medical supplies and scrubbing surfaces clean. We know Ángel doesn't have long, but we'd rather he not get a nasty infection while he's still with us.

Ángel's room is on the ground floor, with large doors that swing open to the patio. We removed the furniture to make room for his hospital bed.

The view from Ángel's room is incredible. He will be able to sit up and look out across the still lake, watch the sun rise and set each day. When he can no longer go outside, we will fling open a wall of windows to bring the outside in.

Yesterday we bought a stack of soft blankets that we can warm in the oven. TJ checked in at the clinic again, to be sure he would know how to contact the staff if we need them. It's simple—nothing like the ICU. But they're nice, and they're willing to offer us support.

In truth, this isn't technical work. TJ researched it extensively: "end-of-life care." He says we are ready, and I believe him. All we need to do is keep Ángel comfortable and surround him with love.

As long as he makes it to us, we can do that.

Everyone was so generous before we left. Prashanti organized a supply drive at the hospital. My mom planned "Ángel's Art Walk," a night when all of the local gallery owners in St. Augustine donated their proceeds toward his care. We have everything: a hospital bed, a wheelchair, oxygen tanks, needles, IV bags, and enough medicine and supplies to last several months—whatever we don't use, we'll donate to the clinic here.

We are ready. All we need now is Ángel.

I stand at the kitchen window, looking out over the still, deep lake.

I feel TJ's arms wrap around me. He presses his body to my back and rests his chin on my shoulder. His skin still feels cool from the lake, and he smells like the minerals that make the water so blue.

"He's on his way," TJ whispers in my ear. "I just got the call."

I turn, throw my arms around his neck, and let out a yelp. "Finally!"

My mom comes into the kitchen.

"You'll get the house ready?" I ask her.

"Yes, yes." She nods and smiles. "I'll take care of everything here. You two need to hit the road!"

Ángel was in detention for a month. They said two weeks, but I guess they lied. Before today he only called us once—we couldn't call there. I sent letters, though, and lots of drawings. When he called, he sounded tired. I asked him how things were in that place, and he said he'd rather not talk about it, so we didn't.

It must have been really bad, if that's how he answered.

But he survived it, and he's on his way.

# CHAPTER THIRTY-TWO

## TJ

**IT'S AN UNMARKED PLANE.** White, with a bunch of numbers printed in black on the side. The rear wing is painted navy blue, with the profile of an eagle in white. I've never seen a plane like this.

Vivi and I sat in the truck bed at the edge of the tarmac for an hour, waiting, watching. We found a McDonald's for Ángel, because we wanted to bring him French fries. They're here in the truck with us, filling it up with the smell of grease and getting cold and nasty.

We weren't the only ones waiting. A bunch of families stood clumped together, staring through the chain-link fence that lines the tarmac. We all kept looking up at the sky, searching for signs of an airplane.

Now, finally, the plane lands and taxis along the runway toward us. We get out of our borrowed truck and head toward the fence. Nobody talks, and the roar of the engine fills our ears.

The rear door opens, and airport workers roll a stairway toward the door. Tons of people come down the stairs and head across the tarmac toward us—mostly men, but a few women carrying little kids. A guy steps onto the tarmac and falls to his knees, kissing the ground. He jumps up and holds his hand to the skies. *"Gracias a Dios!"* he calls out. *"Estoy libre!"*

"What's he saying?" I ask, nudging Vivi.

"He's thanking God for his freedom."

I wonder how long he had to sit in detention before being put on that airplane in handcuffs, but I don't say that out loud. Vivi slips her hand into mine and squeezes. I know what she's thinking. I know she's worrying that we haven't seen Ángel yet.

I am too.

A woman trips down the stairs, holding tight to a baby. A toddler clings to her side, looking down at the ground. When the woman sees a guy with a camera, she lifts her baby's blanket to cover their faces, and she pulls the toddler close.

Fifteen minutes pass, twenty. I'm trying not to stress about Ángel, and why he isn't getting off the plane.

"Are you sure this was his flight?" I ask.

Vivi nods. "I confirmed with ICE, remember?"

"Maybe he got an infection again and they needed to postpone." I try hard to make my voice sound calm, but I'm pretty sure by the look on Vivi's face, that it's a fail. I grasp the chain above my head, staring out at the plane, telling myself not to freak out about all of the things I know could have gone wrong.

The tarmac is empty. Everyone has moved on. We still wait.

"What should we do?" Vivi asks, her voice wobbly.

I shake my head, still staring hard at that plane door. And then somebody appears at the top of the stairs. No, not one person—two.

"Is that . . ." I ask.

"Yeah," Vivi says. I turn around and sprint to the truck, grab the wheelchair from the back. Vivi and I break into a run, rolling the wheelchair toward Ángel, who is being carried down the stairs, cradled in the arms of an ICE officer.

They stop halfway down the stairs, and the cop smiles and says something to Ángel. Ángel turns to see us, and a big, goofy grin lights up his gaunt face.

*He's lost more weight. That's not good.*

When they reach the tarmac, we push the wheelchair to meet them.

"These are my friends," Ángel tells him.

"You have good friends," the ICE cop says.

He puts Ángel into the wheelchair, being more gentle than I would expect. But I'm not really thinking about that, because I'm too busy worrying.

Vivi attacks Ángel with a hug. She's crying, but I know she's not sad. I know they're tears of relief.

"Where's his oxygen?" I bark at the cop. "And his IV—please tell me he had IV fluids on the flight! And antibiotics? Is he on antibiotics?"

My voice sounds pissed, but the cop replies calmly, "He had oxygen on the flight, but we can't bring it off the plane. Once he leaves that transport, he's no longer our responsibility. I'm sorry."

"S'okay, my *vato*," Ángel says. "I'll survive."

I clench my jaw tight, struggling not to go off on the cop, fighting to focus on Ángel instead. I lean in to check his pulse. "How you feeling, homie?"

"Better now. Dude, I didn't think I was gonna make it!"

He smells terrible, like fear and body odor, like decay. But he sounds awesome, because he's laughing in my ear.

"We've got fries in the car—they're a little cold," I say, still holding on to his wrist.

"McDonald's?"

"Yeah, homie! Only the best."

"What are you waiting for, *vato*?" Ángel asks, still smiling big. "Let's get outta here."

Satisfied that his pulse is strong, I release the brakes on the wheel-chair and push Ángel toward the car. Vivi starts to follow us, but the ICE cop stops her.

"He's a nice kid," the cop tells her. I turn around, feeling pissed off again. But then I see him touch her forearm and hear him say, "I'm sorry for what he's going through."

*That's unexpected.*

"Yeah," she replies. "We are too."

"He told me about you two, and your mom, right?" The ICE cop looks across the tarmac toward me and Ángel. "You came all the way down here to be with him?"

Vivi nods.

"He's lucky to have you," the ICE cop says.

If it were me back there, talking to that cop, I'd have a mouth full of choice words to spit at him. They'd probably start with my mus-ings on why the hell a heart patient isn't on IV antibiotics during a three-hour flight. But it's not me, and I guess that's a good thing.

Because, Vivi? Here's what she tells that cop: "I'm the lucky one," she says, shaking her head. "I am so incredibly lucky to have Ángel in my life."

That girl is amazing. It's wild, how she can see the good in anyone—from a scrawny heart patient to a burly cop. She even sees the good in me. She thinks she needs me around, and maybe she's right. But I need her too. And I'm pretty sure that coming down here is the first of a thousand crazy-good things we'll do together.

# CHAPTER THIRTY-THREE

## *VIVI*

**"IT FEELS LIKE FLYING."**

Ángel murmurs the words through dry, cracked lips.

"What did you say?" TJ asks, leaning forward so that his ear is beside Ángel's lips.

Ángel repeats the words, his voice not more than a soft breath. I don't need to hear them again. I know exactly what he said.

It feels like flying.

I understand Ángel, and he understands me. That has been Ángel's gift to me. In these last few days, he has heard what I needed to say. I know it's irrational and impractical, but I think that my dad had something to do with this. And, even though Ángel and TJ laugh at me relentlessly about it, I still think my father's here, watching from the papaya tree. I really do believe that my dad knows—he understands how desperately I regretted his last days, and he's given me this chance to say good-bye to someone I love, and to do it well.

TJ, Mom, and I—we *are* doing it well. We are here with Ángel, all three of us holding tight to him and letting him go.

Since the moment Ángel arrived at the edge of this strange, enchanted lake, we have sat with him, cared for him, fed him, laughed with him. Almost every morning, we have carried him to the blue water so that he could dangle his feet from the dock. On moonless nights, we have taken him out on a sailboat to watch the stars. We have cried together at the overwhelming beauty of them. And on all those nights between, we have taken turns sitting beside his bed, watching the moon wax and wane, watching over Ángel as his heart slowly quits.

Now he is leaving us, and I don't want him to go. It seems so wrong that my heart is working this hard, filled to bursting with the pain of it, while his own heart slows to a stop. But Ángel isn't fighting the end; he's simply living it.

I don't know whether TJ was right, when he said I help Ángel feel less afraid, but I hope he was. I hope Ángel's not afraid.

In the papaya tree, the quetzal sings loud and clear, telling us what he knows we need to hear.

*Very good, very good.*

I look outside and watch our quetzal take to the air. His feathers unfurl as he flies across the lake, in all of his resplendent beauty. He calls out across the water.

*Very good, very good.*

I hope Ángel sings that song too. And he flies.

# ACKNOWLEDGMENTS

In part, this book is about learning how to walk with suffering, and how not to turn away from it. It's about the extraordinary, beautiful relationships that we build when we love each other in all of our faults, and through all of our pain; when we stay present to suffering, even though it scares the hell out of us.

For many years, I have worked with a small nonprofit called El Refugio. We support detained immigrants and their families. Often, there is very little we can do to make their situation better. We simply accompany people through their suffering, stand beside them in love, refuse to ignore it or turn our backs to it. This journey of accompaniment has changed my life, again and again. I am grateful to every one of the beautiful people I have encountered in my work with El Refugio. This story would not exist without you.

One of the greatest joys of this project was the chance to work with my oldest friend, Emily Arthur. For many years (decades?), Emily and I dreamed of making art together. We finally did it! Emily, your illustrations brought this story to life for me—each and every one of them was a perfect gift.

Many thanks to the incredible professionals with whom I have the honor to work at St. Martin's Press: Sara Goodman, Alicia Clancy, Brittani Hilles, DJ DeSmyter, Karen Masnica, and Kaitlin Severini.

I am grateful every single day for my agent, Erin Harris, and my publicist, Megan Beatie. You have been fierce and loving advocates, consistent and creative. I appreciate you so very much!

An unexpected pleasure that came with writing this story was learning to pay close attention to the lovely, intelligent, remarkable winged creatures that share our space in this world. I am grateful to Jennifer Ackerman, whose fabulous book *The Genius of Birds* opened my eyes to their abundant presence around me. I owe a great debt to the Cornell Lab of Ornithology and the *Sibley Guide to Birds*. They were both constant companions during this project. I'm especially grateful to my nephews and birders-extraordinaire, Ander and Paul Buckley, whose love of birds is infectious (and who generously corrected a couple of egregious errors in the manuscript!).

Enormous thanks to those kind and generous people who allowed me to pick their brains as I researched this story: PJ Edwards, Marcia Johansson, Marina Monteiro, Marilia Brocchetto, Robin Moscato, Alice Carrera Lopez, Wendy Tatter, and Dorothy Foster. And, to the wonderful friends and family who kept me from losing my mind while I wrote it: Les and Tanya Zacks, Juan and Anja Ramirez, Araceli Martinez, Cynthia Elizondo, Ana Maldonado, Holly Kroll Smith, everyone in the talented and super-fun Atlanta YA and MG writers' group, and all the wonderful neighborhood friends who generously loaned me their kids to keep mine busy. Speaking of kids, my four are more of a joy with every passing year. Mary Elizabeth, Nate, Pixley, and Annie: I love you with every ounce of my being, *and* I adore hanging out with you. Thanks for being so supportive of my work.

Elizabeth Friedmann (aka "mom"), Lee Taylor, and Mayra Cuevas: What can I say? I'd be absolutely adrift without you three. Thanks for keeping me moored.

And to Chris, who chose to walk with me through my most profound suffering. It would have been so easy for you to turn away, but you never did. Thank you for loving me through the pain all those years ago and for loving me even more today. *Vale? Vale.*

# ABOUT THE ILLUSTRATOR

eedyphoto

Emily Arthur is a studio artist and professor of printmaking at the University of Wisconsin-Madison. Her work can be found in museum collections, including the Denver Art Museum, the Tweed Museum of Art, the Crocker Art Museum, the Minneapolis Institute of Art, and the Weisman Art Museum. Her studio practice includes working with scientists who study endangered birds and threatened habitats. Born in Atlanta, Georgia, Emily now lives in snowy Wisconsin, where she shares a home and studio with her partner and a long-haired shepherd dog. Emily and Marie met in the third grade of elementary school and have been close friends ever since. You can follow her at Dark Horse Press or at www.emilyarthur.org.